CITY OF THORNS

C.N. CRAWFORD

For my readers, many of you in C.N. Crawford's Coven. I love providing escapism for you.

CHAPTER 1

I tried not to stare at the frat boy I'd punched last night, but three things were making this hard. One—the bruise around Jack's eye was a deep, shiny purple that caught the glare of the classroom's fluorescent lights. Two—he didn't even belong in this class. And three—he was sitting in the back making a grotesque gesture that involved waggling his tongue through V-shaped fingers.

Suffice to say, my presentation was not going well.

Jack Corwin had been harassing me since high school. I would have expected that by senior year of college, he'd have grown past finger-in-the-hole gestures and fake orgasm faces, but Jack liked to buck convention. Why give up that level of obnoxiousness when it was his defining trait?

I'd prepared so well for today, putting in hours of memorizing the names of the relevant psychological studies. I'd selected a knee-length black dress with a white collar—cute but professional, and only slightly goth. I'd copied down my notes and pulled my bright red curls into something like a neat ponytail. And yet, my preparation didn't matter when confronted by that waggling tongue.

Focus, Rowan. Forget him.

I squared my shoulders, surveying the rest of the class. My classmate Alison twirled a blonde curl around her finger, looking at me expectantly. She gave me an encouraging smile.

I glanced at my notecards and started to read again. "As I was saying, the concept of repressed memories is fraught with controversy." I raised my eyes. "Many psychologists dispute—"

Jack made a circular shape with his finger and thumb, then slid his other index finger in and out, opening his mouth wide in an orgasm face. The lights gleamed off the strange silver pin he always wore, which was shaped like a hammer.

"Sorry. Uh, dissociative fugue..." I started again. "Which is in the DSM—"

In the back of the classroom, where no one but me could see him, Jack was thrusting his crotch up and down in a pounding gesture.

Anger simmered. For a number of reasons, he was the last person I wanted around, and I finally pointed at him. "Is he supposed to be here?" I blurted. "He's not in this class. Why is he here?"

Unfortunately, no one else had seen what he was doing, so I just looked like a dick.

My professor, Dr. Omer, raised his dark eyebrows and stared at me. When he glanced at the back of the room, Jack looked like the picture of innocence. He held his pen in his hands as if he'd been taking notes the whole time, eyebrows raised. *Just a studious kid here, trying to learn.*

Dr. Omer steepled his fingers, then frowned at me. He didn't say anything because he was doing that psychologist thing where they looked at you in silence and waited for *you* to realized that you had done something inappropriate. I swallowed hard.

Here was the thing: Jack had followed me last night and cornered me outside my house. In fact, he'd been stalking me for years. There was a legitimate reason I'd given him a black eye.

But this wasn't a therapy session, and I wasn't trying to be professional. We were here to learn, or at least to get a passing grade on our transcript and move on.

"He's not in this class," I repeated more quietly. "I don't understand why he's here."

I could feel the class's eyes on me, and heat spread over my neck. Considering I was pale as milk, it was hard to hide it when I was blushing.

"He's auditing the class for the rest of the semester," said Dr. Omer in a calm voice. "He has permission to be here." He pressed his fingers against his lips for a moment, frowning. The psychologist stare. Then, "Is there a problem with your presentation? You are usually prepared, Rowan."

Normally, I adored Dr. Omer's calm demeanor, but now it seemed off, like he was calmly ignoring the house that burned around him.

I took a deep, slow breath and tried to center myself by thinking about my feet, rooted firmly to the floor. *Just focus and get through this, Rowan.* Tonight, I'd have drinks with my best friend, Shai, for my twenty-second birthday. Beer, pizza, gossip about her amazing new life. All I had to do was get through this next twenty minutes.

"No problem at all." I smiled. "I was just confused for a moment. I'm actually very prepared." I cleared my throat. "Dissociative amnesia is theorized to be a state—"

Wait. Was he really going to be in this class for the rest of the semester? I had to take this class to graduate.

I glanced through the window at the City of Thorns—the magical city that loomed over Osborn, Massachusetts. I planned to get in there for graduate school, and I wanted to do so as soon as possible.

"Rowan?" Dr. Omer prompted, a hint of annoyance in his tone. "It might be better if you try this again on a day when you're more prepared. I don't think this is the best use of our class time."

Ouch. My hands were shaking, but I wasn't sure if that was the result of anxiety or anger.

"No, I've got it. Sorry. I was thrown off by the projector not working." I swallowed, ready to regain my composure. "What I'm talking about is an inability to access memories in the unconscious..." I flipped my notecards around, trying to weave my thoughts together into something coherent. "Particularly autobiographical memories, the things from your life..."

I looked up at Jack again to see him leaning back in his chair, massaging his nipples with his tongue lolling out of his mouth.

At that point, two ideas became tangled in my working memory. One was the next phrase on my notecard, which was "If you could imagine..." The other was *I'd love to hit that fucker again.* With my brain tripping over the two thoughts, I stared right at Jack and blurted, "If you could love fucker again..."

Which made no sense but definitely sounded inappropriate.

Shocked, half-stifled laughter interrupted the silence.

The class turned back to Jack. He'd immediately adopted his innocent note-taking pose again, looking baffled at my pronouncement. His eyebrows rose, innocent.

My stomach plummeted.

Kill me. I'm praying that the floor could swallow me up now.

I felt the warmth creep over my cheeks as a terrible silence fell. The lights buzzed and flickered above me, and my mouth went dry. "I said the wrong thing." I gestured at Jack. "He was making faces..." I trailed off, realizing how lame this sounded.

Jack's obsession with me had started years ago when he asked me out as a freshman at Osborne High. I'd said no, and that had made him mad. So he'd started rumors that I'd banged the whole baseball team. Everyone had believed him. They'd called me Home Run Rowan for the next four years, and he'd even photoshopped my face onto nude models. That was what my high school experience had been like.

But no one needed to hear that. They wanted to get this over with and move on to Taco Tuesday in the dining hall.

"I just said the wrong thing," I added again.

Dr. Omer pressed his two palms together in front of

his mouth. "Okay, I don't know exactly what's going on here, but I sense there is some interpersonal conflict, and I don't think this is a productive forum for discussion. If there's an issue between you two, we can explore that after class."

Jack looked sheepish and raised his hand for the first time. "I think I know what's happening. Rowan was upset when I turned her down for a date last night, and she didn't know how to handle it. She lashed out." He gestured at his eye. "But I swear, I'm ready to put the physical assault behind me. I'm ready to focus on Abnormal Psych. I'm a very good student. If you'll look at my transcript, I think you'll find that I'm one of the best students you've ever seen."

"Oh, my God!" Alison's eyes were open wide. "Did you really give him that black eye, though?" she asked me. "I'm not trying to be dramatic, but I'm literally physically scared right now."

Someone said something about calling the police. Others guffawed, half shocked and half thrilled. From their perspective, this was probably the best thing that had happened to them all semester. This was better than Taco Tuesday. This was *drama.*

I crumpled my notecards in my hands, and my heart slammed against my ribs. "Wait. I hit him, yes, but he deserved it. He's the problem here, not me."

Already, I could see the recommendation letter from Dr. Omer disappearing before my eyes. Goodbye to grad school in the City of Thorns; goodbye to my lifelong dream of closing an unsolved crime.

Unhinged. I seemed completely unhinged.

They had it all wrong, but nothing makes you seem crazier than trying to scream that you're the only sane one.

"Okay, you know what?" I tossed the notecards in the trash can. "I think my presentation is over."

My entire body buzzed with adrenaline as I rushed out of the room.

CHAPTER 2

I sat on the bed in my basement apartment, sketching the gates of the City of Thorns.

After my shitty day, I'd gone for a long run. I'd pushed the pace hard, and my muscles still burned as I stretched them on the comforter. Running was the best way I had of dealing with stress, losing myself in physicality. It was also the one time I felt really good at something. The only problem was that sometimes, when my feet pounded the leaves in the woods, I'd have glimmers of flashbacks to the night Mom died. I'd hear her voice, telling me to run.

I shook my head, clearing my mind of the dark memory. Instead, I focused on trying to perfect the picture of the gate. This drawing served no purpose, but I'd become completely obsessed with the gate's contours —the wrought iron entrance to the demon city, decorated with a skull in the center, strangely beautiful and forbidding at the same time. Maybe it wasn't the healthiest obsession to draw the same thing repeatedly like a psycho, but at least I wasn't thinking about Jack Corwin.

I exhaled as I shaded in the skull. Living here was all part of my plan to save money for grad school in the demon city. Down here, I was saving every dime I could, living in a cellar with six other broke students. Our rooms were divided by thin wooden walls, and we shared a bathroom and a kitchenette that was mostly a hot pot and kettle.

My phone buzzed—a call from Shai—and I swiped to answer. "Hey."

"Oh! You actually answered instead of pretending you were busy and then texting two minutes later."

I grinned. "Who talks on the phone anymore? It makes everyone nervous except you."

"So what are we doing for your birthday? Because there's this amazing Thai takeout place I want to try, and I could bring it to you with, like, a couple bottles of wine."

I smiled. "My new place is a shabby basement with spiders. And compared to your fancy Belial University dorms, it'll seem like a full-blown shithole."

"Is it really that bad?"

"Hang on." I snapped a few photos to get the point across, then emailed them to her. "Okay, check your mail. See, if we were texting like normal people, this would be going much more smoothly."

After a moment, I heard her say, "Oh, okay. Well, yeah, it's small. Nicely decorated, but small. I don't love the idea of spiders…I wish I could have you here, but I *think* you could be legally murdered by demons if I sneaked you in."

I nodded. "I'd like to avoid that. Maybe just a drink somewhere in Osborn?"

"Hang on…I'm zooming in on your photos to see if I can find anything embarrassing."

"I've drawn thirty-two pictures of the City of Thorns gates, and most are taped to the wall," I said, "so that's fairly embarrassing."

"Yeah, but I already knew you were a weirdo. I was hoping to find you were some kind of secret sex freak, too. For a second, I thought I saw giant red dildos by your bed, but now I can see they're fire extinguishers."

"What's the opposite of a sex freak?" I asked. "That's me."

"Okay, but why do you have two fire extinguishers next to your bed?"

I sat up straighter, getting anxious just thinking about it. "There's no way out of here, Shai. There's a tiny window over the bed, but it doesn't open. So if the house were on fire, I'd have to fight my way out from a far corner of a basement while the walls burned around me."

She inhaled sharply. "Oh, shit. Can you find another place? That doesn't sound safe even with the fire extinguishers. Is that even legal?"

"Probably not, but I installed fire alarms, too. And I stocked up with the stuff stuntmen used to get through flames."

"Wait, *what*?" she cried.

I mentally reviewed what was under my bed. "Fire-retardant clothing and gels to stop my skin from burning, Hollywood-style. I could walk through flames if I had to. Oh! And I bought a gas mask in case I need to get through billowing smoke. I'm pretty much set with the fire stuff."

"Of course. So you're still kind of a prepper, I'm guessing?"

"Yes, so in the event of a demon apocalypse, come here. I've got several large bags of beans and rice and some fish antibiotics."

"Nice," she said. "Are we going to kill the demons with burritos and penicillin?"

"In case the shops and doctors' offices close. And I've got a water purifier in case the reservoir is contaminated."

What I didn't mention was my weirdest prepper item: the fox urine, which was something hunters used to disguise their scent. If the demons rampaged around Osborne, hungry for blood, I'd drench myself in fox pee. They'd never find me. But Shai didn't need to know that. Even with my best friend, I had a line of weirdness I didn't cross.

"Okay," said Shai. "Well, since there's no apocalypse going on right now, let's figure out somewhere for margaritas, okay?"

"I'm happy with wherever. It'll just be fun to see you and get out of the basement. And I definitely need a drink. I gave an absolutely disastrous presentation today in my Abnormal Psych class."

"Shit. Okay. Just give me a chance to call around and see if I can get us reservations, huh? I'll text you in a few."

She hung up, and I leaned back against my pillows. A flicker of movement caught my eye, and I glanced at a spider skittering over the floor. The scent of mildew and mold hung heavily in the air.

I pulled my drawing pad and pencil into my lap, then

finishing the filagree on another image of the gates to the City of Thorns.

There were only two kinds of mortals allowed in the city: the servants born into their roles, and the students like Shai who could afford it. Every year, Belial University in the City of Thorns accepted around three hundred mortal applicants. At Belial, the demon university, they learned to suffuse their careers with the magical arts. Graduates like Shai always landed plum positions in whatever field they wanted.

But in my case, education wasn't the *real* reason I wanted to get into the demon university.

I wanted revenge. I wanted to find the demon who killed my mom.

When the picture of the gate was finished, I flipped over the page and started jotting down some financial numbers. Right now, I owed seventy-five thousand in student loans, with seven percent interest. If I was going to pay that back, and also save up the hundred grand to get into Belial University on what would likely be poverty wages after graduating…

My stomach churned.

Whenever I started making these calculations, the weight of impossibility started pressing down on me. I'd done it a million times, but the numbers never added up. With my loan interest, I'd save up the hundred grand roughly…

Never.

I would never have a hundred thousand dollars to get in.

Increasingly, I was starting to think about plan B:

break into the city, then find a way to blend in. There had to be a way. Even an ancient demon city would have a weakness.

As I started to mull over my more dangerous and unhinged plan, my phone buzzed with a message from Shai: *Cirque de la Mer. Two for one cocktails tonight. Meet me there at 8:30 xo*

Really, it was probably a good time for her to interrupt my breaking and entering schemes before I came up with something that could get me killed.

* * *

SITTING at the white marble countertop at Cirque de la Mer, my red hair drenched by the September rain, I sipped a Guinness and licked the foam off my lip. I still wore my black dress and boots, but I'd accessorized a bit with black nail polish, eyeliner, and silver rings. This was my look: ginger Goth Puritan.

Behind the bar, enormous windows overlooked the Atlantic Ocean, and the sea twinkled under the starlight. Dubstep boomed around me. I liked it here, with the loud music to drown out my own thoughts and a gorgeous view of the sea. Of course, this was probably the most expensive bar on the north shore of Massachusetts, but for tonight, I wasn't going to worry about money. The loans were too ridiculous to worry about at this point, and I might as well owe a billion dollars.

When Shai sidled up next to me at the bar, she flashed me an enormous smile. Her dark hair fell in two long braids over a cream-colored dress. She wore vibrant red lipstick that perfectly complemented her tawny brown skin.

I'd really needed to see a friendly face.

She hugged me. "Hello, birthday girl. What are we drinking? Tequila shots?"

"I swore off them after the Harvard Square incident."

She grimaced. "Oh, right. Okay, well, let's eat and get cocktails so you don't get messy." She raised her hand, and the bartender immediately came over with a smile. Shai ordered us two mojitos and a butternut squash pizza.

With that accomplished, she turned back to me, eyebrows raised. "Okay, what was this about your nightmare of a day?"

I sighed. "Jack Corwin turned up in the middle of my class presentation and made orgasm faces when I was trying to focus, and then he claimed that I punched him in the eye."

Her hand flew to her mouth for a moment. "First of all, fuck that guy. Second, has he lost his mind? Why would he think that people would believe that you punched him?"

I cleared my throat, cringing. "Well, about that part. I did actually punch him."

"What?"

"After he tried to ram his tongue down my throat," I said defensively.

"So he assaulted you first? You need to call the cops. He's escalating things. He's been stalking you for years now."

The bartender slid our mojitos across the bar, and I grabbed mine instantly. I took a sip, letting the mint and lime roll over my tongue. "I reported it at Osborn State and to the police, but they decided a long time ago that I'm overreacting. Apparently, being a douchebag isn't illegal, and I'm not sure they'd see what happened last night on my terms, either. His dad is a congressman or something, so..." I took another sip. "You know what? I'm sick of thinking about him. Please tell me about the City of Thorns. Let's leave Jack out of tonight. I want to hear about the demons."

"Where do I even begin?"

I raised my eyebrows. "Do you think demons can leave?"

She shook her head. "I think so, but not for long. As far as I know, there's some kind of magical spell from hundreds of years ago that keeps them mostly tied to one demon city or another. But occasionally, they can travel between them. Why do you ask?"

"That night my mom was murdered—"

My sentence trailed off. I could already feel the air cooling, the atmosphere growing thorny as I raised the painful subject. There was no easy way to say, *One night, a demon with a glowing star on his head hunted down my mom in the woods and burned her to death.* And since the horror of that night felt raw even now, it was hard to talk about it without feeling like I was drowning in loss again.

Sometimes, I thought the only thing keeping me afloat was the certainty that I'd avenge her death. That I would get into the City of Thorns and find her killer.

But this was too dark and weird, wasn't it? Worse than the fox pee beneath my bed.

CHAPTER 3

We were sitting at the marble bar, with the night-dark sea glittering before us. I didn't want to ruin the evening, and so I waved a hand. "Never mind. I want to hear more about your daily life. What's it like?"

I could feel the tension leave the air again. "Fucking amazing," Shai said. "I might do another year. Any chance you can get the tuition for next year?"

"I'm working on a few ideas for getting in." Wildly illegal ideas at this point. "What's your dorm like?"

"There's a balcony and servants. Even the ocean is more beautiful there. It's not like the Atlantic—it's like this gorgeous tropical ocean made with magic. Okay, so the city has seven wards, each one associated with a demon. And the university buildings are organized the same way. I'm in Lucifer Hall, and it's this enormous stone castle-like place."

Even putting my vengeance plans aside, my jealousy was crippling. "How are your classes?"

"Amazing. They're held in lecture halls that must be four hundred years old, with seats curved all around a stage." She sighed. "I know, it's a huge expense. But I wanted to learn magical arts, and you can't exactly do that at Osborn State. Belial is the finest witchcraft institution for mortals. I'm desperate to stay another year."

"What are the demons like?"

She ran her fingertip over the rim of her mojito. "Well, my classes are mostly with aspiring mortal witches, but there are a few demons, and the professors, obviously. They're beautiful and intimidating as shit. Some of them have horns, but not all. I haven't met anyone who seems particularly evil. At least, no one worse than Jack." She turned and lifted her empty glass, motioning for the bartender to bring us another round, then swiveled back to me. "I've heard the king is evil—him and the Lord of Chaos. They're both terrifying, but I've only seen them from a distance."

My eyebrows shot up. "Okay, start with the king. What's his deal?"

She leaned in conspiratorially. "King Cambriel only recently became king. He slaughtered his father, King Nergal, who'd ruled for hundreds of years. Cambriel cut off his dad's head and stuck it on the gate to his palace."

I shuddered. "That's fucked up."

"The only way a demon king can die is if his heir slaughters him, and Cambriel did just that. Now he's apparently looking for a demon queen, and there's all kinds of gossip about which female he might choose."

As I finished my first mojito, the bartender brought over two more.

"And the women *want* to marry this guy with his dad's head over his front gate?" I asked. "Sounds like quite a catch."

"To the female demons, he is." She slid one of the mojitos over to me. "And the Lord of Chaos is the other eligible bachelor in the city. He's an outsider—a duke from the City of Serpents in England, so he was leader of a demon ward there. No one knows why he left, but obviously, it was a scandal. Dukes don't normally leave their cities. But the most important thing is that he seems to be filthy rich."

"If it was such a big scandal, how come no one knows the details?"

She stirred her drink with her little black straw. "There's no communication between demon cities. Demons can arrive in a new city, but they can never speak about the old one. It was one of the conditions of surrender in the great demon wars years ago, sealed by magic. The Puritans thought that if demons spoke to each other, they could grow strong and rise up against the mortals again, so he can't say a thing about the English demon city."

"Wow."

"So." She leaned closer. "No one really knows anything about him. But here's the scariest thing: on the rare occasion that a demon comes into a different city, they have to pass an initiation called the Infernal Trial. It's supposed to prove that the demon gods have blessed the new arrival. I don't want to say it's barbaric because that sounds judgmental, but it *is* barbaric. In the City of Thorns, the way the Trial goes is that the demons have to run through the forest and try to kill the newcomer. Only those who survive can remain. Most of them die before they can be initiated, but the Lord of Chaos slaughtered fifty other demons. Obviously, all the women want to fuck him because he's terrifying."

I stared at her. "This is all legal?"

She shrugged. "Their city, their laws. They can't kill humans without starting a war, but demons are fair game."

This was *fascinating*. "What does the Lord of Chaos look like?"

"I've only seen him from a distance, but he's shockingly beautiful. Like, fall-to-your-knees-before-him beautiful. He has silver hair, but not from age. It's sort of otherworldly. And he has these stunning blue eyes, devastating cheekbones. He's huge. I have a crush on him, and on a wrath demon named Legion. He has long black hair and these sexy-as-hell tattoos. Both of them are, like… stunning. Legion looked at me once—a smoldering look. Not even joking, I forgot to breathe."

I leaned closer. "What about a star? Have you seen a five-pointed star on anyone's head?"

A line formed between her brows. "What are you talking about?"

And there I was, back to my obsession—my mom's murder.

I shook my head. "Never mind. I just heard a rumor about marks on demons' foreheads. Might be bullshit."

As the pizza arrived, I pulled off a slice for myself and slid it onto a small plate. It looked surprisingly good, even though it was vegan.

Shai drummed her fingernails on the counter. "Why do I get the feeling you're always hiding things?"

"Some things are meant to be hidden." My mouth was watering for the squash and garlic. I took a bite, and while the vegan cheese burned my mouth, it still tasted glorious. I wasn't sure even the magically inspired food of the demon world could compete.

When I swallowed the hot bite, I asked, "Are you going to show me any of the healing magic you've been learning? If I have a headache, can you fix it?"

She wiped the corner of her mouth with a napkin. "I'm not ready yet. And anyway, I'm a veterinary student. I can't treat humans."

I pointed at her, feeling a bit tipsy now. "But if someone shot me in the shoulder, could you fix it with magic, or would you turn me into a cat or something?"

She shuddered. "Probably half-cat, half-human. It would be horrible."

We went quiet for a while as we ate the rest of the pizza.

When we finished, I turned to look behind me and found that the club was starting to fill up.

"Are we going to dance?" asked Shai.

I was now two mojitos and a Guinness into the evening, and so I shouted something about it being my birthday as I took to the dance floor.

They were playing my favorite, Apashe. As the beat boomed over the club, I found myself losing myself in the music. I forgot my college loans, my disastrous presentation, the spiders that crawled over me when I slept. I forgot about Jack and the five-pointed star. I let go of my lust for revenge.

At least, I did so until the music went quiet and tension thickened the air.

Sometimes, you can sense danger before you feel it, and this was one of those moments. Darkness rippled through the bar, floating on a hot, dry breeze. I went still, disturbed to find that everyone was staring in the same direction with an expression of horror. Goosebumps rose on my arms. The warmth felt unnatural, disturbing. I didn't want to turn around.

When I finally did, my stomach swooped. There, in the doorway, was a demon with otherworldly silver hair and eyes like flecks of ice. The Lord of Chaos? His size and breathtaking beauty almost made me dizzy. He looked like a freaking god.

Maybe it was the mojitos, maybe it was his stunning physical perfection, but I felt magnetically drawn to him. I wanted to slide up closer to him and press myself against his muscular body. As I stared at him, my heart started to pound faster.

Divine. His silver hair hung down to heartbreakingly sharp cheekbones. He sported a high-collared black coat that hung open. Under his jacket, he wore a thin gray sweater that showed off a muscular body. It looked soft, but I could tell the abs beneath it were rock hard. I found my pulse racing as I thought of running my fingers over the material and feeling his muscles twitch.

I'd never enjoyed sex—not once in my life. But as I looked at him, I thought *there* was a man who could actually satisfy me.

I clamped my eyes shut. Wait, what the fuck was wrong with me? He wasn't even human. He was another species, one that used to eat humans.

But when I opened my eyes again, I felt like I was melting. In contrast to his pale blue eyes, his eyebrows were dark as night. The effect seemed shocking, mesmerizing.

But when he slid those pale eyes to me, an icy tendril of fear curled through me. His fingers tightened into fists, and he lowered his chin like he was about to charge at me.

I froze. My heart started beating faster now for an entirely different reason. I had his attention, but not in a good way.

This was a look of pure, unadulterated loathing, a look of palpable hatred that sent alarm bells ringing in my mind. He *hated* me.

Holy hell.

What did he think I'd done to him?

CHAPTER 4

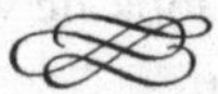

Tension thickened the air, and my knees felt weak.

The demon dominated the room. His eyes locked on me.

Every cell in my body was telling me to turn and run, to save myself before it was too late. He might be beautiful, but this creature was pure death. He'd tear my throat out in an instant.

It felt like ages before the look of raw hatred disappeared, replaced by a cruel, mocking smile. He dragged his gaze away from me. Now, he looked at ease, like all of this was amusing to him. He shrugged. "Well, don't stop the fun, my mortal friends." He spoke with a posh English accent. "One might get the unpleasant idea that demons aren't welcome here."

With a slow, graceful gate, he crossed to the bar, his enormous body seemingly radiating lethal power.

Though I trembled and backed away from him, I found myself unable to stop staring. Shai tugged on my arm, pulling me away, and I nearly stumbled as she dragged me from the bar.

When we were no longer so close to him, she whispered, "What was that all about?"

My mouth had gone dry, and my head was spinning. "You saw that, too? The look he was giving me? I have no idea what that was about."

"Maybe you look like someone he knew." She glanced over my shoulder at him. "That's the one I was talking about. The Lord of Chaos. What's he doing here?"

When I turned to look at him again, he slid his glacial gaze toward me. He arched an eyebrow and lifted his whiskey glass like a toast.

Drawn to him like a moth to a flame, I found myself walking closer to him again.

As I did, a mocking smile curled his lips "Didn't think I'd be seeing you again after all these years."

I cleared my throat. "You must have me mistaken for someone else."

The cold smile he gave me dripped with venom. "Oh, I don't think so, love. I'd know your face anywhere. It's haunted my nightmares for a long time."

The ground seemed unsteady beneath my feet. "I've never seen you before in my life." I tried to steady my voice, but it came out shaky. "Pretty sure I would have remembered a six-foot-five, silver-haired demon."

"Don't stop dancing on my account." He glanced away from me again, dark magic coiling around him. "Why let your horrific past get in the way of your fun?"

For a moment, I wondered if this had something to do with Mom's murder. After all, a demon had wanted her dead. Had he confused me with her? But I quickly dismissed the thought. I didn't look enough like Mom for anyone to mistake us. We had the same pale skin, heart-shaped face, and arched eyebrows, but my eyes were deep brown, while hers had been blue. I had higher cheekbones, a wider smile. Mom's hair had been blonde, but mine was a shocking red with a few blonde strands.

And most importantly, I was sure Mom didn't have a horrific past.

My breath shallowed. The room felt too hot, stifling. I turned to Shai, desperate to leave. "I'm going to go out and get some fresh air. Maybe we can find another bar."

"I'll settle the tab," she said.

"Thank you."

Unnerved, I hurried to the door. When I pushed through to the street outside, my skin started to cool under a light rain. Cirque de la Mer was on a narrow, cobbled street in the old sailor district by the harbor. Across the street stood a brewery, which might make a better option for tonight. They served hot dogs, and for whatever reason, I didn't imagine demons went to places that served hot dogs.

I hugged myself as I shivered. Somehow, I'd made an enemy of a terrifying demon duke, and I had no idea how. One thing Mom taught me before she died was that everyone had a weakness. The Lord of Chaos's weakness —I'd guess—was the woman he'd mistaken me for. The woman who haunted his nightmares.

I took a deep, calming breath. Out here, the salty breeze skimmed over my skin, the scent of the Atlantic heavy in the air. I licked my lips, tasting salt.

Here was the thing: I used to think my mom was deeply paranoid with the way she talked about defending yourself and finding weaknesses. She was a social worker who helped people with traumatic histories. And I had to wonder if she'd had one of her own, because she relentlessly pushed me to take self-defense classes, to learn martial arts. She was obsessed with fighting, convinced that enemies were after us. She was sure that one day, a demon would come calling.

I did everything she wanted me to do. I took every martial arts class in Osborn, and I practiced with her on the weekends. She taught me to search out other people's weaknesses in a fight, to exploit them, to fight back. I always thought she was training me for a war that didn't exist, but the night she died, I learned the war was real. I just had no idea why she'd been killed.

As I stared at the glass doors of the brewery, three frat boys stumbled out, already drunk, wearing their Alpha Kappa shirts. I slunk back into the shadows, hoping to go unnoticed.

A slender blonde hurried out behind them, her shoulders tense. She was staggering, clearly drunk. But she looked freaked out, too. I had the sense she was trying to get away from someone.

When the door slammed open again and Jack prowled out after her, I had my answer. I wasn't the only one he terrorized.

His eyes were locked on the girl, and my heart sped up.

"Jen!" he slurred. "Where you going? Jen! Stop being a fucking bitch! You should feel lucky I paid attention to you. You should feel lucky...I'm the best quarterback

Osborne State ever had. I have business plans you can't even imagine, Jen. I'm gonna be a billionaire. A trillionaire! I'm gonna be on TV."

I had no idea what he was talking about, but it was confirming the suspicions I already had about him. Narcissistic personality disorder: inflated sense of self-importance, preoccupation with power fantasies. A deeply insecure foundation badly covered up with pretenses of superiority and exaggerated achievements.

The blonde—Jen—stumbled over one of the cobblestones. That was when he lunged for her and grabbed her arm. She turned to face him, her eyes wide. "Let me go! You're being a dick, Jack."

"Jen!" he shouted in her face. "You were being a disgusting slut. You should be *grateful* I'm even talking to you." With that, he gripped her arm hard and started to drag her toward the alley beside the bar.

"Stop it!" she yelled.

He pulled her in close to his body and clamped his hand over her mouth.

Oh, fuck this. I'd seen enough. My fight-or-flight response had started to kick in, and adrenaline pumped hard through my veins.

CHAPTER 5

I rushed after them and shouted, "Get your hands off her, Jack!"

He whirled around, and the surprise on his face quickly turned into a leer. He wasn't giving up his grip on the blonde.

He grinned widely, moving closer to me with Jen in his arms. "Rowan, baby, are you stalking me? Were you hoping to get another chance with me? I told you, I don't want you to suck my dick. I'd get a disease."

He jerked her along with him as he staggered over to me.

"Let go of her," I said coldly.

He kept moving closer until I could feel his rancid breath on my face. He reeked of vomit, which told me he had probably just been kicked out of the brewery for puking. Classy.

The silver hammer on his shirt glinted under the streetlights.

"Let go of Jen," I said. "I don't want to have to hit you again."

A lie. I definitely wanted to hit him again, but I didn't want to get in trouble for it. I was honestly surprised he hadn't pressed charges already.

Jack, sadly, was too stupid to heed my warning, and he didn't release his victim.

Now, my heart was starting to speed up, and anger coursed through my blood.

Male voices echoed from the left, and I turned to see that his friends had come back to find him. I hoped one of them would intervene so I wouldn't have to get my hands dirty. Instead, one of them whooped at him, delighted. "Jack! You got two. Can we join the party?"

"I asked you once, nicely," I told Jack. "If I have to ask again, I'll hurt you."

"You know what your problem is? You're too uptight. I swear to God," he slurred, "you should never have turned me down. I could have fucked the bitchiness out of you."

At last, he dropped his grip on Jen, and she started to sprint away. But then he lunged for me. He grabbed me by the throat and pulled me close against him. His grip on my neck was crushing.

Mom was right. The world was a dangerous place, and we had to find our enemies' weaknesses.

Fortunately, Jack's wasn't hard to find. I brought my knee up hard into his groin. His eyes went wide, and when he hunched forward, I slammed my elbow into one of his kidneys. He let out a quiet moan and fell back.

I was shaking with the realization that I might have done serious damage.

"Whoa," one of his frat brothers shouted. "What the fuck is happening?"

Jack, now incapacitated, was on the ground. But his three brothers were rushing over, surrounding me.

"Holy shit, Jack," one of them yelled. "Is this the chick who punched you last night, too? The one you turned down?"

Someone shouted that they were calling the cops.

Unfortunately for me, if anyone was going to get arrested here tonight, it would probably be me—the crazy woman who'd beaten the crap out of a congressman's son. The one who'd had an outburst in class. The one who already had a questionable file at the Osborne Police Department.

Where the hell was Shai?

I clutched my phone, hesitating, until one of the frat boys smacked it out of my hands. He grinned at me. "Oopsie!"

"Dude!" one of them shouted, though I wasn't sure who he was shouting at, or if he even knew.

All of them were wasted, which made them more dangerous. I wasn't scared, though. Just angry.

Jack pushed himself up on his elbows, grimacing. "You can't keep attacking me just because I won't let you suck my dick. It's kind of funny how pathetic it is, though."

Lying sack of shit.

One of his brothers wrapped his arm around my shoulders. "Come with us, Ginger. If you're that desperate, I can find something for your mouth to do."

I slammed my elbow into his ribs, but another guy was already grabbing for my arm. My panic surged as I realized how badly I was outnumbered. Frantic, I was ready to land another punch when something in the air seared my skin.

Time seemed to freeze. In slow motion, a hot, dry wind rushed over me, toying with my hair. Slowly, the frat boys around me staggered back, eyes wide, and then the world returned to normal speed.

I gaped as the nearest of the brothers fell to his knees, blood dripping from his nose.

What the hell?

Looking around, I found that the four other frat boys had fallen, too. They moaned, gripping their skulls. Jack whimpered, and blood gushed from his nostrils onto the cobblestones. My stomach swooped.

Just as the frat boys started screaming in agony, I turned...and there, just as I'd expected, was the Lord of Chaos. He loomed over the dark street, and my heart skipped a beat.

The air felt warm, electrified. A high-pitched scream rent the air, and I turned back to see Jack's face contorted in pain.

Holy *shit*.

As much as I hated these guys, I didn't want to stand there and watch their heads explode. This was sadism, and the agonized noises they were making turned my blood to ice.

I whispered, "Stop." Then, louder, "*Stop*!"

The Lord of Chaos flicked his wrist, and his pale eyes slid to me. "What was that?" he asked in a mocking tone. "Do you want me to believe that you feel mercy?" The wisps of dark magic snapped back into his body. "That's a fun idea. I like to see you trying new things, no matter how absurd."

I looked away from him at the frat boys, who moaned as they began to pick themselves up. At least two of them were sobbing, blood still pouring from their noses. They started to stumble away—slowly, at first, then trying to run.

My body shook with the horror of whatever *that* had been.

When I looked back at the demon, I caught an amused glint in his eyes. "I thought you'd enjoy that."

"Thanks for helping?" I said. "I guess?"

His smile faded, and he moved closer to me with preternatural speed. Peering down at me, his piercing eyes sent a shiver through my body. "Oh, I don't think you want to thank me," he murmured. "Do you? I think you must know what exquisite punishment is in store for you now, love."

I could hardly breathe.

What the *fuck*?

I *had* to get away from him, but it was a mistake to turn your back and run from a predator. It was a mistake to act like prey. Right now, I was fighting an overpowering instinct to lower my eyes in submission. "You're going to have to tell me what you mean, because I have no idea what you're talking about."

His hot power thrummed over my damp skin, raising the hair on the back of my arm. "You must know why I'm here." He leaned down and whispered, "I'm here for revenge."

His scorching magic snaked around me, a slow brush

of hot power over my skin. He was freezing me in place, taking complete control over my body. All of my muscles froze.

"Stop it," I hissed.

But I could already feel his magic sliding inside my mind, and my vision began to dim. I was in his hands now.

CHAPTER 6

I woke in total darkness to the sound of dripping water, my back pressed against a cold stone floor. My dress had ridden up around my hips, exposing my legs, and my right thigh lay in freezing cold water. My teeth chattered.

Down here, the air smelled stale and mildewy, though not wildly different from the basement where I lived.

Shivering, I sat up straight, my mind whirling.

From what I'd gathered, the Lord of Chaos had kidnapped me, and he'd locked me in a basement. I hadn't expected an amazing birthday, but this certainly fell far below my worst expectations.

My heart thundered in my chest. I shot to my feet, searching for my phone. Only then did I remember that one of the frat boys had smacked it out of my hands.

Swallowing hard, I wrapped my arms around myself. "Hello?"

My own voice echoed back to me. The only other noise was the sound of dripping water.

After a few minutes, I started feeling around in the darkness. My fingertips brushed over a slimy wall, moss, ivy, and then iron bars.

Okay, I wasn't in a basement. I was in a jail cell. Or a dungeon, perhaps.

"Hello?" I called again.

As I stared into the darkness, flames burst to life in the torches on a stone wall across from me, making me jump. But since no one was around, I could only imagine that magic had lit the torches. Now, warm light wavered over my cell, illuminating the iron bars that locked me in.

I surveyed the dim space. Vines grew over three of the walls around me, and across from my cell was a crude stone wall with the torches. That was about it.

As my heart raced, I crossed to the bars and gripped them, waiting. Down here, it was cold enough that my breath clouded before my face.

A few moments later, I heard the sound of footfalls.

Then the Lord of Chaos arrived before my cell, his perfect features gilded in the torchlight. It was too bad he was a demon and an unrelenting asshole because he was heartbreakingly beautiful. He stood with an eerie, demonic stillness that made goosebumps rise on my skin. The amygdala—the part of my brain that assessed a threat —instantly picked him out as *predator, not human*. My brain was telling me to get the fuck out of there, and it didn't seem to care that there were bars.

"There you are, love," he purred.

I stared at him, trying to remember how to form sentences. "Don't lock someone in a dungeon and then call them *love*."

He chuckled softly, taunting. "Sorry, is that bad manners?" His smile faded fast. "I guess I don't give a fuck, Mortana."

"Why am I here?"

"Because I loathe you more than any other living person, and I've always wanted to see you on the other side of these bars." His cruel gaze brushed slowly up and down my body. "It's fucking delicious. Especially seeing what a sad little life you've been living among the mortals. Oh, how the mighty have fallen."

I pointed at him. "You need to understand that everything you're saying is wrong."

He stepped closer, his eyes piercing in the gloom, and gripped the cell bars. "This night has been delightful. I never quite imagined it being this good." Despite the fact that he was threatening me at every opportunity, his voice felt like a soft, seductive caress. It brushed over my bare skin, sending a hot shiver through my body—a deeply confusing sensation. "This might be the greatest thrill I've ever experienced. Don't you remember what it was like when you used to come see me?"

Panic was stealing my breath. "I'm not the person you think I am. How can I make you see that?"

An ice-cold smile. "Oh? Have you had a change of heart in the past few centuries? Are you *nice* now?" His voice dripped with sarcasm. "Shall we have a bake sale to fund sports for underprivileged mortal children?"

"I'm not two centuries old. I'm *mortal*. Can't you tell the difference? I'm from Osborn. I went to Osborn High School. I was Lady Macbeth in one of the plays junior year, and I fell off the stage. Jared Halverson asked me to the prom as a joke, and I got dressed up in a black gown, and he never showed up." I blurted these last few tidbits of information in a desperate attempt to explain how utterly nonthreatening I was.

His smile only deepened, his beauty making my chest ache. "Well, this *is* a rather sad display. You're really going to play it this way? The night before your execution, Mortana, and you're going to pretend to be a mortal who's pathetic even among the other humans? This is fascinating."

I ignored the degree to which he was insulting me and focused on one word: *Mortana*. There, I had a name. I pointed at him. "Okay. Let's start here. Mortana. That's not me. My name is Rowan Morgenstern. If you'll check my wallet, you'll see my ID. I'm twenty-two years old. It's my birthday tonight. I gave a presentation about repressed memories today, and I fucked it right up. I live in a basement with spiders." It seemed I was unable to stop spewing irrelevant information.

What were the chances an ancient terrifying demon would accept a Massachusetts license as proof of identity? Not great, I thought.

My heart was racing out of control. "There's got to be some way that I can prove I'm not Mortana." Never before had I felt so desperate to be back in that spidery basement.

He gave a bitter laugh. "Here I was, hoping for remorse. I thought you might want to unburden yourself before your death. But I see I won't get that particular pleasure."

My mouth went dry. "Before my death?"

"You must remember the prison gallows," he said quietly. "I certainly do."

I shook my head, my heart thundering. "No. I don't!" I shouted. "Because for the last fucking time, I'm not Mortana!"

Shadowy magic spilled around him, then shifted in the air. "You've been out of the city gates long enough that you will die quickly. You will die like a mortal if I kill you tomorrow morning before your magic returns. It's not really the death you deserve, but it's the one you'll get. You can thank me tomorrow, love, for your mercifully quick death. Assuming you're not ready to thank me now."

And with that, he turned and strolled away, shadows coiling around him.

As I watched him leave through the cell bars, the torches flickered out, and darkness filled the prison again.

Forcing myself to take a deep breath, I tried to corral my racing thoughts into a plan. Screaming and begging would do no good. In the darkness, I searched out a dry part of the cell and slid down into one corner. And as I sat in the silence, I realized my first mistake. Dr. Omer would have called me on it right away. You can't just *tell* someone they're wrong—they'll just argue back. You have to gently guide them to the conclusion themselves so it seems like their idea.

I dropped my face into my hands, my chest tight.

On the cold cell floor, a sense of loneliness hollowed me out. Was I really going to die in this place? Buried with all my secrets? There were so many things I'd never told anyone. Things that were too dark, too scary.

I hadn't told anyone that the night mom died, I'd been covered in ashes. My senior year of high school, the police had found Mom's charred body in the Osborne Forest. They'd found me by the side of the road half a mile away, shaking and covered in soot. When I talked about her murder, I could always sense the change in the air. I could feel muscles tensing, breath sucking in. No one wanted the absolute horror of having to hear more about a mother incinerated in a forest. People looked at me differently after learning about what had happened, as if the tragedy had cursed me. And it had.

I didn't tell anyone how I'd been nearly catatonic, with confused memories of the night. I hadn't told Shai that when the police had interviewed me, I'd been incoherent, and that I'd been a suspect for a while. All I could remember was that Mom had injured her ankle. She'd told me to run, fast, to get help. I'd known we were in danger, and I'd started to take off in the dark woods. But then I'd heard it—the inhuman sound like a growl. The smell of flesh burning, and her screams. That's when my memories became muddled, but I remembered a five-pointed star burning bright in the darkness.

The only thing still clear to me from that point on was the bone-deep terror.

After the police interviewed me, they came to the conclusion that I was delusional, possibly on drugs. Demons hadn't killed mortals in centuries. It wasn't even possible, they were certain. *Have you lost your mind, Rowan?*

Eventually, they'd come up with a half-baked theory

that the murder was probably drug-related. But that wasn't Mom. She never did drugs.

At school, the rumors had gone wild. People who didn't know a thing about Mom had said she was a prostitute, a drug addict. Some had said I'd killed her in a fit of rage—that I'd poured gasoline on her and lit a match.

When I found the real killer, I'd know what actually happened.

"Fuck," I muttered. Then, louder. "I am not Mortana!"

A sigh sounded from the next cell. Was someone there?

"Hello?" I tried again, this time more quietly. I felt oddly relieved to have company. "I didn't know anyone else was here."

The only response was another sigh. *Definitely* someone there.

Hugging myself, I swallowed hard. "I'm not supposed to be here. I know, right, everyone probably says that, but I'm mortal. I don't think demons are supposed to imprison mortals. Don't suppose you know how to get out of here?"

No response.

"I guess you wouldn't be here if you did. Have you ever heard of someone named Mortana?"

Water dripped into the puddle next to me.

I dropped my head into my hands, my body still buzzing with panic. "I'm not her. I'm not a demon, and I'm not two centuries old."

Somehow, my new prison friend's silence only made me want to tell him more. Because the Lord of Chaos was right. I *did* want to unburden myself, but not because of guilt. My secrets were weighing me down, stealing my breath, and I wanted to be free of them.

"Let me tell you something, prison mate," I started. "I'm twenty-two. And I can't die tomorrow. In fact, I *refuse* to die tomorrow. Do you want to know why? I've never even been in love. I had one boyfriend my freshman year of college. He was into comics and played the piano, and he was tall and cute. But he always told me I needed to exercise more, and I started to resent him, and when we finally had sex, it was...so boring. I remember reading the spines of the books on his shelves, waiting for it to end. I remember a mosquito biting my butt cheek. Then he broke up with me for a girl from his town, and that was at. That was my only relationship."

My mind was racing. I'd never actually told anyone this before, and it felt good to get it out. And I didn't actually give a fuck what this stranger thought, so he was the perfect person to unburden myself with.

This was *freeing.*

"I think we need to talk about Jack," I went on. "You're a good listener, you know that?"

I launched into a diatribe about Jack in high school, the "Home Run Rowan" nickname, how Jared Halverson had posted my confused texts on social media the night he stood me up. Then I rambled about every indiscretion, every embarrassing thing or terrible thing I'd ever done. The time I'd written a friend a bitchy email about my math teacher's sweat stains and accidentally sent it to him. My weird snack of microwaved tortillas with sugar and butter. The time I'd thrown up repeatedly in a trash can in Harvard Square Station after too much tequila. The cab driver with mutton chops I tried to hit on in Cambridge. How I'd peed outside a Dunkin' Donuts because they wouldn't let me use the bathroom. How I'd never actually had an orgasm, and I wasn't convinced they were real—the idea seemed like an elaborate hoax. I explained how I'd given up on men and started wearing granny panties from Rite Aid because what difference did it make?

For at least an hour, I unleashed every embarrassing or selfish thing I'd ever thought or done.

"...and can you explain to me why the *one* guy who seemed like he would actually be able to sexually satisfy me is also a demon, and also he kidnapped me and threw me in a prison? That's how I know there's no God. It's too cruel. The sexiest person I've ever seen, the guy who'd make me want to wear lace underwear instead of the pharmacy stuff—he's the Hannibal fucking Lecter of the supernatural world. Are you *kidding* me?"

Silence filled the cells, and I realized my eyes were growing heavy.

A man's voice came from the next cell, hardly a whisper: "Are you done?"

I sighed, only now realizing that I'd pretty much run out of material. "Yeah, I think that covers my life pretty much," I said, and dropped my head into my hands, exhausted.

But there was only one thing I didn't cover—my mom's death at the hands of a demon with the mark of a star. Because I was still determined to find my way out of this. And I wasn't ruling anyone out. Not the Lord of Chaos, and not my quiet prison friend.

Any demon could be guilty.

As I sat on the cold floor, I was sure of three things.

One, I was going to find a way out of here.

Two, I'd find a way to stay in the City of Thorns.

And three, I would get revenge on the demon who killed my mom.

CHAPTER 7

I usually couldn't sleep when I was anxious about something. And lying in a demon prison the night before I was supposed to be executed *should* have made me anxious.

But strangely enough, I closed my eyes with a sense of peace.

Maybe it was the certainty that I could fix this. Or maybe it was the freedom I felt after finally unleashing my secrets on the demon next door. Whatever the case, I woke up with my head resting on my arms. I stank of sweat and mildew, and I desperately had to pee. But I'd slept.

A few flecks of light streamed in through cracks near the ceiling.

I sat up straight, hugging myself. "Are you still there?" I asked.

Silence greeted me.

Apart from the little sunlight, it was still dark as night in there. I hugged my knees close to my chest, teeth chattering. As I surveyed the dark cell around me, my eye fell on a point on one of the walls, just between the vines. A thin stream of light illuminated a carving in the stone, tucked behind the leaves.

I scooted over and started tugging at the ropes of plants, but it was still hard to read with the darkness. Instead, I traced the letters with my fingers, feeling their contours.

L...U...C...I...F...E...R...

Shuddering, I kept going. It took me a minute because the carvings seemed old and faded, but eventually, I had a phrase mapped out in my head.

Lucifer urbem spinarum libarab...

The rest of it had faded. But if my high school Latin translation was correct, it said something like *Lucifer will set the City of Thorns free.*

Interesting. But not helpful for my release, was it?

I shifted away from the wall and hugged my knees again.

In the silence, I could concentrate on my game plan for getting out of this situation. It hinged on being able to convince the Lord of Chaos that I was not who he thought I was. All I had to do was sow doubt in his mind. Once I bought myself some time, if I could stall this execution, I'd work on making him realize I wasn't Mortana. Whatever his deal was, I was sure that he didn't want to start a war by killing a mortal. Our two species had managed to keep the peace for hundreds of years.

When I heard the footfalls echoing through the prison cells, my body became alert, and my pulse raced. I shot to my feet, ready to convince him. As the visitor moved closer, the torches sprang to life again, and warm light danced over the stone wall across from me.

The Lord of Chaos crossed slowly before my cell, eyes ice blue. He was wearing a white button-down shirt with the sleeves rolled up to his elbows, exposing a disturbing tattoo of a snake formed into a noose.

The warm power radiating off him made my breath quicken. I'd never before been this close to a demon, and everything about him was unnerving. He looked similar to a human, but too tall, too perfect, and too eerily still.

And now it was time for me to present my case.

"I don't suppose I get a trial?" I asked.

He shook his head slowly.

"You mentioned she hadn't aged in two hundred years," I began. "How long has it been since you've actually seen Mortana?"

Curiosity sparked in his eyes, "Is this your defense?"

Lead him to the conclusion. The problem was that this was hard to do when he was hardly saying anything. I needed to use *his* own words. "You're certain that you want revenge by killing Mortana? And that your memory couldn't be wrong after all that time?"

He just stared at me for a moment with that unnerving stillness. I wasn't sure this was going well.

Then he replied, "When I say you look like her, I mean you look *exactly* like her. My memory isn't faulty. I haven't forgotten a single contour of her face. I do not forget things," he said in a clipped tone.

My heart started pounding, but with hope. He was now referring to her as a separate person. "You haven't forgotten a contour of *her* face. Did you notice how you spoke about her in the third person?"

Without another word, he pulled a key from his pocket and unlocked my cell. Looming over me, with magic that brushed over my skin, he stepped inside.

I found myself moving away, cold dread skittering up my spine. In the days before mortals had weapons to fight back, we were simply the demons' prey. When they weren't seducing mortals, they'd drink our blood. Tens of thousands of years of evolution were telling me to get the fuck away from him.

A million terrible thoughts flitted through my mind, and I stood with my back pressed against the wall. "The Osborne police are very good," I lied. "If you killed me, they'd find out."

He cocked his head and spoke in a velvety murmur. "Oh, I doubt that very much."

CHAPTER 8

My breath caught in my throat. "Do you still think I'm Mortana?"

He studied me so intensely that I felt he was seeing right into my very soul. "I listened to everything you said last night."

I stared at him. God, what had I said to him? "That was you in the next cell?"

"You've managed to plant a seed of doubt in my mind. Mortana had far too much dignity to engage in a charade like that. The prom situation. Crying alone in your basement apartment at night. The fear of ladybugs. Having a lucky pen that you hold to feel a sense of security."

"I'd like my pen back, please," I whispered.

"Practicing karaoke songs alone in your room even though no one has ever invited you out. I don't think I ever understood the desire some mortals have to end their lives until I listened to the details of yours last night."

I narrowed my eyes. "Look, I might be a bit of a weirdo, but I've never wanted to end my life."

"Not you. I mean me. I have seen darkness that you couldn't imagine, horrors that would twist your soul. And yet, never before in my several hundred years of existence have I been so ready to shuffle off this mortal coil as I was listening to your sad monologue." He pressed a finger to his lips. "I think it was the bit about the yogurt pouches you keep in your purse because you have no one to eat lunch with. Even though they're meant to be consumed by infants."

This was just insulting. "At least I don't kidnap people like some kind of Buffalo Bill psychopath. Call me crazy, but I'd say that's a worse flaw than purse yogurt. And by the way, they have probiotics, so my microbiome is fucking pristine."

He stared at me, shadows thickening around him.

"My point is, you're not perfect, either," I added. "And you're weirdly obsessed with Mortana."

A ruthless look slid through his eyes. "I never said I was perfect. Frankly, I'm an absolute arsehole with an unhealthy revenge obsession. I'm not *depressing,* though, and I have never made my shirt into a bowl for dry cereal to eat alone on a Saturday night."

Revenge. I'd managed to keep him talking, and he'd brought me back again to what he wanted. This was what I could use. And as it would happen, an unhealthy obsession with revenge was something I understood very well. It seemed this demon *arsehole* and I had something in common.

Dr. Omer's teaching played in my mind. *Build rapport by reflecting back your client's words to him.*

"Okay, so you have a seed of doubt," I started. What would Dr. Omer say? "Let's explore that."

He shook his head slowly. "I admit you *might* not be a demon. You do look exactly like her, though, which is perplexing."

"Maybe she's a distant ancestor."

He shook his head. "Demons rarely procreate. And when we do, we only sire other demons. You can't be a mortal and a descendant of Mortana."

I bit my lip. "Coincidence?"

He considered the notion. "Every now and then, a demon has a mortal doppelgänger. It's rare but possible."

I sighed, relief unclenching my chest. "Good. Yes. That must be it."

"But to prove it, I require two pieces of evidence."

A little spark of hope. "Whatever you need."

His gaze swept down my body. "To start, Mortana had a small scar on her upper thigh. I will need to see your legs."

"You want me to lift up my dress?"

"Yes."

"Fine."

But at that point, I remembered exactly what I'd told him last night—about how he was the only man I'd ever seen who'd make me want to wear lace underwear. How he was the only one I thought could ever give me an orgasm. Mortified, I felt heat creeping over my cheeks.

"Go on," he said softly.

My nostrils flared, and I glared at him as I lifted up the hem of my dress to a point just below my underwear.

The Lord of Chaos cocked his head, staring at my thighs as the cold dungeon air raised goosebumps on my skin. He looked riveted, his eyes growing brighter. Then he moved closer, and he reached down to lift my right leg from under the knee, pulling it up outside his thigh like we were engaged in some kind of dungeon tango. He was just inches from my hips now, examining my skin. With his free hand, he traced his fingertip over the very top of my thigh, and shivers of heat rippled through me.

Holy *hell*, that was distracting. The magical pulse coming off him was seductive, intoxicating. Warmth radiated over my skin from the point of contact. I'd never seen anyone so fascinated with a little bit of skin, nor had I ever realized that a single touch could be so powerful.

"See?" My voice came out in a whisper. "No scar."

He dropped my thigh. When he stepped back, I felt cold again.

He frowned. "Interesting."

I exhaled. "And what's the other thing?"

He curled his lips and bared two sharp, white fangs, then licked one.

I shivered. "What?"

"Mortal blood tastes different than demon blood."

Primal fear slid through my bones. "You want to drink my blood? Like the old days?"

"All I need is a little taste."

My heart pounded hard. "You realize this seems terrifying. Is there not a more clinical way to do this? A syringe, maybe?"

"I don't have a syringe. But you might find it's not as

terrible as you imagine. Mortal women once flocked to offer their necks to demon males," he murmured. "They loved it."

"Sure, they did."

He gave a slow, infuriating shrug. "I have told you that I'm an arsehole, right? So I don't really care if I imprison an innocent person, and frankly, I don't think your life here would be much worse than your life in the Osborne basement. I'll feel no guilt about leaving you locked up here. So you can let me bite your neck, or you can stay here in the dungeon forever. Those are your options."

Maybe it was time to start bargaining. "Okay. I'll let you taste my blood. But when you're done, I'm not going back to Osborne. I want to stay in the City of Thorns."

He frowned. "You can't. If you *are* mortal, then you don't belong here. The only mortals who can stay are students and servants who inherited the role."

I folded my arms. "I'm sure someone called the Lord of *Chaos* can find a way to bend the rules."

He flashed me a crooked smile. "What is it, exactly, that makes you think you have leverage to make any sort of demands?"

I knew his weakness now—a lust for revenge. Something I understood implicitly. And the thing about a sense of vengeance as burning as his was that it could spread like wildfire. You didn't just want to end the life of one person—you wanted to kill anyone who helped them, anyone who let it happen. You wanted scorched earth.

"You want revenge, yes?" I asked. "You said Mortana haunts your nightmares. That's a pretty intense loathing.

So is she the only one, or is there someone else you want dead?"

His eyes were glowing brighter, and I had the sense he understood where I was going with this. "She didn't work alone."

I took a step closer, tilting my head back to look up at him. "So I could pretend to be her. Get information from these other people you hate. I could be your spy."

His body had gone as still as the stones around us, sending a chill dancing up my nape. At last, he said, "Assuming this isn't all an act, I don't think you'd make a convincing succubus. You're not seductive."

I winced. *Ouch.* "Anything can be learned. Even how to be seductive like a succubus." Whatever that was.

He looked transfixed with me. "I will consider it once I've tasted your blood. I need to know for sure that you're mortal before we continue any further."

I opened up my arms. "Okay. Go ahead. *Bite me.*"

Instantly, his warm magic slid around me like a forbidden caress, heating my blood. He had me completely pinned with his piercing gaze, and I felt my nipples going hard under my dress. To my shock, I found that he was right. I *wanted* him to bite me. I wanted him to grab me, shove me against the wall, and clamp his teeth into my throat. In fact—bizarrely—I wanted him to do all kinds of filthy things to me.

He stared into my eyes, and dominance emanated from him. His seductive scent wrapped around me, earthy like burning cedar. There was something more powerful than fear snaking around my ribs: the instinct to submit.

This instinct, forged by thousands of years of evolution, was telling me to give in to him if I wanted to live.

He reached for my waist and pulled me closer. The next thing I knew, I was pressed against his body, his muscles as unyielding as the stone walls around us. Then awe slid over me as I watched his pale eyes go dark. He moved so smoothly that I'd nearly missed that he was pressing me against the wall. I felt the cold stone against my spine, chilling my skin through my dress. His knee slid between my legs.

It was hard to ignore how dangerous he was, how otherworldly. How he could end my life in a single heartbeat and move on to his next victim.

"Arch your neck," he said in velvety voice.

I couldn't resist the urge to submit to his command. My eyes closed, and I tilted my head to give him access, making myself vulnerable to him. I felt his breath warming my throat, and a pounding heat swept through my body. My breath sped up, and my nipples felt exquisitely sensitive under my dress. I didn't want to feel turned on by my supremely arrogant demonic abductor, and yet, here we were. The heart wants what it wants.

When I felt the brush of his canines over my throat, my breath hitched. Liquid desire slid between my thighs. I didn't tell my arms to wrap around his neck, but they did anyway, welcoming him to my body. He felt as solid as the wall behind me. My pulse pounded, and I waited for the sharp sting of his teeth puncturing my skin. Instead, what I felt was a warm kiss.

Oh, *God*, that felt good.

A pulsing, sensual heat was spreading from the place

where his mouth met my throat, and his tongue swirled over my neck. Then a sharp stab of pain curled my toes, made my heart slam against my ribs. His fingers tightened on my waist as his fangs sank into me, claiming me. Pleasure washed over the pain until all I could feel was the sexual ache building in me.

This was supremely fucked up.

I only tilted my head back more, giving him more access. I was tightly coiled with desire now, and I fought the urge to pull up the hem of my dress again. But I *needed* release, and he was the only one who could give it to me.

After a moment, he pulled his canines from my throat, and I started to fall against his chest, arms still wrapped around his neck. I'd never wanted someone so badly in my life. Clearly, my body had terrible taste in men. Really, just the *worst* possible taste. He was arrogant, insulting, a self-professed asshole who'd locked me in a literal dungeon. Oh, and he was a centuries-old blood-drinking demon.

"There," he whispered, brushing a hand down the back of my hair. "Mortal."

I leaned against the hard, muscled wall of his chest, and when I looked up at him, I saw that he looked nearly as dazed as I felt.

"That was horrible," I lied. "I hated it."

He leaned down and whispered, "I don't believe you. But I suppose I am sorry about the abduction."

I glanced down at the powerful arm wrapped around my waist, at the eerie snake tattoo. Then I pushed him away. "Okay. Let's discuss how I'll stay in the City of Thorns as your spy."

"Is that what we're doing? Because I detest mortals nearly as much as I hate Mortana." He tilted his head. "But you do taste fucking delicious, so that softens the hatred a bit."

I touched my neck, surprised to find that the two puncture wounds were already healing. There was hardly any blood at all.

"But you're tempted by my plan, aren't you?" I smiled at him. "Because you're the Lord of Chaos, and you know that a mortal twin of a succubus can turn this city upside down."

"And why do you want to stay here so desperately?"

I shrugged. "You summarized it yourself. My life is desperately sad. The yogurt pouches, the T-shirt cereal bowl. It fucking sucks, even for a mortal, and I can't go back."

"Here's what you have to understand. There is, in fact, one circumstance in which demons are allowed to kill mortals. In which we can drain your blood with impunity or throw you into a fire pit. And that is if you enter the City of Thorns without permission, or under false pretenses. If the king or his soldiers determine that you're actually mortal, then you will die, and probably in an excruciating way. So are you actually sure about this?"

Not at all. "Yes."

He arched an eyebrow. "And once I fill you in on the secrets of the City of Thorns, once I tell you what I want, there will be no going back. I'm not letting you leave this city freely with my secrets, to wander around telling people what you heard. I'd have to kill you first."

I bit my lip. "Are you saying I can never leave?"

"You can't leave until you've helped me achieve my mission."

"Which is?"

He shook his head slowly. "I can't tell you that yet, can I? You're either in or out. And you need to make your choice now. If I take you up to my apartment to divulge my plans, you will have crossed a threshold that you cannot return from until the mission is complete."

Fear skittered up the back of my neck. But I already knew it was too late, that there was no going back. Because I was so close to having answers now. I needed to know what happened to Mom, and I wasn't going to get another chance after this.

Now or never.

And the truth was, it wasn't just that I wanted vengeance. I also wanted to get rid of the cloud of suspicion that hung over me at all times, that maybe I'd been involved.

With a tight chest, I nodded. "I'm willing to take risks. But since what I'll be doing for you is dangerous, I'm going to need you to pay off my undergrad student loans. And I'd like to transfer to Belial University."

He shrugged. "I can easily pay your loans. I can buy you a mortal degree if you want. But you cannot be at the university because *Mortana* would not be at the university."

My eyebrows shot up. "You can't just *buy* a degree."

He looked at me like I was mad. "Of course you can. You can buy anything."

I nodded, realizing he was probably right. My stomach twisted in knots as I realized I was about to undertake something extremely dangerous. "Okay. Whatever the dangers are, I'm in. Let's do this." I clapped my hands together. "And now I'm going to need you to show me where the bathroom is before your opinion of my dignity falls even further."

CHAPTER 9

Blindfolded, I walked through what I thought was a series of tunnels. The Lord of Chaos held my hands to guide me, and it kind of felt like we were on the most fucked-up date in history.

After a minute of walking, I whispered, "What's your actual name?"

"Orion," he said quietly.

I found the sound of his name dark and intoxicating.

And as we walked in silence, I could only feel a wild exhilaration that I was actually getting what I wanted. Forget saving money. Forget breaking in.

Now, I would get to stay in the City of Thorns.

After a few minutes of walking in the cool air, we reached a set of stairs. With his hand in mine, Orion led me up the stairs until I heard the creaking of a door.

When he pulled the blindfold off, I found myself standing in what looked like a heavily columned Mediterranean palace. Everything seemed to be made of pale, golden marble. A splash of blood-red poppies bloomed in an ivory vase by one of the open windows. When I glanced at the ceiling, I found it painted blue and dotted with stars that glowed with magical light. On two sides of the room, glass windows overlooked a sea that glittered like blue topaz. This place looked nothing like the grim Atlantic. This place was *paradise*.

On a third side, the wall was open to the air, and a covered balcony overlooked the sea. There, an overhang shaded a bed with a white duvet. On the other side of the seaside balcony, a table was had been set up with two chairs. A warm, salty breeze filtered into the room.

Holy shit, his life was amazing.

I managed to close my gaping mouth, and I turned to Orion to find that he was on his cell phone. "Morgan? Please bring breakfast and coffee for two." He hung up, then gestured to the balcony. "Let's discuss my proposal out here."

Before I followed him into the buttery morning light, I lingered for a moment to survey the rest of the room—the books lining the walls, the cream-colored sofas. Would I get to stay here?

A warm breeze rushed into the room, and I followed him onto the balcony. Out here, the sun dazzled over the sea.

As I took my seat at the table, the door opened, and a man with a salt-and-pepper beard and a crisp white shirt entered. He looked like he might be about fifty, in excellent shape, and sporting perfectly applied eyeliner.

Orion smiled. "Morgan."

"Orion, darling! You're up early, aren't you?" He spoke with a lilting Welsh accent.

I smiled at him as he slid a tray of fruit, yogurt, and coffee onto the balcony table. But before I could open my mouth, Orion introduced me. "I have Lady Mortana with me. Former advisor to King Nergal. She was living in the City of Serpents, and she has returned here after a long time away."

Morgan smiled at me. "Welcome, darling. I can see why you'd return to the most amazing city in the world. No mystery there." Morgan nudged a bowl of fruit in front of Orion. "You're not having the donuts today. You can't eat junk and look nice forever, even if you *are* an ancient and powerful demon."

Orion draped his arms over the back of his chair. "I like the donuts. They're the zenith of human civilization. Especially the ones with the raspberry jam in the center."

"That's not the bloody zenith of human civilization." Morgan looked at me, shaking his head. "Honestly, he can be so patronizing sometimes. There's plenty of other achievements to choose from. The Great Library of Alexandria comes to mind."

Orion plucked a strawberry. "And do you know what happened to the Great Library of Alexandria? A mortal mob burned it down, destroyed its contents, then flayed alive the scholar Hypatia because women who knew things were apparently witches. Yes, that's a great example of mortal civilization, I'd say."

If I spent enough time with Orion, I was worried I'd actually start hating mortals, too. He really did have a knack for making us sound terrible.

Morgan held up his digital watch. "Okay, forget the ancient world. We've grown better since then. We have

Apple watches now. I know exactly how many steps I walked today, and that I've stood up twelve times so far."

Orion let the silence drag, just staring at Morgan. *There* was the Dr. Omer technique in action.

Morgan looked increasingly uncomfortable and adjusted his shirt sleeves. "Look, I'm going to have to come in prepared with a better answer after doing a bit of research. The zenith of human civilization isn't something you can just come up with off the top of your head. There's a lot to choose from. A *lot*."

"While you're mulling that over, I have another favor to ask of you." Orion turned to look at me. "I'm sure our new king will want to see Lady Mortana soon, but obviously, she can't meet him dressed like a peasant."

I was wearing the best outfit I owned.

Morgan nodded at me with concern. "Dolce e Malvagia opens at ten. Gorgeous clothes. Do you want me to pick out some things and send them up?"

He nodded. "Select a bunch of dresses for Mortana to try on, bathrobes, pajamas, everything she might need. You can put it on my account."

"Right." He looked me up and down. "Lovely hourglass figure. Favorite color?"

I had no idea what Mortana's favorite color was. But if she'd been out of the city several hundred years, what were the chances anyone else would know? "Black." Seemed a safe answer for a demon.

Orion steepled his fingers, and he looked between the two of us. "Morgan, there's something else important I should tell you about Mortana. She is a succubus. You may warn the others."

I watched the color drained from Morgan's face. "A succubus?"

By his reaction, I gathered that this was a big deal. I smiled at him and shrugged, deciding it was probably best to say as little as possible at this point—particularly since I had no idea what was going on.

"The last remaining succubus," Orion added. "She will be taking up residence in the Asmodean Ward after she meets the king."

Morgan's gaze flitted nervously between the two of us. "Can she kill me?"

"She won't kill you," Orion said in a soothing tone. "It's against the rules, isn't it?"

Morgan still looked horrified. "But the whole Asmodean Ward is abandoned. I thought the Lilu were extinct. I was told they're very dangerous."

Orion lifted the coffee pot and poured two steaming cups. A lock of his silver hair fell before his eyes. "*Nearly* extinct."

He nodded and backed away, then hurried out of the room like a ghost was on his heels. The door slammed shut behind him.

I stared after him. "A mortal servant, I take it?"

"Yes, and he is under the mistaken impression that I care about his views on nutrition. But I do value his help." Orion sipped his coffee. "I must fill you in on a few things."

"Agreed. What's this about being the *last* succubus? What happened to the rest?"

He poured a bit of cream in the coffee. "The Lilu were hunted into extinction hundreds of years ago."

I scooped some berries into a bowl of yogurt. "Why?"

Every time his eyes met mine, I felt an unnerving jolt, like an electric pulse in my chest. I hoped that he had no idea what effect he had on me—he was arrogant enough as it was.

"The Lilu were killed for two reasons," he said. "You know about the war between the demons and the Puritans, yes?"

I nodded. "In the 1680s, yeah." It was how demons had ended up locked up in this city in the first place.

"As part of their surrendering terms," said Orion, "King Nergal agreed to kill the Lilu. The Puritans hated all demons, but they *really* loathed the Lilu. They feared being turned on by a demon more than anything." He stared out over the glittering sea. "And Nergal agreed because other demons hated the Lilu, too. The Lilu had a power that threatened the rest—the ability to compel others of their kind, to control their minds, to seduce them to do what they wanted. They're also the only demons with wings. They were simply too powerful."

I squinted in the sunlight. "And how did Mortana manage to survive?"

"By being cunning, calculating, and evil as sin. King Nergal was a dull, tedious man, and Mortana was the opposite. She was witty and captivating, and nearly everyone fell in love with her. Including the king. She made a deal with him—she would help him round up and slaughter all the Lilu, and she would get to live. He kept her in a room in the Tower of Baal, and she became known as the Seneschal."

I wondered what she'd done to Orion. "The king was in love with her, then."

"Yes. Like many others." He stared at me over his coffee cup. "I confess, I marvel at the poor judgment of all those human males who rejected your beauty. Demons have better taste."

CHAPTER 10

Was that a compliment? I could feel myself blushing now, but I had no idea how to respond.

"Mortana," he went on, "demanded that the king make a blood oath. She made him pledge that the crown would always keep her safe."

"What's a blood oath?" I asked.

"It's an oath sealed by mingling the blood of two people. If someone breaks a blood oath, it will result in an excruciating death based on the magic of a curse. The problem is, only the monarch made this oath. The rest of the demons in this city will probably still want to murder you for being a succubus."

I was losing my appetite for the berries and yogurt, and starting to feel like I was in slightly over my head. It seemed there were so many ways to die here in the City of Thorns. But I'd made my choice, and like Orion had said, there was no going back now. "How much danger will I be in?"

"It would be a lot more if you weren't with me. We will be spending a great deal of time together." A smile played over his sensual mouth, but it didn't reach his eyes. "I'll need to keep you closely guarded."

I swallowed hard. "Who is it that you want me to spy on?"

"King Cambriel."

Oh, good. I'd be spying on a murderous king. My stomach fluttered, but this had been, after all, my idea. "Cambriel cut off his dad's head and stuck it on a gate, right?" I paused with my spoon in midair. "You want me to get close to him?"

Steam from the coffee curled before Orion's face. "He will be looking for a wife. If the real Mortana were here, she'd be a strong candidate. She's the duchess of one of the wards. Some think she had a claim to the throne. I mean, she was mistress to his father. She's also widely rumored to have killed his mother, Queen Adele, centuries ago, but I'm not sure that he holds a grudge."

I stared at him. "Okay, slow down for a second. Mortana probably killed the king's mother, and I'm supposed to convince him to marry me?"

Orion shrugged. "It was never proven. Just rumors. They say Mortana hoped to take the queen's place, and one day, Queen Adele's body was found in a vat of wine with her heart cut out."

I frowned over my coffee. "Do you think Mortana did it?"

"Probably. That was her style. Queen Adele didn't drink alcohol, and that irritated Mortana, so the wine was a nice touch. Anyway, water under the bridge now, I'm sure. Charm the king, flirt, get him close to you. As long as I can teach you to act like Mortana, you'll have the chance to try to pry his secrets out of him."

My chest felt tight. "What, exactly, are you looking for?"

"I want you to find what makes him weak." Sunlight glinted in his pale eyes. "Because everyone has a weakness."

It was like he'd ripped the phrase from my own thoughts.

I raised my eyebrows. "Are you telling me you want to kill the king? I thought that only an heir can kill the king. So unless Cambriel has a child who wants him dead, he can't be killed, right?"

"Did your friend Shai tell you that?"

My throat tightened. I didn't want to get Shai involved in this. "What are you talking about?"

He looked out over the sparkling ocean. "I saw her with you in the bar, and I noted the Belial University insignia on her handbag. So while you were sleeping in the prison cell, I found her wandering around Osborn and interviewed her."

Oh, *shit*. I slammed a hand on the table and leaned forward. "You interrogated Shai?"

"Interviewed. I wanted her to tell me what she knew about you." He sipped his coffee. "And as for the king and his weakness—it's true that only an heir can kill the monarch, but the king can be imprisoned. There's more than one way to get revenge."

The coffee was starting to give me a little buzz. "Okay. You want to get rid of the king. And I take it this requires a high degree of secrecy so your head doesn't end up on his front gate alongside his dad's."

His icy gaze bored into me. "Precisely. A high degree of secrecy. You are the only one who knows what I plan to do." He leaned over the table. "And now you know why there is no going back. I cannot allow you to leave here until I've achieved my goal, and if this secret got out, it would be all over for me. Until I'm rid of the king, you are mine. And if you cross me and tell my plans to anyone else, I will murder your dear friend Shai."

Ice slid through my blood. Mentally, I tried to untangle the morality of this situation. I was going to help a demon imprison a king, but he wouldn't be able to *kill* him. And the king had murdered his own father...really, it could be argued that I was doing the right thing. My only deep regret at this point was that this situation put Shai's life in danger.

I finished my coffee. "I like to think of myself as being quite skilled at finding people's weaknesses."

"I believe that." He narrowed his eyes over his coffee, and I felt the air growing hotter around us. "You know, it's unnerving looking into the face of my worst enemy, even if you're only a doppelgänger. It's hard not to reach across the table, rip your heart out of your chest, and throw it into the sea."

Yikes. I'd definitely lost my appetite at this point. "Please try to resist the impulse."

"I'll do my best."

I bit my lip. "Are you going to tell me what she did to you?"

"I don't think that's necessary." For a moment, I caught

a glimpse of vulnerability in his pale eyes. "But I'll do anything to get revenge. I will kill whoever I have to in order to make this happen. I have no moral code, only a burning lust for vengeance. Do you understand?" His words made my heart skip a beat, and the air burned hotter.

Got it loud and clear. No moral code. He was a psychopath.

He rested his arms on the table. "If this is going to work, you'll need to know about demons and the City of Thorns. You'll need to know a bit about what Mortana was like when she lived here, but not what she did in the past two hundred years. We're forbidden from sharing information between demon cities. And if this plan is going to work, your friend Shai is a loose end. She could identify you."

I took a deep breath. He wasn't going to suggest killing her, was he? "I'm sure she'll agree to keep the secret."

"Not good enough, I'm afraid. I'll need a blood oath from her."

I poured myself another cup of coffee from the carafe. "That doesn't really seem fair to her, does it? You get information out of this. I get to live in the City of Thorns and thereby have a less pathetic life. What does Shai get for the risk she's taking with a blood oath?"

He shrugged slowly. "Anything can be bought. I'm sure she has a price."

"Do you just have unlimited money?" I asked.

"Pretty much."

"Can I have a new cell phone, then? Mine was knocked

out of my hands last night in the fight with the frat boys." I raised a finger. "Oh! And I'd like my lucky pen back."

A smile tugged at his lips. "I just told you I have unlimited money, and that's all you ask for?"

"I'd like my student loans paid off, like we talked about. And to get the undergrad degree. And while I'm at it, a hundred thousand dollars." Why not?

"Ah, that's more like it."

I stirred the cream into my coffee. "But will you need a blood oath from me?"

He shrugged. "I'll need a blood oath that you will keep my secret."

I blew out a long breath. "Okay."

"But just in case you don't value your own life sufficiently—and frankly, why would you? Given how sad your life—"

"Can you get to the point?"

He gave me a wicked half-smile. "Please consider Shai's life as well. I want you to do your best work for me."

I dropped my head into my hands, starting to get dizzy. "Do we really need to get Shai involved? I don't want to put her in danger."

He gave me that *you're an idiot* look again. "Then don't fuck anything up. It's really that simple."

I pulled my hands from my face. "And when this is over, Shai will be perfectly safe, right?"

"Yes, and you should try to learn the king's weakness as soon as possible. It's the best way for you to keep Shai safe, and to ensure that none of the demons slaughter you.

If you stay here too long, you'll make a mistake, and then you'll be found out and killed."

My chest tightened. There went my hope of staying in an apartment like this. But more importantly, if I couldn't stay here long, I'd be kissing goodbye to my hope of finding my mom's killer. I wasn't going to do that overnight.

I sighed. I'd have to find out as much as I could, I supposed. "I'll do my best."

He scrubbed a hand over his jaw. "You know, you might not want to stay in Osborne after you leave. It's too close to the City of Thorns, and you could also be in danger at that point."

My mind was whirling. "Well, there isn't really much keeping me there."

"Yes, I did get that impression."

I gave him a sharp look. "But how do I know you'll keep your end of the bargain with paying off my loans and degree?"

"I wouldn't expect you to take my word. You can call the loan servicing company today to confirm."

Holy *shit*. Of all the things that were happening, the most thrilling aspect of it was the idea of seventy-five thousand dollars of debt cleared in one fell swoop. No more monthly payments. No more interest. No more lifetime of debt.

Wild euphoria rushed through me, and I grinned. "I want to be there when you pay the FedLoan Servicing people. I want to listen in. I want to *hear* it all."

I realized I was gripping his arm, and I must have looked a little maniacal because he was staring at me like

I'd just announced my legs were made of ocelots. Obviously, Orion was deeply alienated from the mortal challenges of student loan interest, or he would have understood this elation immediately.

I released my grip on his arm, still unable to believe this was happening. "Before I get too excited, can I get an idea of what would happen if King Cambriel discovered I was a fraud?"

His eyebrows rose. "Well, let's just say it wouldn't be pleasant. It would be even worse than your life in Osborne, if you can imagine such a thing. Torture, a slow death in a fire, and your ashes thrown in the sea. Let's try to avoid that."

A shudder rippled up my spine. But after four years of dreaming of getting within these city gates, this was my chance to find out *something* about Mom's death.

Orion stood and pulled a dagger from a sheath. Eyes twinkling, he held out his hand for mine. I rose from the table and shoved my hand toward him, and as he gripped the knife, he looked into my eyes. "I need you to repeat after me. 'On pain of death, I swear a sacred blood oath to keep my mission a secret from other demons.'"

I inhaled deeply, then repeated the pledge verbatim. As soon as I finished the final word of the oath, Orion tightened his grip around my hand. He drew the blade across my palm, and the sharp sting of the cut made me wince. A line of red gleamed from my skin, and my blood dripped onto the table.

He then cut his own palm and pressed our hands together.

I wasn't sure if it was the sight of the blood or something about the magic of the oath, but as our hands clasped, my head swam. In my mind's eye, I saw a crystal-clear vision: stone walls, cracked to expose a bit of the stars. Then a shadow swinging over the stone—the bloodied, swaying feet of a hanged body. Wood creaked above, and a pain pierced my heart to the core.

Unnerved, I pulled my hand away again, and the vision cleared. I stared at Orion, my blood still dripping onto the table.

He frowned. "What?"

I shook my head. "Nothing. I just felt…pain."

He held out his hand again. "Let me heal you."

When I touched him again, I immediately felt his magic washing over my skin, a warm and pleasurable tingle.

But I hadn't been talking about the pain from the knife. I'd meant the absolutely heart-shattering sadness from the vision—the feet swinging over stone.

Had I somehow seen into Orion's mind? He had unfathomable darkness in him, I thought. But for now, he was my ally. And like Orion, I would do anything to get my revenge.

CHAPTER 11

Orion's bathtub was on a second balcony, one floor up, set into a golden marble floor. The ceiling was held up by columns, and the sun slanted in over my naked body.

It felt completely weird to be nude out here in the light. I could say with some certainty that sun's rays had never hit my nipples before. But when I looked out across the sea, I couldn't see a single person out swimming or surfing. It was just me, the gently bubbling bathwater, and the sun.

I loved it out here, but I couldn't stay too long. I'd guess that succubi never got sunburns, and I had about ten minutes before the jig was up on that front.

The plan for today was that I would get new clothes, and then Orion would teach me about Mortana and the City of Thorns.

I grabbed the soap from the side of the bath and ran it over my legs, clearing off the grime from that horrible prison cell. In some ways, I couldn't believe my luck.

What I thought was the worst night of my life was now turning out to be the answer to many of my problems—assuming I could do what Orion wanted and keep Shai alive. And myself.

Before I'd come upstairs to the bath, we'd called FedLoan Servicing together to pay off my loans. That had truly been one of the best moments of my life. I'd given my account information and PIN number, then handed the phone to Orion for him to provide his bank information. He'd passed the phone back to me so I could explain how much I was paying off—all of it. The guy on the other line had never taken a call like that, which had only delighted me more.

But now I could turn my full attention to the City of Thorns. So far, I hadn't seen what the city looked like, only the bright blue ocean. After so many years obsessing over this place, I would finally start to learn its secrets. As soon as we left the apartment, I was going to start collecting as much information as I could about every demon in the city, scouring the place for signs of someone with a five-pointed star on their forehead.

When I'd washed myself completely, I rose from the bath and grabbed a soft white towel off the rack. I dried myself off, then pulled on a black bathrobe. It was quite clearly not Orion's, as it was black silk with sheer lace sleeves and a slit up the thigh. In fact, the tag was still on it. It was *La Perla*—fifteen hundred dollars.

Holy *shit*. Morgan had expensive taste. I yanked the tag off as I adjusted the robe. The silk felt glorious against my bare skin, and I tied the belt around my waist.

I was so stunned by the luxury that I suddenly realized

I hadn't seen the robe arrive. My skin prickled with heat as I wondered if Orion had seen me bathing, and I swept through his guest room into the marble stairwell. When I crossed back into his living room, I found Shai there, bandaging her palm. She looked so refreshingly normal in overalls and braids, and it was a relief to see her.

Orion was simply staring at his own hand, watching as it healed before my eyes.

I grinned. "Shai!"

She beamed at me. "Guess what?"

Wrapped in the silky bathrobe, I dropped down into a cream-colored armchair. "Please tell you me bargained for something good, because he has nearly unlimited money."

"All my expenses at Belial are covered for as long as I want to learn, which might be for the rest of my life."

She *was* good at bargaining.

Orion met her gaze. "And you do understand that the blood oath means you will die a horrible death by magic if you talk to anyone about Rowan's real identity? I mean *anyone* besides us."

She wrinkled her nose. "Yeah. Got it. I won't let anyone know she's human or that I know her. And I honestly have no idea what all this is about, so I couldn't let any other secrets out, even if I wanted to."

"Best if you know as little as possible." His eyes gleamed. "For your own sake."

She gave me a tentative smile. "I have to run to my feline healing class. But text me if you can, okay? I want to know everything's fine with...whatever you're doing here."

"I'll be fine," I said with much more confidence than I felt.

As she hurried out the door, Orion leaned back on the sofa. He was a prick, but with the cut of his cashmere sweater, it was hard not to notice how gloriously strong his body looked.

"We have a week," he began, "to prepare you for your introduction to the king. Then you will take up residence in the Asmodean Ward."

I took a deep breath. "Just a week? Will I be ready?"

"The city is already abuzz with the news of the one remaining succubus. The king demanded an introduction this evening. I had to negotiate." He frowned. "But we'll have a lot of work to do if you plan to fool them."

When I crossed my legs, one bare thigh came into view from under my robe, and Orion's gaze slid to it. The feel of my thighs rubbing against each other was also my reminder that I still wasn't wearing underwear, which made me think about how Orion had perhaps seen me naked. And *that* reminded of the disturbingly pleasurable feel of Orion's mouth on my neck, and how my body had responded to him dominating me. With those thoughts roiling in my mind, my pulse raced. I tugged down the silky bathrobe over my thigh, hoping that he couldn't hear my pounding pulse.

He arched an eyebrow at me. "Why is your heart racing like you're about to die?"

Well, there went that hope.

I pulled the robe tight. "Did you see me naked in the bathtub?"

His body was so still that I could feel the hair raising

on my nape. Beautiful as he was, these eerie differences in body language marked him out as a predator. "Your heart races when you think of me seeing you naked?"

His implication was bang on, but I rolled my eyes anyway. "You don't need to phrase it like that. I was just annoyed, that's all. Do you know that being annoyed can make your heart race? It's the raised cortisol levels. Anger."

A reminder to yourself, Rowan: he is a different species with fangs, lethal magic, and eyes that turn black. Do not forget.

"Well, you needn't be annoyed," he said quietly. "Morgan dropped the bathrobe off for you, plus several bags of clothes in the guest room. I'm deeply aware of how uptight mortals are with their bodies. I was alive during the Puritan days. But as Morgan is not interested in females, I thought it was fine for him to enter the bathroom."

I resisted the temptation to argue that I wasn't uptight because, truth be told, I *was*. And I was especially uptight around Orion because he made me want to open my robe in front of him.

I frowned and tried to change the subject. "You were alive during the Puritan days? I thought you weren't from this region."

A wry smile. "There were Puritans in England, too. I knew one named Praisegod Barebones who led their parliament. In fact, when I first met you, your outfit reminded me of his clothing."

"Goth-Puritan is my look," I said defensively, still clutching the robe closed.

"You're looking very flushed."

I cleared my throat. "It's hot in here."

"Morgan will return soon with the rest of your new clothes. Mortana always dressed beautifully."

I was still holding my bathrobe together as if I'd burst into flame if he saw an extra inch of my skin. "Okay. I guess I need to start learning as much as I can about Mortana and this world."

"You will need to learn to appear less uptight, or you'll end up thrown into a fire. She is a *succubus*."

I raised my chin. "I'll do fine." I mean, I had to. "Will I get to see the city itself today?"

"As soon as you're dressed. But for now, I'll start with the background of the City of Thorns. What do you know?"

I closed my eyes, trying to remember my history lessons. "The city gates were erected after the Infernal War in the 1680s, when the Puritans and the demons tried to murder each other in the Massachusetts woods. I always thought the point of the gates was to keep the demons in, but apparently, you can leave."

A hot breeze flowed into the room from the open balcony windows. "King Nergal negotiated the terms when he lost the war. Demons can briefly leave the city, but our magic fades after a few days. We become vulnerable if we live outside the city. Weak, slow-moving, and dull. No better than mortals, really." There it was—a sharp little barb delivered in a velvety tone.

My lip curled. "Do you have to keep putting in the digs? It might get in the way of our professional relationship."

"You need to understand how we think. We view

ourselves as superior to mortals because—" He lifted a finger to his lips like he was thinking. "Oh, because we are. Demons are smarter, faster, and more graceful. For thousands of years, you worshipped us as gods. Sacrificed to us. Livestock, sometimes even your children. We're basically divine. Even the tedious American demons are superior to mortals."

I cocked my head. "And yet, here you all are, locked up behind city walls because you lost a war to us. Quite the conundrum."

The corner of his mouth twitched. "I'll admit that mortals have impressive military technology, which has made it harder to compete. They developed guns and learned magic they could use to bind us here. But mostly, there are simply more of you since you reproduce like mosquitos." He gave me a charming smile. "You infest the planet with your shrieking, yogurt-guzzling offspring, taking up more and more space every year and driving out all the other species like a plague of locusts."

I narrowed my eyes. "I'm fascinated that you all could lose a war to us so thoroughly, surrender so completely, and still convince yourselves of your superiority." I smiled back at him. "Have you heard the term 'cognitive dissonance'?"

"In a one-on-one fight without weapons, a demon would win every time. Do you have any idea how easy it would be for me to kill you?"

My smile faded. "Well, we have weapons now," I said sharply.

He arched an eyebrow, and he leaned closer. "Except you sense it, too. No mortal man has ever sexually satisfied you. Whenever I'm near you, you can feel my superiority to your men. You said I'm the only man you'd ever suspected was up to the task." His silky voice was like a sinful caress over my skin. Now, he'd moved close enough that his mouth was next to my ear. "And I do think you're right about that, Rowan."

A forbidden heat shivered through my body, and my thighs clenched under my bathrobe.

Oh, fuck.

As long as I was near Orion, I was in trouble.

CHAPTER 12

I couldn't tell if he was hitting on me or trying to get a rise out of me. But if he was flirting, it was with the utmost condescension, so I wasn't going to reciprocate. The man's sense of superiority burned hot enough to suck the oxygen out of the room.

"Do you know the mortal expression 'beer goggles'? I had that when I first saw you, except with mojitos." I wondered if he could tell when I was lying. "You do nothing for me. Now that I'm sober, I view you as a kind of grotesque alien species. Freakish, really."

He leaned back, then went very still again, staring at me, and I felt like he was using one of Dr. Omer's tricks—waiting for me to admit that I'd said something stupid. His face was a mask of indifference.

Well, he could wait all day, because I could live with my obvious lies. I raised my eyebrows. "Were you going to teach me about something beyond the staggering dimensions of your ego?"

He spread out his arms over the back of the sofa,

ignoring my jab. "Let's begin with the Lilu, the incubi and succubi. They are the lust demons, the seducers of our world. They feed off desire. Before demons were locked here in the City of Thorns, the Lilu would roam freely among the Puritan cities, seducing uptight mortals. They seduced demons, too. But for a mortal, sex with a Lilu means death. It was one of the major reasons for the war in the 1680s, the lusty Puritans dying of pleasure in their beds."

What a way to go. "So Mortana—wherever she is—would be trying to seduce mortals at any chance she got?"

He shook his head. "Mostly demons these days. We're no longer allowed to kill mortals without repercussions. She can draw power from demons just as easily without starting a war."

I still gripped my bathrobe like a chastity belt. "So I need to seem seductive."

"Flirtatious. Sensual. Seductive. Comfortable in your own body." He pinned me with his gaze. "Clearly, we will have to work on those things."

"When were the Lilu executed? After the war?"

He shook his head. "Not right away. For about ten years, they lived in the Asmodean Ward. Each ward worships a demonic god, and for the Lilu, it was Asmodeus, god of lust."

"Which ward are we in now?"

"Luciferian. He is the god of pride."

So Orion lived in the ward for the most arrogant demons. "Yeah, that checks out."

"In a densely populated city, it was harder for the other demons to tolerate the Lilu. They ruined marriages, manipulated people. Other demon females loathed the succubi, and demon males hated the incubi. Their mind control powers were forbidden, but they used them anyway. And that was a threat to King Nergal's rule over the populace. What if they controlled his mind? So in the 1690s, when Cotton Mather asked for sacrifices from the City of Thorns, King Nergal was happy to oblige. The other demons were happy to rid the city of the Lilu, and Nergal sacrificed them in the dungeons. They were hanged and their hearts cut out."

A shudder rippled over me. I'd just *been* in that dungeon, not realizing it was a place of unimaginable horror. "And Mortana was able to survive because of her blood oath."

"Exactly. She's always been impressively cunning. But she disappeared a few hundred years ago, and no one has seen her since."

I bit my lip. "Is it going to be a problem that I don't actually have any magic? I can't control anyone's mind."

He shook his head. "No, you'll just tell people you had a change of heart over the centuries. You won't do anything forbidden by King Cambriel. But the sexual magic...you'll need to make people think that you've been feeding off desire."

I closed my eyes and shook my head. "Sorry, exactly how do I do that?"

"That's simple, Rowan." His low, husky voice dripped with a seductive promise. "You and I will use our body language to make people think we're fucking." He quirked a smile. "Assuming you can feign attraction to a grotesque alien species."

I folded my arms in front of my chest. "I'll do my best to fake it, but if I'm supposed to be getting close to the king, won't it be a problem if he thinks I'm with you?"

He shook his head. "Not at all. Cambriel always wants what someone else has."

"I suppose that's why he killed his own father."

"He's from the Beelzebean Line. Envy. He already envies the attention I've received for killing so many in the Infernal Trial. And if you seem to want me, he'll use his position as king to take you. We'll just have to make it look real."

A hot electrical tension buzzed in the air. "So you'll be playing along with this charade, too. Pretending to want me."

He shrugged. "I'll do my best to fake it."

"Is there anyone here who knows Mortana well?"

A sly smile. "Everyone *hated* Mortana. They called her the king's whore. Her only ally was Nergal himself. I suspect she left here when he finally grew bored and refused to marry her, and she realized she no longer had a protector."

"Do you feel any empathy for her at all? Maybe she was just trying to survive while her kind was being slaughtered."

His brows knitted like I'd just said something insane. "No. I don't have empathy. And if I did, it certainly wouldn't be for Mortana."

"Right."

The door opened, and I turned to see Morgan striding into the room with bulging bags of clothes. He looked between the two of us nervously and dropped the loot.

"Everything you need is in here. I have to run, I'm afraid." He backed away, staring at me. "Please be careful with her, sir, would you? No offense, darling," he added, glancing at me, "but I don't want you twisting his mind all up."

No one had ever been scared of me before. Was it... was it bad that I liked it? He saw me as fearsome.

I dropped the grip on my bathrobe and glared at him, then flashed a smug smile—the kind Orion had been giving me since I'd met him. "I'll try to be gentle with him, Morgan, but I make no promises." My voice sounded icy, cruel.

His face paled, and he pointed at me as if to say, *I'm watching you*. With that, he backed out the door, then let it slam behind him.

I turned to see Orion staring at me, his eyes a pale, heavenly blue. "That was disturbingly convincing. It was like I was watching the real Mortana come to life before me."

The thing was, it was easy to act in the ways that were expected of you. When people thought I was crazy during my presentation, I became flustered and desperate—I started to act crazy. When I was treated like an outcast at Osborn High, I couldn't help acting weird.

And if people thought I was terrifying—maybe I could rise to the occasion.

But instead of explaining all that, I just shrugged and said, "I contain multitudes."

His gaze pierced me, and he waited for me to give a better explanation.

I sighed, and my mind started turning academic, as it often did when I was unnerved. "In the world of social psychology, there's something called a self-fulfilling prophecy, or a behavioral confirmation. It means that people's behavior changes depending on what's expected of them. A person's expectations actually elicit certain behaviors."

"Right..." He ran his finger over his lower lip, studying me. "You're a bit of a nerd, you know that?"

I nodded. "Oh, believe me, I'm aware."

"Does this mean that if I treat you as if you're seductive, you'll suddenly be able to act like a succubus?"

I swallowed hard. "Well, we can certainly try."

CHAPTER 13

I lay naked on the bed in Orion's guest room. While I was supposed to be practicing *not* being self-conscious, even alone, I felt deeply uncomfortable as the breeze rushed over my bare skin. The fact that it was dark outside and I was lying beneath a ceiling fixture that glowed like a spotlight wasn't helping my mood.

I'd be staying here for another week, in a guest room overlooking the sea. While the place was gorgeous, between a floor-to-ceiling window and the *missing* wall beside it—shielded from rain by a balcony, but still a nasty spot to trip—the room seemed to lack a certain degree of privacy. I didn't *see* anyone out in the ocean, but I still felt like I was naked in front of the world.

Plus, I couldn't help but wonder if Orion was thinking of me naked in here. We'd spent the day trying to work on my seduction skills—the walk, the flirt, the eyes that flicked down and up again, the dirty jokes.

I was shit at all of it. Problem was, Orion was hot as hell. If I let myself fall under his seductive spell, I'd burn up. When his fingers had brushed against mine at breakfast as we'd reached for the cream, I'd felt an indecent jolt of excitement. Unfortunately, I was a blusher, and as succubi did not *blush*, Orion had come to the conclusion that I was uptight and uncomfortable in my body. Hence, I was lying here, trying to get comfortable.

And it was true that I was uptight, but my unease was far worse around *him*. He was as dangerous as a forest fire.

When I closed my eyes, I could see his sensual, curved lips.

I glanced at the sea in the moonlight and pulled the blanket over myself, wondering if I could actually pose as a succubus.

With a deep breath, I surveyed the room, trying to ground myself. I needed to get out of my own head.

The decorations in here were simple—a white bed, a bare hardwood floor. The beauty of the place wasn't in the decor, but rather in the blue of the sea and sky, or the glittering of the stars. A warm, briny breeze rushed over the room. Feeling slightly less self-conscious with the beauty of nature all around me, I dropped the blanket and rose to my knees.

Except I could hear Orion's deep, seductive words playing in my mind. *You said I'm the only man you'd ever suspected was up to the task. And I do think you're right about that, Rowan.*

My eyes snapped open again, and I ran to the light

switch. Darkness fell, and I crawled into bed and pulled the covers over myself.

Maybe I couldn't lie around in the nude, but I could sleep naked.

* * *

"HOW DID YOU SLEEP?" Orion asked me over coffee.

He had a book spread out before him, and his eyes were on the pages.

I cleared my throat. I didn't want to tell him about the filthy dream I'd had in which he'd kept me as his prisoner, tied to his bed. "Fine. I slept fine."

His gaze darted up to meet mine. "Why did you say it like that?"

"Like what?"

A smile tugged at the corner of his lips. "Like you wanted to climb over the table and throttle me."

Damn it. He could see right through me. I could feel myself blushing, and I shook my head. "There's nothing wrong. I slept fine, just had some weird dreams."

"About what?"

You, kissing me all over. "Just, um, monsters. What are you reading?" I took a sip of my coffee.

Orion's eyes gleamed, and he lifted the book so I could see the cover.

Fifty Shades of Grey.

I choked and spat out my coffee, then wiped the back of my hand across my mouth as he snickered.

* * *

He sat across from me in his living room, arms folded. I was getting the impression that he was losing patience. "You meet the king tomorrow, and your body is still full of tension and nerves. Do you see how you grimace when you're nervous? How your neck muscles are tight and strained?"

I sighed, trying to focus on relaxing the muscles around my mouth. I took a deep breath. I couldn't help but wonder where Orion had spent the last two nights, and where he'd been at dinner.

"Let's see the Mortana walk you've been practicing," he said.

I rose from the chair.

It wasn't any of my business where he went when he wasn't here. But I'd been learning his patterns—a very early wakeup, as soon as dawn broke. Coffee, fruit in the mornings. Sometimes he dove off his balcony straight into the sea for a morning swim. He spent half the day trying to teach me how to act like Mortana—how she spoke, how she held herself, the kind of jokes she'd make. One afternoon, he'd told me to swim naked by myself, and I was supposed to think about how it felt to undulate under the water, how beautiful I was.

The other half of the time, he'd leave me by myself. I ate all my meals, delivered by Morgan, alone on his balcony. Once I'd eaten, I'd pull out Orion's smutty romance novels. The books that filled his shelves ranged from literary classics and Greek epic poems to full-blown modern fuck-fests with whips and spanking and lots of mind-shattering orgasms. Which, let's face it, couldn't be that good in real life. In the interest of learning, I chose the fuck-fest books to read over my dinners of scallops or salmon. And they were educational.

I did wonder, though—who was he eating with when he wasn't with me? And where was he sleeping?

Not that it was my business.

From the sofa, he arched an eyebrow. "You don't seem like you're focusing."

I straightened the way he'd taught me, then flicked my hair over my shoulder. I curled my lips in a smug smile.

He cocked his head. "Good. You've got the facial expression."

"I'm mimicking that smug 'I think I'm better than everyone' facial expression you always have."

He shrugged. "And now you need to believe it, too. You need to believe that you're the most beautiful person in the city, that others are privileged to be around you. That's what Mortana would think, that she blessed others with her presence. That she's a gift to the world."

I lifted my chin a little higher, just as Mortana would. *A gift to the world.*

"Let me see how you walk. This time, try keeping your footsteps in a single line, like a cat. Shoulders back, hips forward."

I straightened my back and lengthened my neck, and then I started to move the way he'd told me to, one foot directly in front of the other. I found that my hips swayed as I walked, and I strutted around the room in my new little black sundress. I could feel his eyes on me, watching the way I moved—or rather, the way Mortana moved.

"Shoulders back," he said quietly. "You need to look and act like you're thinking about sex at all times."

I pivoted, walking across the room again.

With his instructions, I found myself walking like a total sexpot—tits out, hips swaying from side to side. Maybe I was uncomfortable in my body, but Mortana was not. Mortana had done all the things I read about in those books—fucking men against walls, dragging her nails down their backs, biting the headboard while someone banged her from behind.

I twirled, thinking of how Mortana would feel swimming naked in the sea, or how she would feel with Orion watching her. Mortana would want his eyes all over her naked body. She'd get turned on, and she'd want him to know exactly how turned on she was. She'd want to torture him, tease him.

I spun again and decided that Mortana wanted to sit in Orion's lap. So I did that, wrapped my legs around his waist, my hem riding up to my hips. Instantly, his eyes turned dark as night. With a low, appreciative growl, his hand moved from my lower back all the way up to my hair. He threaded his fingers into my curls, pulling my head back a little. "Good girl," he said quietly. "Very good." His low voice rumbled over my skin.

But this was going too far, wasn't it?

I cleared my throat and jumped up from his lap, smoothing out my dress, tugging down the hem. "There." I exhaled slowly. "See? I can be Mortana. I don't have to do it all the time."

Orion's eyes were still pinned on me, filled with primal shadows. "Of course not."

Tomorrow night, I would meet the king, and that should be the scariest thing in my life right now. But truthfully, what scared me most was Orion.

CHAPTER 14

Today was D-Day.

I wasn't actually clear what the D stood for in the World War II version, but for me, it stood for *demon,* and possibly *disaster*. It was the day I'd be entering the demon world for real, leaving the safety of Orion's apartment. Most terrifying of all, it was the day I'd meet the demon king who'd severed his father's head and stuck it on a gate.

What kind of outfit did one wear for an introduction to a regicidal, patricidal demon king?

I frowned at my new underwear, which looked barely large enough to cover my nipples and ass. But I was, after all, a succubus now. Might as well get used to it. And with a little jolt of satisfaction, I realized I was actually quite comfortable standing stark naked in this glass-walled room.

Among the dresses, there were some more casual clothes, too. Black leather leggings, sleek pantsuits, little skirts and tops. But Orion had suggested that for my grand entrance back into the city today, I was supposed to dazzle people. Apparently, all eyes would be on me.

I plucked a camisole from the bed, one with sheer black lace and embroidered snakes. Its neckline plunged below the breasts at the center. Dark, sexy, demonic. I slid it on, and just as I'd expected, it barely covered my nipples.

I picked up the tiny matching panties and slipped into them.

Then I scanned the dresses. Lots of black, gray, gold. All of them were revealing in some way—tight bodices, slits all the way up to the hips, plunging backlines, short hemlines. First, I picked up a pale silver gown in a Grecian style, with a high waistline and delicate criss-crossing ropes around it. But the neckline went right down to the waist, and I wasn't sure I was ready for that.

Instead, I chose a short, silky red dress with a fitted top and long sleeves, and I wriggled it over my hips. It had a looser skirt, but the fact that the hem stopped just below my ass was definitely new to me. Then I slipped into a pair of thigh-high boots, which had small enough heels that I should be able to walk in them reasonably well.

When I turned to look at myself, I had to admit I looked hot as hell. With the boots on, I only had a small amount of skin showing—the tops of my thighs and my décolletage. And yet, somehow, this was a much sexier look than I was used to. My hair had dried, and it hung in waves over my shoulders, orange on red. It wasn't a *bad* look, I thought.

Fully dressed, I pulled open the door to the living room. Orion was still sitting on the sofa, leaning back with his arms unfolded over the sofa. And he was still as death, eyes burning like stars as he took me in.

Inhaling, I crossed closer to him. He slowly stood, his gaze boring into me. Dark magic whipped the air around him, and a low growl rumbled from his throat and skimmed over my body. I wondered if he was thinking of when I'd straddled him yesterday.

Then a wicked smile ghosted over his lips. "Good. You look like a succubus. Let's just see you move like Mortana one last time. I know you have confidence in your body in some ways. You can land a punch—I saw you take on those mortal fucks." His eyes had an otherworldly silver sheen. "That man who cornered you outside the brewery —was his name Jack Corwin?"

I'd forgotten how much he knew about me, as I'd spilled nearly all my secrets. "That was him."

"After everything he did to you, why would you tell me to stop hurting him? When I was twisting his mind with pain?"

He was doing that dominating demon stare that made me want to submissively drop my gaze. But I held his stare because Mortana would hold it. "I'm a normal person who doesn't want to watch someone's brain melt on the street. It's that thing called empathy. Even when you hate someone, you don't enjoy seeing them tortured."

"Empathy?" His eyes looked icy, cruel. "Sounds tedious. I'm glad I was never cursed with it."

"Exactly how many people have you killed in your life?"

He moved around to my side. "I'd love to tell you about each one just to see the horror cross your pretty face, but we have only a few hours left to work on your hunched posture."

I frowned. "Did you say *hunched?*"

"We'll try one last thing. I'm going to trace my finger up your spine, and as I do, I want you to straighten your back along with it. Lean into it, square your shoulders."

Already, I could feel the power of his magic tingling over my skin. When he touched my lower back, I nearly gasped at the pleasurable sensation. Just the feel of his fingertip on my back, through my dress, was like a hot, electric vibration through my body.

"Close your eyes. Let your shoulders relax and fall back. Imagine a thread pulling the top of your head toward the ceiling." With exquisite slowness, he stroked upward. My body responded to his touch, spine straightening, pulse speeding, and skin burning.

Holy moly, Rowan. Remember, this is just a job. And the bit about him being a demon. And also the bit about how he threatened to murder Shai.

As his finger brushed my nape, my neck lengthened. Then, with a touch light as a feather, his finger grazed back down again, and heat radiated from every point of contact. He let it rest between my shoulder blades. "Lift your chest. Raise your chin. You're proud of your beauty. It's part of your power."

My breath sped up, and I felt him move behind me, his hands going to my hips. I fought the insane impulse to lean back into his powerful body.

"Move your hips forward a little," he said quietly. "Open your eyes now."

I opened my eyes, already feeling different with my new posture.

"Perfect."

With graceful movements, he crossed in front of me. His beauty was deeply and unfortunately distracting. His gaze flicked to my mouth, and with a jolt of embarrassment, I realized I'd been licking my lips. A blush crept over my cheeks.

He cocked his head, his cheek dimpling with a sly smile.

I actually felt *sexy* for once. And now, I liked thinking of his eyes on me, on the naked tops of my thighs...in fact, I had the most inconvenient desire to show him my whole body.

I strutted across the room, swaying my hips like he'd showed me a million times, one foot in front of the other.

"Good," he murmured. "Now turn to face me."

I spun around, my curls bouncing. His stance was casual, hands in his pockets, shoulders relaxed. But something about the way his eyes burned, the way his jaw looked tight, told me that he wasn't actually calm at all. What was going on beneath that calm, easy exterior? Rage? Lust? Still trying to stop himself from ripping out my heart?

And where had he slept last night?

Whatever the case was, he was looking at me like he wanted to devour me.

"What next?" I asked.

"Now, when you walk back to me, try pretending a droplet of water is slowly moving from your neck down between your breasts. Trace it with your fingertip."

I started walking again, like a cat, and I moved my fingertip from my throat, down my chest. It was just like martial arts, wasn't it? Figuring out how to move my body in the right way.

I stopped when I could feel his hot magic skimming over me. Getting closer than I was now, looking into his eyes, felt like it would be too intense.

He raised his eyebrows. "Very good," he purred. "You need to always communicate through body language that you want to fuck someone. You make it clear through innuendo, eye contact, and touch."

I tossed my hair behind my shoulder.

"That was cute, but for starters, you have to stand closer than three feet. You know, like you did yesterday."

I swallowed hard, then walked closer to him. I stared up at him, imagining how it would feel to have his hands all over my body. *Just a job, Rowan. This is just a job.*

Amusement glinted in his eyes. "Now you'll need to lose the deer-in-the-headlights expression. Try a half-smile, an arched eyebrow."

I contorted my face on one side.

He grimaced. "Oh, no. Don't do that. Remember, you are a gift."

I let my face relax, then tried the smug expression.

His gaze brushed down my body. "Closer. Show vulnerability. Tilt your head back to show me your neck, like you're allowing me to bite you again, like you're inviting it."

This close to him, his sensual power was washing over me like a wave. I found myself staring into his endless eyes, my pulse racing. My nipples pebbled under the silky camisole. What I really wanted was for him to bend me over, pull down my panties, and stroke me—

Stop it, Rowan. He's not even human.

I knew what was happening. My id was taking over—the stupid, animalistic part of my brain that would fuck everything up for me if I let it. But maybe my id was what I needed here.

"Good," he said quietly. "You've got the eye contact down, now try using your sense of touch a little as you talk to me."

I reached out and touched his chest. I bit my lip as I traced my fingertips over the soft material, feeling the hard muscle beneath.

"You forgot to talk," he said quietly.

Ah. That was because my mind had gone totally blank.

He was *very* convincing at looking at me like he wanted to rip my dress off, but that was the job, wasn't it? He'd said that he'd try *acting* like I was sexy.

He reached for my arms and lifted them up, wrapping them around his neck so my body was pressed against his. As I reached up, my short hem rose behind me, and the warm breeze rushed over my upper thighs and the bottom of my ass.

Heat swept through my body. This was flirting? This felt positively indecent, and a hot pulse beat through my core. Looking into his eyes, I felt like I was going to plummet into a dangerous abyss.

My muscles clenched.

Demonic killer. Back away now, Rowan.

I pulled my arms from his throat, my jaw clenching, and looked away. My heart was pounding out of control, which was unfortunate, because now I knew he could hear it. "Okay, enough of that." I swallowed hard. "I think I've proven that I can put on the Mortana act." I plastered a smile on my face. "Why don't you show me around the city?"

"You'll need to stop blushing first."

I smoothed out my hair. "Fine."

"Have you memorized the map?"

I nodded. "I think so."

"Just remember that if you drop the Mortana act by accident," he cautioned, "you will end up in a pit of fire."

"Great way to help me relax."

But underneath the nerves and the fear, I was actually thrilled. Today, for the first time—after all these years—I was finally going to get a look inside the City of Thorns.

I was going to find my mom's killer.

CHAPTER 15

Orion had led me into what I'd thought was a closet, but was actually an elevator. While we rode it down, I kept studying the map.

"You have to put that away when we get to the bottom."

"I know." I'd drawn the gates of the city so many times, but I'd never imagined what was inside it. This was forbidden information and deeply fascinating.

The map showed that the city was divided into seven sections—eight if you included the Elysian Wilderness, south of the Acheron River.

The Luciferian Ward—and the Leviathan Hotel, where Orion lived—were right on the eastern side overlooking the ocean. South of Luciferian was the royal Beelzebub Ward, and the great Tower of Baal where the king lived. Once I had the king's approval, I'd be staying in the Asmodean Ward—west of here, on the river. It was the smallest ward, and I suspected it had grown smaller over the years as the neighboring wards encroached on it.

Curiosity burned bright in me. I wanted to see everything—the old prison, the ancient demon temples, the demon bank. This place not only contained my mom's killer, but it was *magical*.

When we reached the ground floor, the elevator opened into a lobby, and I shoved the map into my new red handbag, next to my new phone.

I stepped into the bright sunlight of the lobby. From above, sunlight poured through a dome of windows like a Victorian greenhouse. The floors were ivory marble, designed with black tiles in an Art Deco style. Sweeping stairs led up to a mezzanine, with a black railing that somehow looked like sexy lace.

I'd never actually been in a place like this before, and I had to remember to keep my jaw closed and not look awed by the grandeur. Mortana would not be impressed by this place. She'd be bored by all of this. So I pulled my eyes away from the beauty of the building, and I focused on my catlike walk, on my swaying hips.

On the way to the door, we passed a handful of people, who gaped at me. Two gorgeous demon women with red eyes and curved ivory horns—one blonde, the other with raven hair—huddled together and whispered as I crossed to the door. I had the feeling that word had already gotten around, and I gave them a confident smile.

That's right, demons. The succubus bitch is back.

Orion pushed through the large glass door, then held it for me. With swaying hips, I found myself stepping outside into a city of golden stone. In the sun, the world gleamed around me, and my breath caught at its beauty.

With its narrow streets—clearly made in a time before

cars—the city looked medieval. The hotel opened up onto a piazza of sorts, where cafés and shops lined a large stone courtyard. Arched passages jutted off from the square. In the center of the square, the stones formed a geometric shape sort of like an upside-down isosceles triangle, with lines curving off it and a *V* on the bottom.

Orion gestured at the symbol. "As you can see, Mortana, the Luciferian Ward is unchanged, and Lucifer's great symbol remains."

I sighed. "Delightful."

Now the real question was, did one of the squares contain a star symbol? And which of these fuckers burned my mom alive using fire magic?

When I surveyed the square, I realized all eyes were fixed in my direction. A shiver of dread rippled over me, but Mortana wouldn't look overwhelmed. Mortana would loop her arm around Orion's and smile smugly—the same kind of wry little curl of lips that Orion had been displaying since I'd met him. So I did just that.

With his body close to mine, his warm magic radiated over me, soothing and seductive at the same time.

Arm in arm, we crossed into one of the arched passages. In here, where it was empty, Orion leaned down and whispered. "I don't think people are thrilled about your return."

"Just the succubus issue?" I whispered back.

"That's part of it. And also, you're with me. The king and I are now the two wealthiest bachelors in the city, and the unmarried demon females have been competing for our attention. Infernal debutantes presented at court in a series of balls and soirées, each of them hoping to become a queen or duchess. Demon females wait years, centuries even, hoping to find the most advantageous match they can."

I looked up at him. "Why aren't you married?"

"I don't see any reason to marry."

"And the king?" I asked. "He's centuries old. Why marry now?"

Orion shrugged. "Before, he could fuck every woman in the city, and he probably has. No one had a claim to him. But a king is expected to marry, so he must choose a wife."

We walked through a series of narrow streets and stone stairwells, past shops and hotels. We swept past a round library belonging to Belial University.

Orion quietly explained to me that in the ancient days, Lucifer—the shining one—was the supreme demon god. Even now, Lucifer's power permeated the city. The temples were mostly abandoned, but some demons still left offerings to the old gods.

"Do you believe in them?" I whispered.

He glanced at me. "I don't know, but I don't really give a fuck if they're real or not."

Ah, of course. His arrogance knew no bounds—not even when it came to his gods.

IN THE MAMMON WARD, we stopped for lunch at a restaurant by one of the river's tributaries, the Erebus Stream. It burbled past us, gleaming in the sun. We sat by a pedestrianized road of amber stone, and I watched the demons stride past in their designer clothes, some of them with metallic horns that sparkled in the afternoon sunlight.

Far across the square, the Bank of Thorns loomed over a square, with towering columns that made it look like an ancient temple. Black brambles grew over the stone.

A few mortals walked past, dressed casually in Belial University sweatshirts and leggings. They moved differently from demons, and their expressions were unguarded, in awe at the beautiful world around them. By contrast, every demon stood out to me as a predator, gliding along with lethal grace. The demons kept their features calm at all times.

None of them bore the star I was looking for.

I leaned back in my chair to sip the red wine Orion had ordered for us. I was no wine expert, but this was *amazing*. I let the dry flavor roll over my tongue, then swallowed. "Delicious."

He returned my smile. "Claret from grapes in the fields of Elysium. One of my favorites."

The waitress returned, staring almost exclusively at Orion. And who could blame her? The woman had functioning eyes, and he looked like a god. Her cheeks flushed as she took his order, and she flicked her long brown hair over her shoulder.

With a smirk, he said, "I'll have the duck breast."

I was pretty sure she actually *gasped* at the word breast. She bit her lip and cocked her head, as if he'd just suggested spanking her. "Yeah?" she said. "Is that all you want?"

Orion had said flirting was all about making it clear you wanted to fuck someone, and this chick was a goddamn expert. Frankly, she'd be much better than me at the succubus role.

I had to admit, I found it a bit irritating. For one thing, I was starving, and she still hadn't taken my order. For another, what if this were actually a real date? I mean it wasn't, obviously. I had no reason to be jealous, so I wasn't.

But *she* didn't know that.

The real question was how Mortana would handle this situation. Personally, I thought she'd be fucking pissed. Mortana liked being the center of attention, and she wasn't getting any right now. Nor did I think she would tolerate this kind of disrespect.

I cleared my throat. When the waitress finally turned to look at me, I narrowed my eyes at her and made my body go as still as possible. Having just experienced this a few times from Orion, I knew how unnerving it was. Plus, this was basically a bitchier version of Dr. Omer's *I'll sit in silence until you realize what you've done* technique.

I watched her rosy cheeks go pale, and then I slowly tapped my fingernails on the table. "Are you quite done with that little display?" My voice came out sounding cold and distant.

"Sorry," she stammered. "I was just taking his order."

"Oh, I don't think so, mortal." I chuckled. "But you know, your desire does give me strength." Never in my life had I sounded so imperious. To tell the truth, I wasn't entirely sure where this was coming from. "Your lust is making me positively ravenous."

I watched her throat bob as she swallowed. "Did you want lunch?"

Orion was picking up the tab, so I might as well get something expensive. "Lobster Fra Diavolo." An appropriate name when I thought about it. "I'm feeling a bit devilish." I bared my teeth. "And if that doesn't satisfy me, I'll need to feed on something fresher, so you'd best tell the chef to make sure it's good."

She stumbled back from me, then turned to hurry to the kitchen.

Shit. Was that what my id was like under all my repression? Did I have an evil side?

When I turned back to Orion, he was studying me closely. "Mortana, you really haven't changed at all."

I leaned closer to him and whispered in his ear, "I like being back."

He raised his wine to me in a toast. "To the most malignant, evil demon to ever grace this city."

Every time I looked around, I realized people were craning their necks, trying to listen in.

I sighed, looking out across the Acheron River to the south bank. "The Elysian Fields. I do remember them fondly. Is it true that during your Infernal Rite, you slaughtered fifty demons?"

He twirled the stem of his wineglass between his fingertips, and the crimson liquid glinted in the sunlight. "Well, I don't like to brag—"

"Liar."

Amusement curled his lips. "Fine. I love to brag. Yes, I killed fifty demons. And yes, I think the others find me terrifying."

Did the king find him terrifying, too?

I sighed, trying to get into my role. "It's been so long since I've seen King Nergal."

"Don't worry." He flashed me a dazzling smile. "You will see *his head* soon. But now you have unwavering loyalty to the new king, don't you? You know how it is here. *Vae Victis*."

Woe to the vanquished. Expect brutal treatment at the hands of the victors. Another reminder that I couldn't fall into enemy hands here.

I lifted my wineglass, smiling, and repeated, "Vae Victis."

CHAPTER 16

When we finished eating, the tour continued—one ward after another of honey-colored stone. The walls wrapped around the city's borders, punctuated by towers that looked out over Osborne.

I was thrilled I'd had the foresight to choose the most comfortable boots, because we walked for miles—through the Belphagor Ward with its Hall of Guilds, and the old Parliament by the river. We saw the haunted prisons in the Sathanas Ward, and the gallows outside where executions took place. A three-headed guard dog snarled at us outside its iron gates. It must have been the magic of the place, but the city was far more enormous than it appeared from the outside.

I noticed that the fashion looked slightly different in each ward. In the Luciferian Ward, there had been a lot of silk dresses and large belts with plunging necklines. In Sathanas, I saw bustiers and men in suits with thin ties.

But the Asmodean Ward was something altogether

different. Here, canals flowed through the city instead of roads, and deserted boats floated in turquoise water. The streets were narrow and deserted, occasionally opening up onto squares with faded grandeur. Classical buildings were adorned with columns and tall windows, and the faded stone looked like it had once been painted bright colors. Many of the façades were crumbling, the windows boarded up. An empty fountain stood in the center, carved with statues whose faces had been smashed.

My heart clenched. Sadness permeated the air here like a dark miasma. I felt the loss of this place viscerally.

Across from us stood a palatial building with arched, mullioned windows. A canal flowed on one side of it. Workers were rushing in and out, carrying furniture inside and replacing broken windowpanes.

Orion pointed to it. "There. That's your home for now. No one has lived in the Asmodean Ward in centuries, but they're making sure it's fit for Mortana."

I turned to look behind me, unnerved to find that three female demons had followed us into the abandoned ward. There was nothing for them here—no restaurants, no shops. No one lived here. They were simply watching us, and they didn't seem to care about being subtle.

A tall, brunette demon with sapphire eyes and black horns was glaring at me, arms folded. The look in her eyes was pure wrath, sending shivers through my bones. In her leather shorts and corset, she looked as sexy as she was terrifying. Two blondes flanked the horned one, all of them statuesque. But the most interesting thing about this trio was that the horned one had tattoos of flames on her arms. Did she have fire magic?

I needed to know how common flames were among demons.

Moving closer to Orion, I wrapped my arms around his neck, and I shot a smug smile at the trio. In response, Orion wrapped his hands around my waist. His intense magic sizzled over my body, heating me.

I reached up and pulled his head down closer to my mouth. "Orion," I whispered, "I can see that people want to kill me already. I need to know what their powers are like."

"What do you want to know, love?"

"What about fire magic?" I whispered.

His arm brushed down my back, and he looked over my shoulder. He reached for my hand, then he led me toward a building that looked like an abandoned brick mansion, the windows boarded up with wood. He kicked through the ancient wooden doors into a room of faded marble and dusty tile floors.

I coughed in the stale air. I could see that at one point, this place had been truly stunning. Busts in alcoves lined the hall, carved with flowing hair and crowns. But their faces were smashed, too. A few of the statues had been pushed to the ground and lay shattered on the marble. An old, dusty diary had been forgotten on the floor, as had a moth-eaten cape. Two crystal glasses and a decanter stood on a table. A maroon stain darkened one part of the floor, disturbingly the color of dried blood.

It was hard not to be curious about an abandoned demon mansion, so I peered through one of the doorways to see something that looked like a ballroom, covered in dust and cobwebs. A harpsichord stood in one corner, and more crystal glasses and plates littered the tables. It was like the Lilu who'd once lived here didn't see it coming. Like they'd left mid-meal. It made my heart twist to see it.

"Why was this all left here?" I asked. "If the Lilu are gone, why did no one take over their palace?"

He turned to look at one of the smashed busts, and he traced his fingertips over its rough contours where the face used to be. "Demons are superstitious. When something terrible happens, a place is thought to be cursed. Haunted."

"Do you believe that?"

He shook his head. "No. Haunting requires a soul, and I don't believe we have them."

But for some reason, since we'd come in here, the shadows seemed to thicken as if this place spooked him. Hot magic warmed the air around him.

"Do you think mortals have souls?" I asked.

His eyes slid to mine, his expression distant. "I've never spent any time thinking about mortals. Maybe you have souls. It's honestly difficult to take interest in fragile little creatures that only live for a few years."

I'd *really* have to just get used to his condescension. "Right. Okay. I suppose none of that matters right now."

"You wanted to ask about fire magic." His gaze pinned me. "Why fire magic specifically?"

I shrugged. "There was a demon woman outside with fiery tattoos. I'd heard a rumor that demons can light people on fire, and I happen to be more than a little terrified of it."

"That's Lydia—Duchess of the Luciferian Ward, House of Shalem. Fire magic is rare. Most of us possess only strength and speed relative to mortals. A few have ice magic. The ability to summon water, or to cause a storm—there are some examples of elemental magic. But fire—only the most powerful can summon fire. Those from a branch of royal lineage. Some say it means you've been touched by Lucifer himself."

Now *this* was the most important thing I'd learned since I'd arrived. "So who's on that exclusive list?"

"The king, Lydia, and Mortana."

And now I had three suspects.

Orion raised his hand, and flames burst from his fingertips like candles. The fire danced in his eyes. "And me."

I stepped back from him, my heart pounding, and the flames disappeared.

He looked at me with curiosity. "You really *are* afraid of fire."

I exhaled slowly. "Yeah. It's a thing I have."

He took a step closer. "You're here with me, working with me. I'll make sure that no one hurts you. Understood?"

Either he was telling the truth or he was a very convincing liar.

He turned, heading back for the door. "Let's go, love. I don't like it in here."

Add Orion to the suspect list, then.

Fuck.

CHAPTER 17

We reached our endpoint in the Beelzebub Ward, where we stopped for dinner at a riverside restaurant called Valac's. The setting sun cast dazzling red and orange rays over the river just to our south.

Everything in the royal Beelzebub Ward, where envy ruled, looked as though it were gilded. Sandstone streets, trees that bloomed with yellow flowers, women in metallic dresses, cheekbones highlighted with gold dust. The setting sun washing it all in amber.

Orion had left me on my own to get dinner. He'd said something about wanting to speak to the king before my arrival. And with him still footing the bill, I ordered crab legs with butter and garlic mashed potatoes, along with the most expensive red wine on the menu. I wondered which kind of wine Mortana had used to drown the queen, and frankly, it seemed like a real waste.

The task that lay ahead of me tonight made my stomach churn: charm a king and convince him I was a succubus. Fail, and my best friend would be murdered. And I'd die in a literal fire.

I let out a long breath, scanning the scene around me. From here, I could see the bridge that crossed the Acheron River—the Bridge of Harrowing, according to the map. On the other side of the river, shadows pooled in the darkening woods. A warm breeze rushed from the south, carrying with it the mossy scent of the wild forests.

Nowhere had I seen the star I was looking for, and I desperately wanted to ask about it. I couldn't just bring it up cold, though. Not when Orion himself was a suspect.

In the City of Thorns, I was like an undercover cop.

I'd once watched an old Keanu Reeves movie called *Point Break* where he played a cop infiltrating a gang of surfer bank robbers. He blended in, got to know their culture, and waited for information to come to him. He didn't just start interrogating the other surfers. Only when he got them to trust him did they reveal their secrets.

As I sipped my wine, staring out at the Acheron, I mulled over the horrible but real possibility that Orion was the killer. What if he'd known exactly who I was when he found me in Cirque de la Mer? What if he'd dragged me here under false pretenses to spy on *me* after killing my mom four years ago?

But the theory didn't really hold up. Why would he spy on me? He had lethal magic at his fingertips and zero empathy. He could torture answers out of me if he felt like it.

My heart kicked up a notch as I realized that Lydia, the tattooed woman, was sitting at the table across from me.

Her lip curled as she stared back at me, and my blood turned to ice.

I couldn't let her actually see that I looked nervous, though, so I kept my expression bland and gazed at the flowing river.

"Mortana?" Orion's deep voice pulled me from my musings, and I turned to see him. In the sunset, his beautiful face was bathed in rosy hues. "It's time to get ready for your meeting with the king. And I'm afraid tonight might be a more difficult than I'd imagined."

My stomach sank.

* * *

ORION and I approached the outer gates of the Tower of Baal, arm in arm. The palace looked ancient, the outer wall carved with arrow slits. A sandstone path led to an arched gateway. From here, I could just about see the former king's head impaled on the outer gates above the first entryway. My blood turned cold as my heels echoed off the stone.

In the past hour, we'd taken a cab back to Orion's house in the Luciferian Ward, and I'd readied myself. I'd picked out a gorgeous dress—long black lace with a slit up the thigh and a neckline so plunging that a bra wasn't an option. I never wore stuff like this, but Mortana did. And you know what? Mortana looked fucking hot.

While I'd been fixing my hair, Orion had dropped the bomb. There was so much controversy about the return of the succubus, I wouldn't be meeting the king alone. In fact, I'd be meeting a whole council of demons, and they would decide my fate. The whole Infernal Quorum would be in attendance—a duke or duchess from each of the city's wards.

Including Lydia.

And if any of them sensed I was an imposter, I'd be thrown into a pit of fire right there in the Tower of Baal.

As we drew closer to the outermost gate, I considered why the king would need the input of a quorum. He had the ultimate power here. But my guess? He wanted to be able to blame other people if Mortana turned out to be a royal disaster. After all, it was their decision, too, right?

Powerful people—even when they had total control—were great at blaming others.

My heels clacked over the stones, and I tried not to dwell on the flames. It was just that of all the methods of execution, *that* was the one that really scared the shit out of me. But I was doing this for Mom, and now for Shai, so no matter what happened, I had to get it right.

When we got closer, I could see that the old king's head looked remarkably well preserved, with a full head of black hair and his skin still smooth. But his eyes were closed, and his facial muscles looked slack. Torches fixed to the walls cast wavering light over the sandstone walls, and the dancing shadows almost made King Nergal's head look like it was moving, the dead lips gibbering. I let out a long, slow breath.

With my arm looped through Orion's, I leaned in to whisper, "Is this normal for demons? The severed head?"

He looked at me with confusion. "Of course not."

Thank God. So they weren't all sociopaths.

Then he added, "There would be no reason for other

demons to keep a severed head above their gate. It's only because he was the former king. It's a reminder to the world that King Nergal was defeated by someone stronger, and that Cambriel is the rightful king. *Vae Victis*, remember?"

"The severed head doesn't bother people who live here?" I whispered. "It's a bit macabre."

He shrugged. "He wasn't very popular."

I found myself staring at Orion, trying to read him. His face showed absolutely nothing, and the head clearly didn't faze him. I wondered if all demons lacked empathy.

In mortal terms, someone with no empathy was called a psychopath. From what I understood, psychopaths had reduced activity in their amygdala, the part of the brain that created anxiety. So psychopaths didn't feel fear as deeply as the rest of us, or any emotions, really. That meant they sometimes went to disturbing lengths to feel things. If they grew up middle class, they could chase a high buying and selling stocks, or go into politics. If they grew up around violence, maybe they'd cut off their dad's head and stick it on a gate.

We crossed through into a stone courtyard, and I realized there was yet another gated wall before we got to the tower. The king had a *lot* of protection. "Orion," I whispered, "do you ever feel fear?"

He frowned. "What would I be afraid of? I could kill nearly anyone."

Oh, dear. "Do you ever feel bad for someone? I'm just trying to understand what kind of people think the decapitated head is a good idea."

His lips curled with a taunting smile. "If you want to

understand what kind of people think it's a good idea, you can read your own history. It's where we borrowed the custom from. Mortals were doing the exact same thing when we closed the city gates in the 1600s. The heads of defeated enemies jutted out of Boston Common in the 1670s." He shrugged. "Demon culture simply moves more slowly."

Well, I'll be damned.

He had a good point. Demons and mortals alike were fairly terrible at times.

At the other side of the courtyard, two hulking, muscular demons stood guard before a door carved with a sigil. It almost looked like an insect with long legs, and it must be the symbol of Beelzebub.

The guards' ivory horns curled from their heads, the color matching their pale, waxy skin. They glared at us and clutched their spears. Silvery magic curled off their bodies, and a low growl rumbled over the stones beneath our feet. The sound rose to a sort of deep, morose song that filled the air.

A shudder crawled up my nape at how unfamiliar this was. But I managed to keep my sexy, catlike walk going. My hips swayed. It was the weirdest thing, as I'd never met Mortana. I hardly knew a thing about her. And yet, I felt like I had an intuitive sense of how she thought. Her confidence, her disdain for others, her ability to control a situation. She was like my ruthless shadow-self coming to the surface. My id. She was the primal part of the brain, unburdened by self-consciousness or anxiety. The id was all desire and aggression, and maybe it was kind of fun letting it come to the surface.

When we got to the door, the two guards shifted out of the way. Now, the gates opened into a field of wildflowers in gorgeous fiery hues—amber, pumpkin, cherry red. A stone path carved through the field, leading to a gilded tower of concentric circular floors, which narrowed at the top. Closer to the tower, a red carpet had been laid out for our arrival.

It was the most grandiose thing I'd ever seen, and clearly, it had been built to intimidate. Around the tower, demons milled about in gorgeous ballgowns and suits. It looked like a Met Gala, with outrageous gowns of crystals and metallic colors. There were red dresses with long trains that trailed over the grass, men in pinstripe suits or velvet with enormous sashes. I could have transposed the scene to New York but for the fact that half the attendants had horns.

Tonight was apparently quite the event. Everyone wanted to be here, possibly to watch a succubus roast in a fire.

I stole a glance at Orion, taking care to maintain my placid expression. His silver hair gleamed in the moonlight, and when he turned to look at me, I felt an unwelcome fluttering in my heart. The thing was, I was starting to feel safe with him, like he was my protector. And that was absolutely stupid, considering he was one of my suspects.

And as we drew nearer to the red carpet, I felt all the demons' eyes on me. The crowd started to close in. My heart was fluttering hard, my stomach twisting. I did my best to look bored, even if I was anything but.

In my black gown, I was wearing one of the simplest

dresses here, but I thought it made sense. Mortana was a badass bitch with the confidence to show herself off. She wouldn't rely on the clothes to do it. Why give all the attention to the designer when it could be on *her*?

Did I feel her confidence? Fuck, no. But I'd be doing my best to fake it.

The demons stared at us as we climbed up the steps to the tower itself. Two more guards stood at the top of the stairs, and they pulled open the doors.

The first thing I noticed was the pit of fire, flames dancing above it like a portal to hell.

And that's where I'd find myself tonight if I wasn't able to master my fear.

CHAPTER 18

The fire pit was set in the center of the hall. Nausea climbed up my throat, and my breath started to grow shallower.

Stay calm. Stay calm. Stay calm.

This would be a *great* time to have my fire-retardant clothing and blankets and gels, although even those things would only last for so long. That pit was eternal.

Panic started to dig its claws deeper into my heart. If I didn't master this worry soon, the jig would be up for sure.

I had to manage my breathing, to keep the breath deep and slow so my body didn't go into panic mode. I was in control of what happened—as long as I could fake it convincingly, I could get out of here with my skin still on my body. I could keep Shai alive, too.

Slowly marshaling a sense of calm, I took in the space around me.

When I'd heard *Tower of Baal* and *demon fire pit,* I hadn't expected the place to look so sleek and modern. It shone with burnished sandy marble. Above us, circular floors reached up to an oculus, through which I could see the moon. And there *was* a fire pit in the center, yes, but there was also a banquet laid out to my right, with civilized canapés and hors d'oeuvres. Behind the banquet, windows overlooked a garden bathed in moonlight. To the left, a pool curved to the side, with a swim-up cocktail bar. Mortal waitresses in short dresses glided around with trays of drinks. All perfectly civilized.

Five demons stood around the fire pit drinking champagne and cocktails—Lydia of the fire tattoos, and four males. Each one of them represented a ward, and the king led the sixth.

From Shai's description, I recognized Legion—long black hair, golden-brown skin, his sleeves rolled up to reveal vicious black tattoos. The leader of the Sathanas Ward, wrath. Shai was right. He was hot, but also terrifying.

Perhaps not quite as scary as Lydia, whose eyes burned with little flecks of fire as she glared at me. The firelight cast dancing shadows over her features, and a menacing smile curled her lips. A cat about to slaughter a mouse.

As a human woman slipped past me with a tray of bright red cocktails, I plucked one off and took a sip. The alcohol would help me calm down, and I could at least *look* like I was enjoying myself.

The king himself sat on a gilded throne on a dais, just on the other side of the fire pit. His long blond hair draped over broad shoulders. Silver horns jutted from his head, and his eyes were dark as night. He wore midnight blue clothes that clung to his enormous body. Firelight wavered over him, further enhancing his otherworldly appearance. His expression was unreadable, his body as still as the stone walls around us. Like Orion, he radiated pure power.

"Mortana, Lady of the House of Lilitu." His low voice rumbled over the hall. "The last succubus. You return to us."

Somehow, having Orion by my side was helping me. I'd been watching him so carefully throughout the day that I'd developed a good sense of how to mimic his overwhelming confidence.

I smiled, then gave one of the lazy shrugs that he would give, as if I were totally at ease. "The City of Serpents started to bore me." I took a sip of my red cocktail, which I think was pomegranate juice with vodka. "And then I thought of the City of Thorns. I did have such *fun* here." I projected my voice over the hall.

I lifted my chin like Orion had told me, and I drained half my pomegranate martini. *Not a care in the world.*

The king's dark eyes landed on Orion. "Do you know why she left the City of Serpents?" His rings glinted in the warm light.

"Now, now, King Cambriel," said Orion, his tone faintly mocking, "you know I can't say what happened there. Our cities are shrouded in secrecy."

He was really going to take that attitude with the demon king? I'd expected deference, but I supposed that was too much to expect from someone with his ego.

"Indeed," said the king in a cold tone. "Which is why we still know nothing of why you left your ward in the City of Serpents, though I'm sure it involved a scandal.

And I do wonder if that particular scandal involved this succubus. But I suppose you're right. These things cannot be discussed." The king turned his dark gaze back to me. "My father was very fond of you, Lady Mortana."

The severed head outside was fond of me. I fluttered my eyelashes and took another long sip of my drink, trying to untangle the weirdness of all this. Somehow, this felt like a test. I sensed that if I showed loyalty to the dead king, I'd fail.

"As you saw on your way in," the king went on, "the former king has been vanquished. *Vae Victis*. Do you grieve his death, Mortana?"

This definitely was a test. How did I respond in a way that would flatter King Cambriel? Orion had said King Nergal was dull and tedious.

I widened my eyes, my hand flying to my chest with mock horror. "Is King Nergal dead? Honestly, given his personality, I'm amazed anyone could tell."

Unfortunately, King Cambriel didn't smile a bit, so that only made my stomach muscles clench tighter. I'd already emptied my cocktail, and the alcohol was starting to go to my head. I dropped my glass on the tray of a passing waitress.

A heavy silence still filled the room, and my pulse raced. After an endless few moments, titters broke out at last, and I relaxed just a little.

Had I gone too far?

The thing was, I had a feeling Mortana would go too far. It was part of what made her interesting. She wouldn't have made so many enemies without shocking and insulting people along the way. She knew how to get attention and keep it.

The king's lips curled just a little. He liked Mortana's cruelty. "You don't mourn his death, then? You must have been fond of him once."

"Well, I was very fond of *one* part of him, but that part seems to be gone now, since there's just the head left."

Holy shit. It was fun to be evil. Was I turning into Orion? *Empathy? Sounds tedious.*

When Orion's pale eyes slid to me, I could see the amusement in them.

One of the king's fingers tapped the armrest. The flames of the fire were gleaming off his golden crown. While Orion's beauty was sensual, the king had a sort of stark elegance. Refined, masculine features and straight black eyebrows.

"What do you intend to do here?" The king's voice boomed over the hall.

There was a question I didn't know how to answer. A bit of anxiety snapped through my nerve-endings, and I felt my fingers tightening on Orion's bicep. Maybe we should have prepared for this question.

In response, Orion slowly reached over and stroked his fingertips over my wrist. His warm magic pulsed into me, and instantly, I felt my muscles relax. *Wow*. He could just *do* that? Mortals spent years training in graduate school for counseling techniques to help people manage anxiety, and all Orion had to do was touch them. Boom. Anxiety gone.

I still had to figure out an answer, though. So far, it

looked like demons mostly went to fancy restaurants and bought gowns. What would my id say? What did I want?

I fluttered my eyelashes as the flames danced between us. "Well, I do intend to use that pool bar of yours, if you'll let me. And perhaps Orion can join me." Drawing more from my id, I turned to Orion, stroking his large bicep. The look he gave me was deeply carnal, which was good, since I was supposed to be inspiring envy in the king. "Oh, do you know what else I'd like to do? I'd like Orion to fuck me hard against a stone wall, since we haven't done that yet."

Holy shit. *Too much id. Too much id.*

With a low growl, Orion's eyes darkened to shadows, and his heated expression seared me.

Was that a warning that I should shut my mouth, or something else?

At that moment, the flames in the fire pit rose higher, burning the air and scorching my skin. Was this Orion's fire magic at work, or the king's?

"You certainly have my attention, Mortana," said the king sharply. "And what, exactly, is your relationship to Orion?"

One thing I'd learned from Dr. Omer was that when you didn't want to answer a question about yourself, you deflected it back to the other person. You made it a question about them.

I jutted one hip and smiled coquettishly. "Your Majesty, I'm delighted by your interest in my love life. What is it, I wonder, that makes you so intrigued? Is this something we should explore, perhaps?"

Explore. That was a Dr. Omer's word, but he'd never used it quite so suggestively.

The king gave me a faint smile. "You are the last of your kind, Mortana. A curiosity. That's all." But now he was giving me the same look Orion had, like he wanted to lick me from head to toe. Considering gorgeous women in the City of Thorns were a dime a dozen, it was clear Orion was right about what attracted the king's attention. Jealousy was the key to his heart. He wanted me because Orion had me.

I turned to Orion, giving him a full view of my cleavage, and touched my finger to his lips, then traced it down his body. I felt his muscles twitch beneath my touch.

"The city could use a succubus again, I think," I said loudly. "Don't you?"

The look in Orion's midnight eyes sent my heart racing. It was hard not to think of how I'd felt with him pinning me to the wall, with his teeth in my throat.

I breathed in deeply, then turned back to the king. He was gripping the armrests hard, leaning forward on his throne. He almost looked like he wanted to leap over the fire pit and grab me.

For the first time, the king stood, and I saw exactly how tall he was—just about the same size as Orion. The two men towered over the other demons. He opened his arms. "The dukes and duchess will advise me as to whether you may stay here in the City of Thorns. But of course, I will make the ultimate decision. And I do think you should stay."

I exhaled slowly. This seemed like a victory, right? It

seemed like no matter what the Quorum said, the king would keep me here.

"Your Majesty." A husky, feminine voice turned my head.

Lydia, the Duchess of Shalem, had stepped forward. She was stunning in a gold dress that revealed her fiery tattoos. Her legs were long and athletic, and her dark hair curled in shiny waves over bare shoulders. For one moment, she shot me a withering look, then she schooled her expression and gazed at the king again. "Your Majesty, as the lone female leader in the City, you know that I do not share the petty and trivial concerns of the rest of the females."

Nice. She's really going to start her speech by explaining she's not like other girls?

She lifted her chin. "Many of our city's females may object to Mortana's presence here because they see her as a rival. They're only concerned with their marriage prospects, the desire to seek wealth, and other superficial matters. They see her as a threat to the attentions they could receive from Duke Orion or from you. Frankly, their preoccupations with celebrity and wealth speak of the decline of our society."

Orion rolled his eyes. "Are you going to get to a point at any time this evening?"

She curled her lips. "But as you know, I see beyond these frivolous feminine concerns, and I am not like other females. My concerns are deeper. May I point out that the Lilu were barred because of the danger they pose to other demons? Once, the City of Thorns chose to rid its streets of them because they used mind control to manipulate others, to satisfy their own depraved needs. They are an abomination among demons."

Well, the claws were certainly out, but the real question was how *Mortana* would feel about that remark.

I didn't think she'd like it one bit. She'd be ready to fight back.

CHAPTER 19

I turned to Lydia and snarled, baring my teeth. The sound came from deep within my chest, and it rumbled over the hall.

Well, *hello,* Mortana's aggression. I'd just become familiar with my animalistic side, I guess.

Looking back at the king, I smiled again. "I think you'll find I don't need mind control to satisfy my *depraved* needs."

The king's sharp jaw clenched, and a dark smile curled his lips. His knuckles went white as he gripped the armrests.

A duke stepped forward—this one with dark hair, copper skin, and deep brown eyes. "We all know what the Lilu were like in the past. They cheated us out of our money using their seduction. Some of us are even old enough to remember." He glared at me. "Mortana lured my brother away centuries ago, and I haven't seen him since. Immediately after his disappearance, his gold disappeared along with him."

Okay, Mortana sucked. But I still had to stay in character because that's how I'd get out of here alive.

Another duke folded his arms. He was tall and thin, with dark curls that fell before his eyes. "If no one else is willing to say it, then I guess I will. Everyone knows *she* killed Queen Adele."

I raised a finger. "Everyone does *not* know that, because I never killed the queen." I could say this without worrying about looking like I was lying, because for once this evening, I actually wasn't. Maybe Mortana once killed a queen, but I hadn't. "Those were merely rumors. Nothing was ever proven."

Orion's face was a mask of calm. "Why let yourselves be swayed by gossip from four hundred years ago?" He shrugged. "I suppose it doesn't matter to me, but I've been enjoying fucking her, and I'd hate to lose my favorite plaything." He arched an eyebrow, his pale eyes gleaming with wickedness. "I'd heard the rumors about succubi, how they'd beg on their knees, but never before did I get to experience the wild desperation of the Lilu."

Shocked murmurs rippled through the room, and a hot tendril of anger coiled through me. Did he really have to put it *that* way? Absolute *prick*. I shouldn't care what the demons thought, and I was only playing a role. But still, I wasn't sure how much humiliation I could take in this place.

And yet…

I could already see it had worked, because now the king looked ravenous for me.

Lydia cocked a hip. "You filthy scoundrel. Lord of Chaos, you weren't here then. You don't know what she was like. And she had the most motive, desperate to be queen. Only Mortana would be cruel enough to leave the Queen Consort in a vat of wine. I don't care about the trivial issues of marriage, but how do we know Mortana won't slaughter the rest of us for power?"

I sighed. "You can't possibly believe I'm the only cruel demon in the City of Thorns. It could have been anyone."

A gaunt duke with luscious brown curls wrapped his bony fingers around his wineglass as he stared at me. The firelight gleamed off his ivory horns. "You may not remember me, Mortana. I wasn't a duke when you left, but I am now." He grimaced at me. "You hardly gave me the time of day back then. A succubus like you was too good for a gluttony demon."

I realized after a moment that his drink wasn't wine at all. It looked like *blood.* He was a glutton for human blood.

Disturbing...

I blinked at him. "Oh, I still think I'm too good for you. That hasn't changed."

I was trying to stay in character. The problem was, staying in character meant pissing people off. And how much did I need them to like me in order to get the approval of the Quorum?

With a furious expression, he knocked back the rest of his blood. "Let me just spell this out. If you become duchess of the Asmodean Ward, that means less tax revenue for the rest of us."

Duchess...*right*. As the last Lilu, I'd be the automatic leader. They'd be sharing power with me. Of course none of them wanted that.

But the king made the ultimate call, right? If he wanted something enough, I was sure he'd find a way to get it. My goal needed to be getting him on board as much as possible, and jealousy was the key to his heart.

I turned to Orion and brushed my fingertips over his abs. As I did, I felt his muscles clench, which was a strangely delicious feeling. My cheeks were growing hotter.

"Look, if you all decide you don't want me here, then I can leave, of course. I can live anywhere. And perhaps I can compel Orion to come with me. I think there's something about him—a very large thing, in fact—that I'm really quite attached to. I can't imagine any other male coming close."

Orion grabbed me off my feet. He moved swiftly but gracefully, and the next thing I knew, he was lifting me against a column. I stared into his hypnotizing blue eyes, and I wrapped my legs around his waist. With a wicked, seductive smile, he pinned me against the stone.

When the air hit the top of my thighs, I realized that he'd pulled my dress up nearly to my hips.

Whoa. Hello.

I stared into his eyes. At this point, I was glad for the wine *and* the cocktail I'd downed, because in normal life, I was never this uninhibited. As Orion had pointed out, I was a bit tightly wound. But it wasn't just the alcohol, was it? Orion had his own sort of intoxicating powers. His seductive, velvety magic stroked my body. As he held me against the stone, his eyes looked dark, dangerous. I stared into his perfect, masculine features, and the world around me seemed to dim. I wanted him to lower his mouth to mine, to kiss me deeply.

God*damn* it. Terrible taste in men, Rowan. Absolute worst.

A breeze rushed through the hall, skimming over my bare skin. The strap of my gown had fallen, nearly exposing my entire breast. In fact, half my nipple was showing, tightened to a sensitive point against the silky material.

In any normal situation, I'd gasp and rush to cover myself up. But in any normal situation, I wouldn't be thrown into a fire pit for being self-conscious, so I took deep breath and let the strap fall even more.

I watched Orion's eyes as they brushed down my chest, and I heard his sharp intake of breath. He pressed in harder between my legs, and I bit my lip. From the feel of him, he wasn't just faking this desire. And what I'd said before about how I couldn't imagine any other male coming close to him? Holy moly, I wasn't wrong.

Orion started to lower his mouth to mine, eyes black as night—

"That's enough!" The king's voice boomed through the hall.

I was horrified at how disappointed I felt at the interruption.

Orion lowered me, and the hem of my gown fell to the floor once more.

I knew my cheeks were flushed and my chest heaving as I pulled my strap up again. It was hard for me to focus. Only the sight of the rising flames, now towering several feet above us, sharpened my senses again. When the flames died down, I could see the king on the other side of them, his jaw clenched and muscles tense.

We'd certainly gotten his attention. The firelight danced over his tan skin and blond hair, making him look like a gilded statue forged from the flames.

My adrenaline was pulsing hard through my body. Had we actually pulled off this act?

The king pulled his gaze from me, surveying the Quorum. Then a smile curled his lips. "I think the City of Thorns could use a succubus."

A silence fell over the room. Just as I thought, the king would be making the call, regardless of what the others thought. Their faces were grim, furious.

One of the dukes, with platinum blond hair and gold rings on his fingers, stepped forward. "We cannot, of course, disagree with your wisdom." He looked furious. And as I stared at him, a golden symbol started beaming from his head—something like a crescent moon.

My heart slammed on my chest. *That* was what I remembered from the night Mom was killed. It was a symbol just like that, shining from a demon's head. Only it had been a star instead of a moon.

My blood was pumping so hard now I *nearly* dropped character. I'd actually made progress.

But when I saw Lydia's eyes on me, the curl of her lip, I made sure my expression looked serene. Mortana wasn't surprised by anything here. This was all business as usual.

The king steepled his fingers as he stared at his quorum. "Don't you agree that the city could use a succubus?" His voice rumbled off the marble. "A duchess for the Asmodean Ward?"

He wanted them to agree with him. He *knew* they didn't—they'd just said so—but they wouldn't argue with a king. And as long as they agreed out loud, he would have someone to blame if the succubus turned out to be a complete disaster. *Why did you all advise me to allow her in?*

The five demons murmured, then nodded.

Only Lydia looked completely stone faced. "We could use a succubus. The king in his infinite wisdom can see this. But any demon who enters the city must be tested in the Infernal Trial, is that not correct? It's how we know that the gods bless someone's presence." Ferocity burned in her eyes as she turned to us. "Orion, you remember your Trial. You killed some good friends of mine, in fact. Now, it must be Mortana's turn."

"That's only for new demons," he replied. "Mortana lived here once before. She's returning to her former home." He was trying to seem casual, but I could tell by the way he'd answered—a little too quickly—that this was *bad*.

Lydia smiled pleasantly. "Yes, but she never passed the Trial because she lived in the city at its founding. There were no trials in the 1680s. The law says that any demon entering the city must pass the Infernal Trial unless they have passed it before. I think you'll find that there are no exemptions stated for those who lived here when the city was founded." Her smile deepened as she looked at me. "You haven't gone soft in the City of Serpents, have you, Mortana?"

Fear settled in my gut.

The king stood, and warm light danced over his sharp jawline. "It is agreed, then. Mortana will join the City of

Thorns as long as she can pass our initiation. Then we will know if even the gods approve of her presence here." He turned to look at me, his crown gleaming. "Your Trial begins at midnight tonight. You have been formally summoned."

I couldn't exactly say no, could I? Mortana would say yes. She would be one hundred percent confident of her ability to get through this.

I could either break character or commit myself to a life-threatening trial.

So I found myself opening my mouth and saying, "I can easily pass an Infernal Trial. Of *course* the gods want me here." I chuckled softly. "I think we all know that."

Lydia was seething at me, her lip curled a little. "But what if Duke Orion tries to help her? Clearly, they have a relationship. We all know how skilled he is at killing. What if they *cheat*?"

The king cut a sharp glance to Orion. "Well, the duke will remain with me on the other side of the Acheron River, just outside my tower. We will be watching for you to cross over, or listening for the victory cry that would herald your death. We will have cocktails."

"And no flying," spat Lydia. "You can't use your wings."

Now there was one rule I'd have no problem sticking to. I didn't have wings, or magic, or really any hope to survive the rest of the night. Not unless I figured out a plan *real* fast. Maybe a quick, secretive exit from the city before anyone noticed.

Except the king wasn't dismissing us. No, he was drawing a dagger from his belt. Dread started to bloom in my chest as I realized what was happening now.

The king held out his palm and carved a slash in it. Crimson blood slid down his hand on to the marble dais beneath him. "Good. We will seal this sacred commitment with a blood oath."

Holy hell. Looks like I'd be working on a plan B.

CHAPTER 20

I paced the floor in Orion's apartment, gripping the bandage around my hand.

We'd managed to rush out of the Tower of Baal before anyone realized that I didn't heal like a demon. Still clutching my hand, I pivoted, pacing across the room again.

By contrast, Orion barely moved an inch as he watched me. Then he leaned back and spread his arms out across the sofa. "I'm starting to think this was all a mistake."

That wasn't exactly what I'd wanted to hear.

"What I would do," he went on, "if you hadn't agreed to the blood oath, would be to rush you out of the city. Then I'd make sure you stayed hidden. But you agreed to the blood oath." He leaned forward, pinning me with his gaze. "Why, exactly, did you do that? You just signed your own death sentence."

"I was staying in character," I shot back, exasperated.

"If I broke character, I'd be dead, right? In a fire. Mortana would never back down from a challenge. Mortana would do the Trial in a heartbeat. I have more of a chance in the Trial than I do in a fire pit. It was just a calculation of the odds."

"Mortana would do the Trial in a heartbeat," he repeated, and his eyes gleamed in the dim light, cold and ruthless. "Why are you talking about her as if you knew her?"

That was a good question. Why *did* I feel like I knew her?

I gripped my injured hand hard. "I don't know. She's like my id."

"Hmm. That sounds like a mortal thing I don't want to explore further because it'll annoy me." Orion's eyes narrowed. "The thing is, Rowan, Lydia will likely kill you with her fire magic. And I'm supposed to stay at the Tower. Even if you manage to survive the Trial by hiding, the other demons will quickly realize you don't have any powers. *Then* you'll die in a fire pit. And if you fail to show up, you'll die from the blood oath."

I stopped pacing to stare at him. "Are you trying to be helpful?"

He rose and grabbed my injured hand. "I'm going to heal you. I forgot quite how long it took for humans to heal. Ridiculous." He pulled me closer to him and sat again, and I plopped on the couch by his side. He unwrapped my bandaged palm, and our heads leaned close together we peered at the deep gash. He brushed his fingertips just to the right of the red slash. As he did, warm, healing magic skimmed over my hand. I stared as my skin smoothed over before my eyes.

"Are you healing me because you feel empathy, Orion?" I asked.

"I don't want blood on my floor," he murmured.

When the skin looked good as new, I pulled my hand away. "What can you tell me about what the Trial will be like? I need to make a good plan."

Our faces were close now, and a line formed between his eyebrows. "A good plan," he repeated, his tone suggesting it was the most absurd thing he'd ever heard.

Orion probably never needed to plan things, did he? He could show up and kill people.

"Just tell me how you think the night will go," I prompted.

"It'll begin in an old oak grove in the Elysian Wilderness. The other demons will be in different locations throughout the wood. They won't know which way you're moving, but they'll try to hunt you down by scent. If you stay in one place or try to hide, they'll converge and kill you. If you try to run, they'll smell you and kill you. They are far, *far* faster than you. And it's not just the five demons from the Quorum, mind you. It's anyone from the city who wants to participate. It could be a hundred demons. In order for the Trial to end, you'll need to survive for a full hour."

Despite the horror of what he was telling me, an idea was starting to form in my mind. "Lydia has fire magic. The others don't. So can fire hurt them?"

"Yes. Some only have strength and speed, and others have forms of elemental magic. You could be frozen to death, although Nama isn't great at hitting a moving target. It's more likely that she'd trap you in a wall of ice or something, then beat you to death and carve your heart out with her claws."

My throat went dry. "How thick is the ice?"

"It's not incredibly thick. I could probably punch my way through it. It's like glass."

My heart pattered in my chest. "Okay. I have a plan. Can we send Shai out to pick up a few things from my apartment?"

He frowned. "You can't use a gun, if that's what you're thinking."

I shook my head. "No. This is specialty equipment. Oh, and do you think Morgan will let me borrow his watch?"

"Yes. But what do you need?"

I closed my eyes, reviewing the items I had in mind. "My fire-retardant gels, clothing, a gas mask, and a fire blanket. Also, I have a knife that can shatter glass. Oh, and I'll need gasoline or another liquid accelerant, but she won't find that in my apartment. Obviously. I'm not insane."

He stared at me. "May I ask why you have these things?"

"Well, you have magic, and I have my own superpower. It's called anxiety. It's a pain in the ass, but I'm prepared for every fire scenario you can think of. And Facebook's algorithms identified me as anxious, so they started advertising things like a knife that can cut through glass if you drive your car off a bridge into a river." I frowned. "I don't even have a car, but I have the knife."

He looked transfixed. "Right."

"I'll also need bleach and ammonia. And a tool belt."

His body was completely still. "Is this just a random list of items? Have you done that thing that mortals do when their minds break from too much stress?"

"Oh! And this is crucial: we need to tell her to get the fox urine from under my bed," I added. "And a Super Soaker."

"Ah." His features softened. "Your mind *has* broken."

I reached out to touch his arm. "It hasn't. Trust me. I have a plan."

"Does this plan involve attacking demons with fox urine?"

I shook my head. "No. I have a better plan."

He still hadn't moved an inch. "The contents of your bedroom concern me."

"I just want to be prepared for the apocalypse, Orion. That's all. And that apocalypse is here, even if it's just for me."

"That's not what *apocalypse* means."

I lifted a finger. "Let's stay focused. Fox urine, bleach—"

"This sounds insane," he said, cutting me off, and scrubbed a hand over his jaw. "I thrive in chaos. I like to watch things burn. But this situation is making me feel something different, unfamiliar. I don't like it," he said in a clipped tone. "This is making my heart beat faster, almost like a...like a *warning*. As if something bad is about to happen."

My eyes widened. "Yeah. That's anxiety. Are you feeling anxious for my safety, or are you worried you'll be caught out?"

His gaze shuttered. "Don't be ridiculous. I'm a lethal four-hundred-year-old demon of chaos, imbued with godlike powers. I fear nothing."

"Not sure I believe you anymore, Orion."

I may not know magic, but I know anxiety.

CHAPTER 21

Darkness surrounded me in the oak grove. Beyond the stench of fox pee, the air smelled of moss and soil, and faintly of gasoline.

For years, I'd been waiting for the demon apocalypse, and now it was happening. At least for me.

My knees shook as I waited for the sound of the klaxon that would herald the beginning of the Trial.

There was only one rule: no flying. As the Lilu were the only type of demons with wings, if I could actually use them, I'd be simply flapping around above the trees the entire time.

I glanced up at the sky. Clouds covered the moon, which was both good and bad. The bad part was that I'd be reliant on the night vision goggles I'd bought last year off Amazon (in case of the apocalypse), and they weren't great. But the darkness was good, too. It gave me a little cover for the ridiculous suit I had on—a navy flame-retardant suit, with the safety stripes covered up. The demons might not notice the night vision goggles, the safety gloves, or the backpack I carried filled with supplies. They wouldn't see the sheen of the flame-retardant gel on my cheeks and chin.

And when this ended, I'd need to get this shit off quickly before anyone could see what I'd been up to.

Sweat ran down my body under the suit. Tonight, the forest air was hot and humid, and heavy with tension.

Demons never considered using tools or weapons. Honed by evolution, they didn't need technology. But me? I could only hope that my little arsenal would help me. And I prayed that the fox pee would disguise my scent, the way hunters used it in the woods.

My heart slammed against my ribs. Any moment now, the Trial would begin.

With my goggles on, I scanned the trees for signs of movement. My vision was black and white, and I could just see the trunks around me.

My plan for now was to get as close as possible to the river as quickly as I could. Before coming out here, I'd installed a compass app on Morgan's Apple Watch, so I knew exactly which way was north, and the river was about four miles. When I got there, I'd spend the rest of the time fending off attackers.

With a thundering heart, I checked my borrowed watch—two minutes until midnight.

In high school, I'd run track and cross country. I'd even made it to nationals. This felt a lot like the start of those meets, burning with adrenaline, waiting for the gun to go off…except in this race, I could end up battered to death by an angry mob of demons, so the stakes were just a *tad* higher than coming in second.

I watched the countdown on my watch for a few seconds, then pulled out my first weapon—the Super Soaker.

When the klaxon sounded, I started to run.

Unlike my high school track meets, I was carrying about ten pounds of weight, encased in a metallic suit, and wearing goggles. I was already sweating into the suit, so speed wasn't on my side tonight. As I ran, I breathed in the musky, acrid scent of fox pee, and my eyes watered.

With my night vision goggles, I scanned the trees for signs of movement. I ran for about ten minutes, sucking in breath sharply, without seeing a single demon. I thought I'd probably made it a mile and a half.

Only fifty minutes to go.

When my foot loudly snapped a twig, it occurred to me for the first time that speed might *not* be the most important thing. If they couldn't see me easily or smell me, they'd be relying on sound. That twig breaking the silence might as well have been a cannon going off.

I froze, scanning the woods around me and catching my breath.

My heart skipped a beat as I saw a demon moving toward me. Unlike me, he moved with shocking speed, his body like wind through the trees. But he was still some distance away.

Before he could get to me, I used the Super Soaker to spray gasoline on the ground between us. I created a wide arc, at least twelve feet, then dropped the gun and snatched the deodorant from my tool belt. I'd superglued a lighter to the can using a plastic binder clip, so it stuck out at just the right angle to form a blowtorch. The lighter itself had a rubber band around it to hold the flame when it was depressed.

My body shook as I flicked the lighter and the flame sprang to life. Then I pressed the top of the deodorant. Four feet of flames shot out into the air, and I lunged forward, angling the fire toward the gasoline. The reaction was instant—an enormous wall of fire surrounding me.

Now the demon was just on the other side of the flames—and by his luscious curls and ivory horns, I recognized him as a duke. The blood-guzzling gluttony demon bellowed in rage, and the sound slid through my bones. It wasn't just the sound itself that sparked my fear—he'd just alerted the entire demon army to my location.

I snatched the Super Soaker from the ground and sprayed through the flames toward the demon. The fire spread in his direction, and he backed away, staring at the flames and roaring.

I pivoted and broke into a run before more of them could find me. I had to put as much distance as possible between the bellowing demon and me.

I usually ran five days a week, often six to seven miles, maybe up to ten, and even with my backpack on, the adrenaline was giving me extra strength. I pumped my arms hard, running faster through the trees than I'd been moving before. But when I stole a glance behind me, I saw movement in the distance. A demon was closing in on me. No—not just a demon. With my goggles, I saw two…three…six?

Fuck. They were all over, and I still had a mile to get to the river.

New tactic.

My hands were shaking as I pulled off the night vision goggles, and I felt blind without them. Vulnerable. But for what I needed to do next, I couldn't have them on.

I unzipped my backpack and found the gas mask. When I slid it on over my face, my sense of vulnerability only increased. I pulled the hood over my head and tightened it as quickly as I could, and the eyepieces fogged a little.

Just like I'd done when I was mixing chemicals earlier, I had to test the filter first. I covered it, checking to make sure no air was escaping into the mask from other gaps. With the filter covered, I couldn't breathe at all, which was both terrifying and what I wanted.

Now I was ready.

I knelt down again and reached into the backpack for my glass jars. I started hurling them at the tree trunks, one by one. Within moments, the demons were coughing, then screaming.

I couldn't see very well through the darkness and the goggles, but I didn't think they were moving any closer to me.

I had no idea if demons were rushing at me from the north, but I hurled another jar in that direction, just in case, until I was surrounded by a cloud of homemade mustard gas on all sides.

Right now, the bleach and ammonia mix would be searing their lungs, stealing their breath, and burning and blistering their skin and eyes.

Was this prohibited by the Geneva Convention? Okay, *technically* yes, but those laws had been written for mortals. The demons would recover, even if the next twenty minutes would be deeply unpleasant.

I grabbed my backpack and started moving again.

With the gas mask on, I couldn't run anymore. For one thing, I could no longer see where I was going, and for another, it was incredibly hard to breathe in that thing. I could only hope the mustard gas took out any demons around me.

I checked the watch, making sure I was still heading north.

Twenty-one minutes. I only had to survive twenty-one more minutes, and I'd be free. Holy shit, this was actually working.

When I thought I'd cleared enough distance from the mustard gas, I pulled off my gloves and took a little breath, testing the air. My skin wasn't burning, and my lungs felt fine. I pulled the gloves back on and tried loosening my gas mask. Lungs seemed okay...

I took a deep breath. My eyes stung a little, but that was it.

I pulled the gas mask all the way off and took a few breaths, then quickly slipped my night vision goggles back on. Backpack hoisted, I started to run. I was closing the distance now, only a half mile or so to the river.

As I zoomed between the trunks, a chill rushed through the air, and the trees became hazy through my night vision goggles. Before I could figure out what had happened, I slammed into a wall of ice. A jolt of pain shot through my skull as the force of the crash cracked my goggles. I ripped them off and stared around me at a large sphere of ice.

Nama had already trapped me in here, and I didn't know how far away she was. But just as Orion had said, the ice was thin as glass.

As quickly as I could, I sprayed the ground around me with gasoline, then reached for the glass-breaking knife in my pocket. It didn't look like much more than a bit of plastic, but hidden within the plastic was a blade that popped out on impact. I slammed it hard against the ice, and it shattered around me.

With a thundering heart, I grabbed my flamethrower. I flicked the lighter on, pressed the deodorant, and blasted flames at the ground. Fire erupted around me, and fear twisted my heart. I *hated* fire.

But Nama was still running for me, and I blasted flames in her direction using the Super Soaker and the homemade flamethrower. In the distance, I stared in a sickening sort of horror as her hair and clothes caught fire from the flames on the ground. She screamed, the sound curdling my blood.

My pulse raced out of control. *She's a demon,* I reminded myself. *She'll get better.*

I only had a half mile left to go, and I checked my watch.

Ten minutes.

I just had to survive ten minutes.

I started to run again, but this time, I couldn't see the trees. I flicked on a light on the Apple Watch—which wasn't ideal, since people might see it. But it was the only way I could see to avoid running into an unyielding trunk. I ran with the flamethrower in one hand, pumping my arms hard as I headed for the river. The backpack bounced behind me, and I bounded over roots and stones. I was sweating *hard* in my suit as my body overheated.

As I moved closer to the city, I could turn off the light on my watch, as the lights from the town square illuminated the forest.

Suddenly, I heard Lydia's husky voice cut through the forest. "Demons, hear me! I'm following her trail! She's by the river!"

So *that's* how they'd been finding me, even through the stench of fox piss. They were tracking me through the woods, looking for the broken branches I'd left behind. And broken demons, too.

And now, Lydia was trying to summon all the demons to attack me at once.

Four minutes left.

Through the forest, I heard the bellowing of demon war cries—a deep, malignant sound that slid through my bones and sent my heart racing out of control. The ancient part of my brain was telling me to panic, that predators were coming for me. And for once, that anxious part of my brain was fucking right.

Get to the river, Rowan. Get there now.

The demons were coming to her call, bellowing for my blood. They were all heading for the river, closing in. Their otherworldly cries turned my blood to ice, and panic scraped up my spine. But I could see the river now through the trunks, glimmering in the lights from the Tower of Baal.

Three minutes left.

And what's more, I could smell the scent of gasoline I'd poured out two hours ago.

It was time for the pièce de résistance—my real shock and awe.

When I reached the riverbank, I pulled out the flamethrower and flicked the lighter. As I touched the arc of flame to the ground, a wall of pure fire raced out from either side. I'd created a mouth to hell.

I leapt through the fire into the ice-cold Acheron River and swam down to the bottom, deep into the murk. Turning, I swam east for a moment and then I unzipped my fire suit. My lungs started to burn as I held my breath and stuffed the suit and tools into the backpack. I zipped it up and let it sink to the bottom, and then, my secret hidden, I swam to the northern bank.

And as I pulled myself out, I heard the sound of the klaxon blaring. There they were—the king standing by Orion's side, waiting for me. My little victory party. A small crowd stood behind them, staring at me.

Holy fucking shit.

Holy fucking *shit.* I'd made it.

Joy surged through me. I'd *survived.* Maybe everything was going to be okay after all. Had I really done this?

Soaking wet, I hoisted myself onto the bank, trying to hide exactly how exhausted I was.

I saw the king raise his cocktail glass in a toast to me, and Orion's pale eyes shone brightly in the darkness.

Under my fire suit, I'd been wearing a sleek black outfit—fitted black pants and a corset. If I weren't soaked in river water, I might *actually* look pretty good right now.

As I stepped into the stony esplanade before the Tower of Baal, I raised my arms in victory and surveyed the demons around me. No one was exactly cheering at my survival, which seemed a bit rude. In fact, they looked a little pissed off.

And as the klaxon continued to blare, I felt a sharp tug at my wet hair, dragging me back onto the stones. I slammed down hard on the ground. The next thing I knew, Lydia was on top of me. She wrapped her hands around my throat and squeezed, fangs bared and a maniacal look in her eyes. Then she raised one of her hands, and gleaming claws burst forth.

She was going to cut my heart out, wasn't she? That was how demons killed each other. They ripped each other's hearts out with their claws.

"There's only room for one queen," she hissed under her breath.

I couldn't breathe. Oh, holy fuck, I couldn't breathe...

CHAPTER 22

Hypervigilance: a heightened state of anxiety and alertness, a tendency to scan the environment for threats.

In my everyday life, it was dysfunctional. In the world of demons, it didn't hurt to turn up the dial, because somehow, I'd missed that Lydia had been sneaking up behind me, and now she was crushing my throat.

As my vision started to go dark, enormous hands reached down and ripped Lydia off me.

The sound of the klaxon died out at last.

I sucked in air, trying to hide exactly how fragile I was. I wanted to gasp deeply and audibly, but I was worried that would make me look too mortal. All eyes were on me right now. Had they noticed how easily she'd taken me down? Did they know I was mortal?

Unwilling to look weak in front of the others, I forced myself up.

But as I steadied my breathing, a rush of movement caught my eye. I turned to see the blood-guzzling demon running for me from the bridge, the wind whipping at his luxurious curls. With a bellowing war cry, he was charging for me at an alarming speed. Moonlight glinted off his ivory horns, and long silver claws shot from his fingers. If I tried to run, they'd all see how slow I was.

"It's over!" called the king. "The Trial has ended."

But the duke wasn't listening, and he was almost upon me. Ten feet away…two feet away…

I froze in place, staring at him. The bloodthirsty duke reared back his arm, ready to strike at my chest—

Fast as lighting, Orion shifted in front of me, blocking the hit with his enormous body. I heard the sound of claws ripping into his flesh, and my stomach tightened.

Horrified, I wrapped my arm around his back to keep him upright and craned my neck to see the damage. The one way a demon could die was having his heart cut out.

The duke's eyes were wide as he ripped his blood-covered claws out of Orion's chest.

"What have you done?" someone shouted. "Did you kill the Lord of Chaos?"

My heart slammed against my ribs. Orion was clutching his chest, bleeding all over the stones.

The world had gone dreadfully silent, and panic tightened my throat. "Are you okay?" I whispered.

Before us, the duke's claws retracted, and his hand flew to his mouth. "Oh, Lucifer save me, I didn't mean to do that. I was aiming for the succubus. Why did you jump in the way, you idiot? You know what it means if she survives."

Orion raised a bloodied hand. "I'm fine," he said at last, and then he darted forward and grabbed the duke by his neck. The duke's eyes bulged, and Orion lifted him by the throat, choking him. Silver claws shot out from Orion's fingertips.

Oh, *God.* He wasn't going to—

Orion's claws sliced into the demon's chest, and one sharp, ruthless swipe carved out the heart. The glutton demon's bony corpse fell to the ground with a *thud,* his chest cavity gaping open and his body still twitching.

Holy *shit.*

My gorge rose, but I couldn't afford to throw up. I had to look like that was normal. All perfectly normal. Oh, *God,* the way it glistened...

Orion shrugged. "What? He attacked me. I was well within my rights to end his life, as I'm sure you all agree."

The crowd murmured. The shocked excitement in their eyes reminded me a little of the glee in my classmates' faces when I'd had my meltdown.

Orion turned to look at me, brow furrowed. Was that a flicker of worry in his pale eyes?

"You're okay?" I asked again. "I think we should get you home." And I had to get out of here before the bruises bloomed all over my throat.

But the king was prowling closer, dressed in a finely cut midnight suit. His dark eyes were locked on me, and a smile curled his lips. "Good. Everyone survived, then, it seems. Lady Mortana, house of Lilitu. Duchess of the Ward of Asmodeus. After tonight, the abandoned ward will no longer be abandoned." He raised his hands to the dark skies. "The council of seven is reunited!"

. . .

INSTEAD OF CHEERS, only silence greeted his pronouncement. Then, the sound of a throat clearing broke the silence. The king lowered his hands to look down at the twitching corpse on the ground.

"OR, nearly reunited We will have to get a new one, I suppose." He raised his hands to the skies again. "Anyway, the celebratory party begins immediately in the Temple of Ishtar!"

Orion had just been nearly stabbed to death, another duke died, and they wanted to throw a party? I was so caught up on that thought, I nearly missed the other part —*Duchess.* That was me now. A demonic duchess.

A few people clapped, but it didn't sound enthusiastic. Orion was standing straighter now, and I let my arm drop from his back.

My gaze flicked to Lydia, who still seemed furious. Darkness coiled around her, curling into the night sky like smoke.

If I hadn't been nearly strangled, I'd probably make a big, cocky pronouncement right now, like Mortana would. But my voice box had been crushed, and I didn't think I'd sound normal when I spoke.

Clearly, I had to watch my back here. Lydia would rip my heart out the first chance she got.

I hadn't really thought about the implications until now, but as the only person in the Asmodean Ward, I would be its leader by default. Lydia was no longer the only female on the council, and she didn't like that one bit. I'd be part of the Quorum now. Close to the king. A rival for the role of queen.

She just had no idea I wouldn't be here that long.

I glanced back at the Bridge of Harrowing and saw that some of the other demons from the forest were starting to stumble out, looking like zombies—bodies scorched, clothing singed. Some had blistered skin and watering eyes.

This night had been brutal for lots of us, but I supposed only a single death was a victory.

Orion pulled me close to him, almost protectively. "My lady will want to dry off, and I'll need a change of clothes after that unfortunate incident. We will soon join you at the temple."

He grabbed me by the hand, leading me to the street on the far side of the esplanade. Within moments, a sleek black car pulled up, and Orion opened the door for me. I slid inside and buckled up while Orion told the mortal cab driver to take us back to his apartment in the Leviathan Hotel.

Now, for the first time tonight, I felt the full weight of my exhaustion. My muscles burned with fatigue, and my throat felt raw. Even without the other clothes, I still smelled faintly of fox pee.

Never in my life had I craved a bath so badly.

When the car started rolling, Orion turned to look at me. "Congratulations," he said softly. "Duchess Mortana of Lilitu."

* * *

THE FIRST THING I'd done upon our return to Orion's apartment was to run upstairs to the balcony bath. As I'd filled it with scalding water, I'd stripped off my clothes. Now, I was leaning back into the hot, bubbling bath as the steam curled around me. I let my muscles melt and scrubbed my body clean.

While I soaked in the heat, I gazed up at the stars. I could just about make out the North Star, I thought, at the end of the Little Dipper. Mom had taught me to find it, another survival technique. I looked for it at night sometimes, centering myself. It was just that the compass app was a lot easier and worked even when there were clouds.

I let out a long, shaky breath. My mind kept flicking back to the demon I'd hit with fire. Hair blazing, clothes flaming...*horrible.*

I shuddered, suddenly struck by the feeling that I didn't want to be alone.

Half of me wanted to call Orion in here while I bathed to keep me company. But like the primal keening of the demons' war cries in the wilderness, I sensed instinctively that it wouldn't end well.

I rose abruptly from the bath. Water dripped off my bare skin in the cool night air, and I started to towel off.

Sex with Orion absolutely could not happen. For one thing, he'd threatened to kill Shai, and I'd just seen exactly how efficient he could be with killing. In under a second, she could be dead. On top of that, he was a suspect. I was sure that the police had rules about not sleeping with anyone under a criminal investigation.

His attraction to me was probably fake, anyway.

I mean...it didn't *feel* fake. That encounter in the

Tower of Baal, with my legs wrapped around him—it *really* felt like he hadn't been faking that desire. The heated look in his eyes, the exquisitely sensual stroke of his magic over me, the feel of his hardness between my thighs…

I started to towel-dry my hair, flipping it over my head. Anyway, he was bad news.

Once dry, I slipped into the clothes I'd laid out for myself—tiny, silky underwear in a deep blue, and a matching lace demicup bra. I stepped into the underwear, doing my best not to think about Orion, and then pulled on a soft black dress. It was kind of a cute 1960s look—short as hell, but with long sleeves and a turtleneck, and smoking hot when paired with thigh-high boots, succubus style.

When I came downstairs again, I found Orion sitting on his cream sofa with a glass of whiskey. He'd changed into a white button-down shirt with the sleeves rolled up to the elbows, exposing his creepy snake tattoo. He wore deep forest pants that looked like raw silk and probably cost ten thousand dollars.

"The duchess returns," he said as I sat beside him. "You know, love, I didn't think a mortal could do what you did. It seems you're capable of great surprises." His voice was a velvety caress. "Your not-so-adoring crowd will be expecting you soon. Mortana doesn't tire, I'm afraid."

"How's your chest?"

"Same as it ever was." A sly smile. "Fine on the outside, dead on the inside. Fortunately, only metaphorically."

I crossed my legs, and his gaze flicked to my bare

thighs for just a moment before he rose. "Stand up. Let me heal your bruises."

I pulled down the high neck of my dress. He frowned, then touched me lightly, just beneath my chin. I closed my eyes as the sensual feel of his magic washed over me. Simmering waves snaked around my throat, making my muscles relax.

He pulled his hand away. "There. good as new."

Sighing, I sat again. "Don't you want to know everything that happened?"

He took a seat across from me. "I saw the ragged remnants of your enemies. Did I mention that there's something kind of terrifying about you?"

"You killed fifty demons, didn't you? That means you ripped out fifty demon hearts in the forest. I think you're more terrifying."

He gave an easy shrug. "But I'm obviously dangerous. People can tell that as soon as they meet me. You disguise it. You're a lion dressed as a lamb." He frowned. "And then in a second lion disguise, since you're also supposed to be Mortana."

"I have layers." I raised my eyebrows. "And maybe a dark side."

"About that." He leaned forward, his blue eyes piercing me. "You told your secrets, Rowan, in that prison cell. But you didn't tell all of them, did you? There was something you kept hidden."

Even from myself. That thought rang out in my mind—a voice that wasn't quite my own.

Hidden from myself.

What the fuck?

I gave Orion a tired smile. "No, I don't spill my darkest secrets. They make people uncomfortable."

"I doubt you'd find that to be the case with me."

I doubted that, too. My darkness would be nothing to him. He held a world of shadows within himself.

But I wasn't about to spill my guts to one of my suspects, and I had a very important question to ask him. One that related to *my* investigation. "Orion, when we were in the Tower of Baal, one of the demon males had a symbol on his head. Like a crescent moon. What is that?"

He shifted into the cushion and spread his arms out across the sofa back. When human men took up space like that, it was a defensive posture. Was it the same for demons?

"Sometimes, we shift to a more bestial, darker form. Black eyes. Sometimes, scales emerge. And we'll have a demon mark. When we shift, it can appear."

"What makes a demon shift?"

"We feel emotions very, very intensely. And when that, happens, it can reveal our true selves."

Fascinating. "But you don't feel empathy."

"I don't. Some of us shut things down. It makes it easier to think logically in the haze of emotions."

"Okay." I bit my lip. "But back to the mark—"

His eyes were growing darker, weren't they? This topic was making him shift a little. Weird.

"Does every demon have their own unique mark?" I asked.

"Yes."

I drummed my fingertips on my knees. I needed to be

an undercover cop about this and not push the point too much, but the desperation was building in me. "So do you know what everyone's mark is? Have you seen them all?"

"No, most demons keep them hidden. Sometimes, the marks betray things about people they'd rather keep secret. Powers, the truth about their lineage…"

"What about a star?" I asked, gripping the armrests.

As soon as the shadows slid through his eyes, it was clear I'd struck a nerve. He was shifting, wasn't he? And it wasn't just his eyes that changed. The room was going darker around us, and his mood swallowed up the light. "Why, exactly, are you asking about that?" His voice was a low, quiet warning.

What the hell… Maybe demon psychology was different than humans', but he was definitely defensive. I'd stumbled into some kind of dangerous territory.

I inhaled sharply. "No reason. I just thought if there was a moon, there must be a star."

He sucked in a deep breath. "A star identifies the Lightbringer, our destined leader. No one has seen that mark in a long time."

An ice-cold chill rippled through me. "Not on the king, then?"

"I've never seen his mark. No one has." The shadows around him seemed to sharpen into blades, growing darker.

And all of this was a *fantastic* reminder of why I couldn't be seduced by his beauty. Did he look perfect? Yes. Was he sketchy as fuck and possibly a murderer? Also yes.

"It seems like you killed that duke very easily," I said. "Was it really necessary?"

"He wanted to kill you so badly, he wasn't playing within the rules. He seemed like a liability."

I frowned. "So when you have a difficult interpersonal situation…do you often just kill the person to make things easier?"

His eyebrows rose. "'Difficult interpersonal situation'? Is that what you call it when someone tries to kill you?"

"Okay. Point taken." My head was spinning, and I wasn't quite sure I was keeping up with the level of danger in this world.

I glanced at the macabre tattoo on his arm—the noose made from a snake. "Since you're not going to tell me about your mark, how about this: why did you get that tattoo?"

A muscle tensed in his jaw, and he rose, towering above me. "We should go to your victory party."

Wow. Another off-limits conversation. "Give me a second to do my hair and makeup."

I could be allied with my worst enemy. But at least I'd learned something new. If I wanted to identify my mother's killer, I'd have to try to provoke strong reactions from every demon. I needed to see their marks.

Unfortunately, I'd have to anger a *lot* of demons in the process.

CHAPTER 23

When our cab arrived at the Temple of Ishtar, another red carpet stretched out to greet us.

The temple was just north of the Tower of Baal and south of where Orion lived. Small crowds of demons flanked either side, snapping photos on their cell phones. It was after one a.m., and I was starting to get the impression that no one here slept. As I stepped out of the car, I felt underdressed for this crowd of onlookers. But Mortana wouldn't be self-conscious, so I just gave everyone that smug demon smirk. When Orion was by my side, I made sure to walk with a swing of my hips over the carpet.

A humid ocean breeze rustled through my hair, and I licked the salt off my lips. The Temple of Ishtar was actually a bar now, but it still looked like a temple, with Doric columns and carvings of a beautiful, winged woman jutting out from the roof.

With Orion, I ascended the steps and passed through

the towering open doors. There, I found myself in an enormous hall of golden stone. Demons in gowns and suits stood on a floor of blue and gold tiles. On the walls to the right and left, mosaics formed images of golden lions. Directly across from us, the columns were open to the sea, and a balmy breeze rushed in. Sparkling phosphorescence made the waves glitter under the night sky.

I glanced at the golden-brick cocktail bar to my right, where row upon row of liquor bottles stood before the mirror. God, this place was amazing. It was unfortunate I wasn't actually a succubus.

When I glanced at Orion, a shiver of unease rippled through me. For a number of reasons, I didn't want him to be my enemy. But given how he'd reacted to the star question, I'd have to keep my eyes open to the possibility.

I watched as he crossed to the bar and chatted with the bartender. Was he avoiding me?

After today, my nerves were completely shot. But *Mortana,* my shadow-self, wanted a drink. So when a server brought over a tray of bubbly cocktails in champagne flutes, I plucked one off and took a sip, tasting gin and lemon.

When a hush fell over the room, I turned to see King Cambriel arrive, his golden hair falling over a gorgeous velvet suit. He walked arm-in-arm with Lydia, who wore a black leather jacket over a silky gown with slits in strategic places. The dress showed off little glimpses of her waist, her ribs, and part of her thigh. She looked cool as hell.

What was *not* as cool was the way she snarled at me when she met my gaze.

She didn't know this, but I was probably the one person in this bar who didn't actually care that she was on the king's arm. At least, not beyond the fact that I had a deal with Orion.

I had two goals here tonight. One was to get the king's attention so that I could start to learn about his weaknesses. But the other was my own. Could I sufficiently rile up this crowd that I saw some of their demon marks? Could I churn up emotions powerful enough to make some of them shift?

Orion had said that he, the king, Lydia, and Mortana all had fire magic. That meant three marks I needed to see in order to rule them out.

Right now, Lydia had the king's attention. I *thought* I had an idea of how to enrage her and provoke the king's emotions at the same time. I watched as Lydia grabbed a champagne flute, then leaned in, whispering to the king in a conspiratorial way.

Time to get his attention, and that meant getting Orion's attention. Jealousy would be my friend tonight.

But before I could find Orion, a female demon with a halo of white curls caught my eye. Her cheekbones shimmered with pale glitter. With a tight smile, she sauntered over to me. "Well, Mortana. Congratulations are in order." She touched her throat and swallowed with a grimace. "I've never met a demon with your powers of poison before. Quite intriguing. Miasma magic."

I gave her a fake smile and a shrug. "I don't often have a reason to poison people."

"I'm Nama."

Ah…the one with the ice powers.

When her glance darted over my shoulder, her expression changed. She licked her lips, and her pupils dilated. I stole a quick look behind me to see Orion.

So that's why she'd approached me. *Keep your enemies close...*

Her gray eyes locked on mine again, and the look she gave me sent a chill through my body. "It's interesting to see the duke getting close to someone new. Before you arrived, he and I were going to be quite good friends." She flicked her white hair over her shoulder. "I'll admit we haven't had the chance to become properly acquainted yet, but I think I'm considered one of the best marriage matches for him."

"Oh?" I took a sip of my cocktail, trying to get into the bitchy Mortana mindset. "Considered by whom?"

Her lips thinned. "By many. He and I both come from wealth. You know, we have a lot in common. We both love the sea."

My shadow-self found her irritating, so I lifted my cocktail glass and stared into it. I swirled my drink, looking disinterested in her. "Everyone loves the sea. Why would you possibly think that would make you well suited? It's akin to liking sunlight."

"He likes pastries, and I'm an excellent cook," she said sharply. "And when I injured my thigh in a sea cave, he healed me. Listen, Mortana, have you been spending a lot of time around mortals, by any chance? You seem as dull-witted and unsophisticated as they are. There's something really not right about you."

I gave her a patronizing smile. I was starting to find that it wasn't hard at all to come up with what Mortana would say. "Maybe I'm unsophisticated, but I'm going to guess that you hurt your thigh on purpose, then ran to Orion crying that you needed help. Don't you think he could smell the desperation?" I sipped my cocktail, watching as her cheeks went red. "Don't mistake pity for affection, my dear."

Wow. Mortana was a bitch. And maybe it was kind of fun.

Nama's eyes darkened to shadows, and her jaw went tight. She leaned in and whispered in my ear, "You're older than I am, Mortana. But I've been told why the king wisely rid the city of your kind. The succubi whores like you brought disrepute to our city, begging for cock like you did. Disgusting. Dirty. I heard what he said about you. How you beg for it on your hands and knees. And you might charm Orion for a week with whatever tricks your twat can manage, but he'll quickly see that you are *all* used up. No better than a mortal whore. He'll want someone younger. Cleaner. They always do. Tell me, harlot, do you know what happened to the succubus Jezebel in the ancient world?"

I kept that serene smile on my face, but I had no idea. "Of course."

"Maybe you'll find yourself thrown from a palace window, trampled by horses, then eaten by stray dogs," she hissed. "Just like Jezebel."

Ah. Learned something every day.

CHAPTER 24

I kept my face calm and raised an eyebrow. "Is that a threat, Nama?"

"None of the demon males stepped in to protect your kind when you needed it. They fucked you, then left you to die. All it takes is one look at your harlot-red hair and the repulsive way you move to know you're not wife material. You're an easy, available hole." She backed away and fluttered her eyelashes at me. "Nice talking to you, Duchess." Then she spun on her heels to walk away.

Her words were directed at Mortana, but there was enough personal stuff included there to make my stomach tighten with anger anyway. No better than a mortal? *Harlot*-red hair?

Had to say I didn't like Nama very much.

And when I turned to see that she had sashayed over to Orion, that she was giggling up at him, I felt a tiny little ember of my own jealousy burning. But that was absurd. Orion and I didn't have a *real* relationship, obviously. He'd hired me to do a job, I was treating him as a suspect, and that was that. But I found myself staring as Nama looked up at him adoringly, lightly stroking his tattooed arm. My id—my shadow-self—was getting angry.

I glanced behind me and found that the king's attentions were occupied with Lydia.

It was time to turn all this annoying shit to my advantage, *now*.

I turned back to Orion and Nama. Now, Orion was looking at me, the corner of his mouth quirked in a half-smile. It was almost like he knew I'd felt jealous. But there was no way he could have sensed that, so that was probably me being paranoid.

I summoned my id. With a seductive smile worthy of Mortana, I beckoned Orion toward me.

If I said it wasn't satisfying to watch him brush Nama off and walk closer to me, I'd be lying. She was giving me the look of death, like she was going to rip my head off any second now. The unfortunate part was that she probably could.

Orion prowled closer with languid movements, eyes locked on me. When he was just inches away, I reached up and pulled him down closer, whispering, "Let's make the king jealous."

"Hello, love." His low whisper was a seductive stroke up my spine. My pulse started to race. "Are you ready to leave your inhibitions behind?"

Just being close to him and feeling his magic pulse over my body made my breath hitch, even if all this was just for show. "Yes." *Must...remember...he's my suspect...*

Taking me by the hand, Orion led me to a chair near the king. In the next heartbeat, he was pulling me into his lap. I could feel all eyes on us now, but my attention was on Orion. His exquisite beauty was still shocking to me. His lids looked heavy as his eyes darkened. I felt a blush creep over my cheeks.

"Your friend Nama seems to think I'm taking something that belongs to her," I said quietly.

His fingertips brushed up my leg just above my knee, and heat rushed through my body. "I belong to no one." With excruciating slowness, his hand moved further up my thigh, then slid under the hem of my dress, his touch scorching. He leaned in, lips lightly brushing over mine. The Lord of Chaos had an excruciating capacity for restraint. The graze of his lips against mine was making my nipples go hard in my silky bra. His hand moved higher, dragging my hem with it. He fingertips stroked slowly up and down my skin…

God, I wanted to take him somewhere alone.

This is just a job.

I wondered if he could hear how fast my heart was beating now. Did he realize that when I told him I didn't find him attractive, I was lying through my teeth?

For his part, his muscles seemed tightly coiled. Maybe this restraint wasn't so easy for him.

Unable to contain myself anymore, I pressed my lips against his. Under the hem of my dress, his fingers tightened on my flesh. He kissed me back slowly, deliciously, his tongue brushing against mine. When he pulled away from the kiss, my heart was racing out of control. I ached for him. And if all of this was happening in front of other people—that wasn't my fault. That was *Mortana's* fault.

I could feel everyone watching us now, but to my shock, I found that I actually didn't care.

He moved his mouth close to my ear. "Why do I get the feeling that you want more?" His deep purr made me melt into him.

I could feel my cheeks heating. "Just doing my job," I whispered back.

The brush of his fingertips was a slow, maddening touch that left a trail of heat in its wake, now near my panties. I felt as if there was something reverent in the way he was touching me, and my core pulsed, aching for him. Slowly, he moved his hands over my panties, brushing his fingertip down the front. I gasped at the sensation. I was sure that he could feel *exactly* how turned on I was through the silk, and I felt my cheeks going redder. From him, I heard a quiet growl that seemed to reverberate over my skin.

I should probably stop this now. Succubus or not, I wasn't going to fuck him right here in front of a crowd.

"I think that's enough," I whispered.

When he pulled his hand away from me, out of my dress, I rose from his lap. I felt my cheeks and chest flushed with heat as I looked around, seeing everyone's judgmental eyes on me. Nama looked like she was about to crush the glass she was holding.

But there was *her* demon mark—a byzantine golden symbol that beamed from her forehead.

Several females gaped at me, seething, their marks blazing. One had the mark of a serpent, the other a triangular shape. It seemed that Nama wasn't the only one who had designs on Orion.

But Lydia and the king? The ones I actually hoped to see? No demon marks on display.

I was still catching my breath when I caught the king's eye. That had gone a little far, hadn't it? But I'd gotten what I'd wanted—his attention.

He crossed over to me swiftly, his eyes dark as night, pale hair draped over his velvet suit. His jaw was set tight, and he boxed me in until my back was against a column. He pressed his hands on either side of my head, his crown gleaming in the lights of the bar.

My heart skipped a beat. I'd *definitely* gotten his attention.

His stance was possessive, dominating. And since I was supposed to be an ancient and powerful demon, I couldn't shrink from it. "I hope you will find your new accommodations in the Asmodean Ward to your liking. I had my mortal servants working day and night to get it in good condition. I had my best magicians working on it, too. I can give you *anything* you desire."

I smiled serenely. "I haven't had a chance to see it yet. I was at Orion's apartment earlier."

His muscles visibly tensed. "Why be with a duke when you could be with a king?" He sounded almost pleading. This was driving him mad. "I don't understand."

I looked into his chiseled features. "I could be with a king?"

"Don't you remember, in those days when you were with my father," he said through gritted teeth, "don't you remember how much I wanted you?"

Of *course*. Motivated by jealousy, the little prince wanted what his father had. The succubus mistress.

"Did you?" I asked with a smile. "It seems so long ago. It's just that I notice Orion more. He pays so much attention to me. He tells me things, all about himself. You haven't really told me about yourself. It's hard for me to desire someone unless I know what makes him vulnerable."

Over his shoulder, I could see Lydia fuming. Unfortunately, I couldn't see her mark.

"Tomorrow," he replied. "I'm having a party in my penthouse suite in the Tower of Baal. You must be there. I will *not* take no for an answer. Come by yourself. There's no reason to bring the duke."

But the duke, paradoxically, was the key to his affections. All my power over the king depended on his jealousy.

"I'd love to come, but Orion will be joining me. Once you tell me more about yourself, we can get to know each other better."

He nodded curtly, then dropped his hands. With the look he was giving me, I had the sense that he didn't hear "no" often. "Fine. Bring the duke," he muttered. "He isn't a threat to me."

Good news for Orion's spy mission: the king wasn't a very good liar.

CHAPTER 25

It was nearly dawn by the time we reached my new home in the Asmodean Ward. Orion and I jumped in a cab, not saying a single word about our very public kiss. I only told him we had party plans for the next night, and he seemed pleased at my progress.

When we arrived at my house, a man in a black suit and hat opened the cab door for me. A second doorman opened the building's front doors into a hall with pale blue and gold tiled floors. High above, arches of a pale buttery stone swept over us. Sweeping staircases led up to a mezzanine floor.

In the center of the lobby, the ceiling was painted with an image of a nude woman, a snake wrapped around her legs and body. Lilith, I thought. While most of the hall was gleaming, restored through magic, the ceiling had faded and chipped over time.

To my surprise, Orion stared at the fresco for a long time, his body completely still. He normally seemed so bored with things, but either the naked woman or the snake had caught his attention. In fact, I sensed him shifting a little, the shadows bleeding into the air around him.

While he studied Lilith, I crossed to the far side of the hall, where arches opened onto a courtyard with an enormous pool. Beyond the pool, I could see the river through a set of columns, the dark water glinting with just a hint of morning light. And just on the other side of the river was the forbidding Elysian Wilderness. I shivered, not wanting to remember the hour I'd spent there, fighting for my life.

Orion said the Puritans thought the natural world was dangerous. Right now, I felt their fear. I understood why the devil scared the shit out of them. The primal power of these demons, their bestial side—it was terrifying.

"You need sleep." Orion's deep voice pulled me from my worries.

"No arguments here." My body was exhausted at this point, and I desperately wanted rest. I followed Orion up a flight of stairs, and we stopped at a door that had once been painted a deep maroon, the color now faded with time. He slid a skeleton key into the lock, then opened the door, handed me the key, and flicked on a light. I found myself staring at the key in my palm, then tracing its shape.

I owned a key like this. It was one of the few things that I'd always kept close to me until the night Orion had abducted me. My heart raced as I stared at it, and then I slid it into my pocket and followed him into the apartment.

The walls within were stone, like a medieval castle,

except they were smooth and gleaming. Enormous windows overlooked the pool, the water of which had started to glitter a little with peach light as the first blush of sun began to tinge the sky with gold. Stairs led to a loft floor, which must be where the bed was. A chandelier hung from the ceiling, a circle of wood that looked as if it had once held candles, but now boasted electric lights.

"The king must have had this place wired today," said Orion. "He's desperately trying to impress you, I think."

"He told me that he used to lust after Mortana when she was with his dad." My lip curled. "He really has a lot of Oedipal stuff going on."

"Of course he wanted his father's lover." Orion crossed to an open archway and peered in. "He's made everything modern. *Ridiculously* so. He's put a cappuccino machine in the kitchen, and even I don't have one of those. I'm wondering if I need to seduce the king now."

I crossed to the stairs, then turned to look at him. "Will you stay? I mean, you said I might be in danger."

Amusement shone in his pale eyes, and he dropped down on one of the leather sofas. He stretched out his arms across its back, and I had a feeling that he was *well* aware of how hot he looked as his shirt clung to his magnificent body. "I'll be here."

Somehow, he'd made that one sentence sound like an indecent invitation.

"That kiss in the bar was just a job, of course." Why did I say that? I sounded desperately defensive.

"Of course. I'm glad we're in agreement." A smile played over his lips. "Go to sleep, Rowan. I'll be here."

* * *

EVEN AS THE sun poured into the room though the arched windows, I continued to sleep on the softest bed I'd ever touched. By the time I woke, the afternoon sun was already high in the sky. I'd slept in my underwear, and the sheets felt silky against my bare skin.

I sat up and rubbed my eyes, taking in the sun-drenched space around me. The loft above the suite included a large bedroom with a railing on one side and a marble bathroom and bathtub on the other. I rose from the bed and crossed to the bathroom to splash water on my face. Mentally, I tried to reorient myself. Night and day seemed mixed up here.

I pulled off my underwear and turned on the shower. Steam started to billow around the tiles, and I grabbed the soap and washed.

My pulse raced whenever I thought about Orion's lips brushing over mine. When I thought of what he'd look like without his shirt on...

Insanely, I wanted him in there with me.

Everything about him distracted me. I turned down the temperature of the shower until a blast of cold water started to clear my head and sharpen my senses.

Tonight, I was supposed to go to a party in the king's penthouse. I was *pretty* pleased with how well I'd been able to get the king's attention. But what if I learned his weakness before I solved my mom's murder? I hadn't seen a single star, and I'd need to be here a while to hunt the killer down.

Could I just...lie to Orion until I got what I needed?

Shit. No. Not when he'd threatened Shai's life.

Goosebumps covered every inch of my body in the freezing shower, and my nipples were hard as rocks. With teeth chattering, I turned the shower off.

I grabbed a towel and began to dry off, only to recall that I had no clean clothes upstairs.

Chilly, I crossed to the balcony. When I peered over the edge, I saw that someone had delivered all my new clothes from Orion's apartment.

Gripping the towel around myself, I headed downstairs. A knocking sound echoed into the room, and I watched as Orion moved to open the door, his silver hair ruffled.

What I didn't expect to see—what I really didn't *want* to see—was Nama sauntering into the room with a basket of fresh-baked goods.

She'd come to prove herself to him with croissants.

CHAPTER 26

Her white hair cascaded over a thin white dress. On the one hand, it looked like an innocent sundress. On the other, I didn't think it was an accident that when the afternoon sunlight hit the material, it became almost translucent. I could see the shape of her breasts through the fabric, the nipples standing at attention, and with the angle of the light hitting the doorway, she practically glowed.

She shot me a look of death, then smiled at Orion again. "I was bringing you some chocolate croissants at the Leviathan Hotel, but your doorman told me you were here. I must say, I found it a bit shocking. I wanted to make sure no harm had come to you, given what we know of her kind."

With my chin held high and proud like a demon's, I descended the stairs. "As you can see, he's fine."

Orion grabbed one of the croissants and dropped back into a chair. He met my gaze and gave me a wicked smile, eyes twinkling. "She didn't leave any marks that will last forever."

I bit my lip, watching Nama's reaction. Her demon mark beamed from her forehead. If all the demons were so easy to provoke, I'd find the murderer in no time.

Clutching my towel with one hand, I plucked a warm croissant from the basket. "Thanks for the breakfast. You can go now." Ahhh...my id was a fucking bitch, but definitely fun. "Feel free to pop by tomorrow morning, Nama. We might have worked up an appetite again."

The mark blazed from her skin. She pressed her lips into a thin line, and she turned to go. But before she left, she whipped around and grabbed me *hard* by the back of my neck. I dropped my towel as she yanked me close to her ear, and she whispered, "There's something not right about you. Something besides you being a whore. I saw you in the forest, dressed in that strange suit. I smelled that putrid scent. You smelled like animal piss. No one believes me because they think I'm mad, but I plan to find out what your game is."

"Get your hands off her, Nama," Orion snarled from behind.

She released my neck and hissed at me. An actual hiss, like a snake.

With a furious blush crawling over my cheeks, I scrambled to pick my towel off the floor. I wasn't sure what was more horrifying right now, being fully exposed in front of these two demons, or the fact that Nama might know I was mortal.

The door slammed behind her, and I hastily wrapped

the towel around myself. When I turned to Orion, I could feel that my cheeks were burning red.

For his part, he looked fucking delighted. Infinitely amused.

"What?" I snapped.

He just shrugged. "That was a gorgeous view I wouldn't mind seeing again. That's all."

My jaw tightened. "We have a problem."

"We do," he agreed, his smile fading. "She's watching you too closely because she's threatened. But I don't think you need to worry about her. She doesn't have a lot of credibility here. Everyone knows she's unhinged. She's never learned to control her emotions." His eyes lingered over my bare shoulders. "I liked you better without the towel."

"Can you turn around so I can get dressed?" I asked.

With a sigh, he turned to face the other direction. "When we're at the king's penthouse tonight, he may want to see you alone, but I want to stay close to you. The king, as you might have gathered, can be dangerous."

With Orion's back to me, I dropped the towel to the floor. When it hit the tiles, I heard a quiet growl rise from his chest, nearly imperceptibly. He wanted me.

What would it take to make *his* demon mark come out? To see if he really belonged on my suspect list?

Stark naked, I crossed to the bags of clothing on the sofa, then glanced at him from behind. "What should I wear? Sheer black panties or the white ones with the ribbons and garter belts?"

A sharp intake of breath. "Sheer black." His voice

sounded low, husky. His hand at his side was now clenched into a fist.

"You're sticking with me at the party tonight," I said, slipping into the sheer black underwear. "So you *are* my protector, then." I pulled them up over my hips, then grabbed the matching bra. "As long as I don't betray you or fuck anything up, in which case, you'll murder my best friend."

"That's a good summary."

I looked through the bags again until I found a silky red sundress. I slipped it on, and it hit my thighs just below my butt. "You can turn around now."

When he pivoted, his deep gray eyes shimmered like stars, but for the first time, I saw something like sadness in them. "You really look so much like her. It's disturbing."

"Well, I'm not her." Weirdly, that didn't feel entirely true. Last night, I'd inhabited her character so easily that she'd felt like a part of me. And worse, I liked being her. It was oddly freeing. "You haven't actually revealed anything about yourself, though. You haven't told me what Mortana did or why you're so desperate for revenge."

His eyes seemed to be searching mine, and silence spread out between us. At last, he said, "Mortana was involved in my mother's death. When she died, I made a blood oath that when I found Mortana again, I would slaughter her."

Something sharp pierced my heart. All this—the spying, the rage, it was all to avenge his mom. He and I had way more in common than I'd expected.

"And her close blood relatives," he added. "To stamp

out her family line forever. Except I think everyone in her family is already dead, except her."

Panic twinged in my chest. "I look *exactly* like her. Are you sure I'm not her descendant?"

He sighed. "If you're mortal, you're not her descendant. We don't breed mortal offspring. Hardly breed at all, really, which is why it's unlikely there would be any family line to destroy. She killed all her own relatives when she helped King Nergal with the Lilu purges."

My chest unclenched a little. "I'm sorry about what happened to your mom."

His brow furrowed. "Well, it wasn't your fault. You're not actually Mortana."

"No, that's just something mortals say." I took a deep breath. "Someone killed my mom, too." As soon as the words were out of my mouth, I was surprised I'd actually uttered them.

"Ah." He cocked his head, going very still. "That's what you weren't telling me. Your mother was murdered."

"Someone burned her to death in the Osborne Woods. I was there..." My chest went tight, and it started to feel hard to breathe. "I was with her, but I don't remember most of it. Just the scent of burning flesh, mostly, and..." Emotion tightened my throat, and I trailed off. I shouldn't be sharing so much with one of my suspects. So much for being an undercover cop.

He reached up and brushed a tear off my cheek. "What?"

"Some thoughts that are a bit too dark for other people to hear," I said.

"Not for me." His eyes were an endless blue. "I think you'll find I don't have any limits in that regard."

The guilt was eating at me from the inside out. "Okay, well, here's a question for you. Why am I still alive when she burned to death? Why did I keep running?"

His eyes darkened to shadows. "We're compelled to keep ourselves alive. It's the law of nature. And as your mother, she was compelled to keep you alive. That's the law of nature, too."

"So you don't feel any guilt for surviving when your mom didn't?"

The air was growing hotter around us, nearly scorching. "I didn't say that." His voice was barely a whisper.

I nodded. "That's why you want revenge so desperately, too. Isn't it? To make it right."

"Or maybe my rage drives me because it's all I have. It defines me and burns away the guilt. There's nothing else left in me but wrath."

I felt like my chest was splitting open. In my hunger for revenge, would I become like him? "Do you feel guilty for anything?" I ventured. "Or have you found a way to turn that off?"

Shadows darkened around Orion. "I told you." A ragged edge under that seductive voice. "Beyond a hunger for revenge, I feel almost nothing at all."

My pulse sped up as I sensed something changing around me. When psychologists looked for signs of lying in mortals, they looked for indications of anxiety. In most people—those who aren't psychopaths—lying makes them nervous. It's why polygraphs show increased heart rates, or why a liar pulls eye contact. People lying might fidget, look away.

Demons didn't show emotions in the same way. They never fidgeted or lowered their eyes out of nerves. But they could shift, and their bodies seemed to change the air around them, making it hotter or colder.

I'd moved closer, just inches from him now. "I'm not sure I believe you. But I think you should know that there's something I would want revenge for. If you lay a finger on Shai, I'll find a way to kill you."

Demonic stillness, eyes dark as night.

Not my protector. Not really. Must remember that.

A dark chuckle. "Do you still think it's wise to threaten me? As fragile as you are?"

"You forget, Orion, I passed the Trial all on my own. I don't break that easily." I delivered these lines with a lot more bravado than I actually felt.

His lips were curled with a dark smile. "No, I don't suppose you do. I suppose I can feel something besides a lust for revenge, and that's a surprise."

Was that nearly a compliment from Orion?

But his eyes were still dark as night as he was starting to shift. A demon's black eyes conveyed a message to mortals: *If you were smart, you'd probably run.*

And maybe that was something I should keep in mind around this predator. "Can I have a few hours to myself? I need to clear my head."

And you make that very difficult.

CHAPTER 27

With a margarita in one hand, I dipped my legs into the pool outside my room. Since I'd slept through most of the day, twilight was already spreading its coral mantle over the sky, and the shadows were growing longer. The setting sun bathed the golden stones in blood-red light, and it dazzled orange off the flowing Acheron River. On the far bank, shadows pooled in the wilderness.

As requested, Orion had left me alone—with his number programmed into my new cell phone. If Nama or Lydia, or anyone else, cropped up looking for trouble, I was supposed to hit *star seven,* and my protector would appear in a whorl of shadows.

I also had the doorman and mortal servants looking out for me, one of whom brought me a pitcher of margaritas and vegan tacos. And most importantly, Shai was on her way over for a dip in the pool with me.

This would continue to be *my* pool, if I had my choice —if I didn't have to leave here, and if Shai's life weren't at risk. This place was intoxicating in a way that started to make me wonder if I'd lose my mind here. I wanted to sink my claws into this city. I wanted to take it over like an invasive species. When I thought of Nama, a sense of competitiveness started to rise in me.

I had an insane impulse to stake my claim on this city —permanently. I wanted to *actually* be the demon duchess, to bring the Asmodean Ward alive again. The incubi and succubi didn't deserve their fate. Whoever Jezebel was, the woman probably hadn't deserved to be thrown from her palace window and eaten by dogs. I wanted to plant my roots here as a succubus just to spite the rest of these judgmental fuckers.

So clearly, the intoxicating powers of this city were making me go mad, because none of that could happen. I had very limited time here.

And why was I starting to care about the fate of the Lilu? I sipped my tart cocktail, letting the taste of lime roll over my tongue.

I suppose, for one thing, people thought I was a Lilu, so I was starting to feel like one. Behavioral confirmation. For another, it was just the injustice of it all. It seemed like the Lilu had been murdered because of others' raging jealousy and insecurity.

"Mortana!" Shai waved at me as she crossed through one of the arches. She wore a yellow sundress, and her hair in a halo of curls. "Nice place."

I grinned at her. "Come in the pool with me."

"As long as I can eat tacos in the pool."

"Of course." I pointed at her margarita waiting by the side of the pool. "And you have a drink."

Shai pulled off her dress, revealing a bright red bathing suit, and slipped into the water.

In the City of Thorns, it seemed like the weather was permanently tropical. Another reason it would be great to sink my roots into this place.

I let out a long sigh.

"What? Why do you sound like you're not enjoying this paradise?" Shai took a bite of her tacos.

"I'm feeling guilty that I got you dragged into all this."

"Dragged me into all what? Tacos and margaritas in a pool? It's not your fault you look exactly like some succubus."

"I know," I whispered. "But if I fuck anything up, Orion says he'll kill you. Your life is in danger, Shai."

She snorted. "Do you think I'm an idiot? I made him swear a blood oath to keep me safe."

I stared at her. I'd never considered just extracting promises from him like that. "Wait, *what*?"

She took a sip of her margarita. "It's all about leverage, darling. My mom taught me that during the divorce. You figure out what they want, and you threaten to destroy it if they don't meet your terms."

My jaw dropped open. So her life wasn't at risk... "Sorry, what did you threaten to destroy?"

She squinted in the sun. "Well, don't take this the wrong way, but I knew he needed you for whatever his plan was. So I threatened to get rid of you if he didn't agree." Another bite of tacos.

"*What*?" Shai once got mad at me for killing an ant. "You threatened to kill me? You're a vegan!"

"Well, he doesn't know that," she whispered. "And you

always go on about psychopaths. I feel like I learned a few things from you. I know you said psychopaths don't get nervous, but I don't think he realizes that, either. Because my palms were sweating and my heart was beating out of control. But I kept my voice totally calm, and it worked." She smiled at me. "I sounded really scary, I think."

"What did you say?"

She shrugged. "I watched a true crime show once about a psychopath who murdered his mom by cutting off her head. So I just said that if he didn't do what I wanted, I'd cut your head off."

"How does he know you're not going to murder me now?"

She waved a hand. "It was a whole thing. He made me swear a blood oath in return—not to hurt you or tell anyone what you really are. He felt like he was actually getting a good deal out of that. Since I have no intention of actually murdering anyone, I've really never made an easier deal in my life. I've got my tuition paid, plus I got a much better apartment than the one I had before. And he has to keep me safe. And I got a really great cappuccino machine. This has all worked out nicely for me. You have literally nothing to feel bad about."

"Holy shit, Shai. He never told me any of that."

She shrugged. "Of course he didn't. I'm his leverage. He can get you to do what he wants as long as you think my life is at risk. He should have asked me to keep quiet during the blood oath, but you came down and interrupted, and then I think he got distracted."

I bit my lip. "Well, this is a very interesting development. So I can...stay as long as I want here."

She frowned at me. "I'm not sure I like the look on your face. What are you scheming now?"

"I don't want to leave."

She shook her head. "But you can't keep this lie up forever, can you? What would happen if the king found out you were lying?"

I cleared my throat. "Well, that *is* a little hitch in my plan."

"No, really—what does happen if the king learns you're lying? Demon dungeon?"

"Fire pit."

Her eyes widened. "Fucking hell, Rowan. Obviously, you can't stay."

I lifted my finger to my lips. She couldn't say my real name that loudly.

She had a point, except I think I was so scared of the fire pit, my brain refused to consider it was a possibility. I was in some kind of advanced state of denial. "But what if I can keep the deception going? Orion will keep me safe until I can find the information he wants."

She rested her elbows on the side of the pool. "I mean, I can see why you'd want to stay here. You're living like a queen, and this is heaven. But is it really worth the risk of a fire pit?"

"It's not just the pool and the luxury. Shai—I'm almost positive a demon killed my mom. One with fire magic. And I want to find out who it was." I left out the bit about avenging the Lilu, and the feeling that my shadow-self was growing more powerful, because she'd think I'd lost my mind.

She frowned, her dark eyes piercing me. "I can understand the temptation. But then what? What does it get you?"

"I want to know the truth." And I wanted to murder the fucker, maybe.

"Have you found anything out so far?"

I let out a long breath. "I have a short list of suspects. Orion is one of them."

Her eyes widened. "Fuck. Why would he have killed your mom?"

I shook my head. "I don't know why *anyone* would. I only know two things—I think it was someone with fire magic, and I think it was someone with a demon mark shaped like a star. You know, the shiny forehead things?"

"I've seen one once. Not a star."

"I haven't seen that particular mark yet, either, but I keep looking. That's all I remember from that night. And Orion is one of just a handful of demons with fire magic—along with Lydia, the king, and Mortana herself. Orion says the star mark means that you're destined to be the demon leader, blessed by Lucifer. So my guess is that the king is the top suspect. But no one knows what the king's mark looks like, so I'm not sure."

Shai stirred her drink with her straw. "Maybe if you want to find the killer, you need to learn more about your mom instead of learning more about demons. What was her connection to this world?"

"I searched all her things after she died, looking for clues. I couldn't find anything." I closed my eyes, running through my memories until something sparked in my mind—something I'd seen recently. "Except a key." My eyes snapped open. "It was a skeleton key like the ones they use here. Like the one Orion used to unlock my apartment door. I found it hidden in a drawer, but I never knew what the key went to."

"Do you still have it?" she asked.

I nodded. "She didn't leave much behind. Just the key, some clothes, old books, and enough money for a few months' rent. So I kept the key." In the gathering shadows, as darkness fell, it was hard not to feel a pang of sadness. Mom had a whole life she'd never told me about.

"I can go in and out of the city," said Shai. "I can grab the key. If you can find what it goes to, maybe that'd be a clue."

I smiled at her. "Thanks, Shai."

She grabbed her cocktail off the side of the pool. "What do you have planned for tonight?"

I took a deep breath. "Spying for Orion, of course. In the king's penthouse."

Her eyebrows rose. "But you'll be careful with all this, right? Because everything you're telling me sounds dangerous as hell. Particularly the fire pit situation, considering the king is one of your suspects."

"Yep. And Orion, too. I don't trust him at all."

"Is that right?" Orion stepped from the shadows, his pale eyes burning like stars. He wore an expensive-looking charcoal-gray suit. "And here I was imagining we might be friends."

My stomach flipped.

He cocked his head. "We have a party to get ready for, don't we?"

CHAPTER 28

In the Tower of Baal, we stepped into the elevator to ride up to the penthouse floor. I wore a dress made of a sheer material that showed off my legs, but with strategically placed blue filigrees to allow a bit of modesty.

As soon as the elevator started, Orion turned his piercing blue eyes to me. "I'm curious what you and Shai were talking about. You said you don't trust me, which makes sense, because I'm a dick. But there's more to it than that, isn't there? There's something specific."

I crossed my arms. "Fine. You want revenge, and I do, too. I want to find my mom's killer. Someone killed her with fire magic in the Osborne Woods, and I want to know who it was."

His eyes went wide. "Ah." He turned and pressed the emergency button, stopping the elevator. "There we are. You think I could have killed your mother."

I shot an irritated glance at the door. "Do we have to have this conversation trapped in an elevator?"

"I'm afraid so."

I crossed my arms, looking impatiently at the door. "You have fire magic, so yes, you're on my short list of suspects."

He slid his hands into his pockets and shrugged, looking up at the ceiling. "I'm ruthless, lethal, lacking in empathy. I don't hide my flaws or lie about what I am, so that's no secret. I'd murder a mortal woman if it got me what I wanted." He met my gaze. "But I didn't burn a mortal woman to death in the Osborne Woods. I'm not morally against the concept, it's just that it wasn't me."

Either he was really good at lying, or that was the truth. As I stared at him, I felt my chest unclench. "Okay."

His eyebrows rose. "I take it Shai told you that I can't kill her."

"It did come up. She's not actually a psychopath, by the way. She just used that to get you to agree to the blood oath."

He narrowed his eyes. "Hmm. Finding another person you care about that I could kill would be the easiest way to bargain…"

"That's not really what a bargain is. That's a threat, Orion."

He shrugged, his expression cold. "Well, clearly, it would be the easiest option, but it won't work. From what I understand, you don't actually care about anyone else. Shai is your only friend, and your family is dead."

I swallowed hard. "That's a depressing summary."

"How about a new bargain, then? You get me what I want, the truth about what makes the king weak, and I'll help you find your mother's killer. Once I get what I need, you'll get what you need."

I bit my lip, staring at him. This all came down to a single question—did I actually believe him? It was hard to say. But since I didn't have many offers of help here in the City of Thorns, I'd accept for now. "Fine. I'll take this deal before you come up with something worse."

"And then you'll need to leave the City of Thorns as soon as we are finished. Every hour that you're here is another hour that you risk ending up in the fire pit."

He turned and pushed a button to make the elevator move again. We started rising, and within moments, the elevator doors opened into the penthouse apartment.

Holy moly... It was like nothing I'd ever seen—a pool inset into a marble floor and towering glass windows that opened onto a balcony. Beyond the balcony, the sea glittered under the stars. A balmy breeze rushed into the apartment, toying with the demons' long, silky gowns.

The king stood on the other side of the pool, martini in hand. Subtly, people swarmed around him like moths to a flame, eyes flitting to him, fingers reaching out to touch his arm. But his attention was locked on Lydia and one of the dukes.

When my eyes met Nama's, my pulse started to race. She wore a long white gown that matched her wavy hair, plus earrings that looked like dripping icicles. But despite the delicate beauty of her outfit, her lip was curled, exposing her teeth like an animal about to attack. She pulled her gaze from mine, then smiled at Orion. When he didn't seem to notice her, she stalked over to him. "Hello, my duke." Her voice sounded shaky, angry.

Orion seemed to be looking right past her. "You again, is it?"

When a server crossed to us with a tray of cloudy purple cocktails, I plucked one off for myself and took a sip. This one was gin, lemon, and the faint hint of violets.

And as I surveyed the room again, trying to catch anyone's eye, I was starting to get the impression that people were ignoring me on purpose. This was a demonic cold shoulder.

No one wanted a succubus duchess here. The demons had tried killing me in the woods, and when that didn't work, they'd try a social freeze.

I pretended I wasn't listening as Nama started talking to Orion again, but I absolutely was.

"Your new succubus friend reminds me of a mortal sometimes," she said, as though I weren't standing right there. "The way she moves. Her slowness." Her jaw tightened. "You know the fear that mortals have, since they were our prey for so long? I sense that in her. She was wearing something strange in the woods, and she smelled like animal piss. What's she so afraid of?"

Nama was a twat, but she was a perceptive twat.

Orion flashed her a taunting smile. "She's afraid of me, I should think. And you should be, too."

Nama pouted at him, then lifted her chin. "But we're going to be great friends, you and I. We are alike. Do you believe in a soul bond?"

"I'm afraid I don't have a soul, Nama," said Orion. "I'm divine on the outside, I know. But I'm absolutely empty inside."

I was starting to think this was the mask he wore—

cold and uncaring, devoid of emotions. Underneath his sarcasm, under the sensual smile, was a well of buried pain.

Nama's smile looked twisted and strained at his comments. "I don't believe that for a moment. We're fated to marry. You can pretend to deny it all you want, but I've foreseen it." Only now did she shoot me a withering look to acknowledge my presence. "And if you're not going to look into the truth about this one, then I will. She looks... fidgety. Anxious. *Mortal.*"

My stomach clenched. What if she started asking around about me in Osborne?

I couldn't worry about that now while Nama was scrutinizing me for signs of anxiety, so I tried to summon my dark side—which, as it turned out, involved finishing the cocktail fast.

I closed my eyes as I drank it down.

I'm not Rowan. I am Mortana, succubus, seductress, devourer of souls. I will eat the weak for breakfast.

When I'd finished the drink, I had a nice little buzz. Despite my new anxieties, I had to keep up the seductive charade while I was here in front of the demon crowd. With a little smile on my face, I started walking toward the king, crossing alongside the pool. I imagined the trickles of water running down my body as I walked, my eyes locked on him. The warm lights of the room cast a flattering light over his masculine features and sharp jaw.

He slid me a curious look as I approached, and I could see Lydia tensing, her eyes going dark.

I wanted him alone. If I were going to learn his weakness, it would have to be away from the others.

When I was standing next to him, I leaned in to whisper, "There's only one thing you could do to turn my attention from Orion to you."

Then, with that catlike walk. I headed onto the balcony. Out there, the briny sea air rushed over me, and I stared out at the sparkling sea. I'd feel fairly stupid if I did all that and the king failed to join me, but I supposed I had to stand there with the confidence of my shadow-self.

And when I turned to look back, I found that the king *was* stalking outside to join me, a cocktail in hand. The salty air toyed with his blond hair. "As always," he said quietly, "you intrigue me, Mortana."

I leaned back with my elbows over the railing and smiled at him. I was tempted to look inside to see what Orion was doing, but that wasn't my job here. Jealousy was a game I was playing with the king; it wasn't for me to indulge in.

I sipped my drink. "You know, this city is even more beautiful than I remember. They say a king is tied to his land, so I'm sure you've only enhanced its appeal."

"I think the City of Thorns has been missing its last Lilu. We can't be whole without your kind. We're a city of seven wards, seven gods. We made a promise to the mortals, and you are the single living exception." He raised his glass. "Exactly how did you extract such a deal from my father?"

I shrugged and let the strap of my gown fall just a little. "I made him happy. You know, I always thought I should be queen."

"So did I." There was something fierce in his voice, a desperate edge to it. "Maybe I still do."

"Well, it's not too late." I sipped my drink. "But if our relationship is going to progress, I need to know the real you."

He put his drink down on the railing, then moved closer and planted his hands on either side of me. The wind whipped at his pale hair. "In what way do you want to know me?"

I reached out to stroke his jawline. "The thing is, Your Majesty, everyone has a weakness. Even a king like you."

"I'm not sure that's actually the case, Mortana."

"*Everyone*," I repeated. "If we're going to be equals, then I need to know what makes you vulnerable. If you only know someone's strong side, you don't really know them at all."

"And what makes you vulnerable, Duchess? Is there anything that you fear?"

Dammit. A deflection. It's like he'd been studying with Dr. Omer.

Maybe I could answer. What made my shadow-self feel vulnerable? I closed my eyes, trying to tune in to what Mortana would feel. If I were answering the question for myself, there'd be a wide array of fears to choose from, spanning the gamut of likely to nearly impossible: fire, dying alone, childbirth, imprisonment in North Korea, choking on a stray zipper that got into my cereal, bug infestations, making selfish choices, getting trampled by a moose…the list was pretty much endless. But Mortana? She was different. She was a survivor. She didn't agonize about being selfish or flawed—she just survived.

"Being hunted and trapped." I opened my eyes. "For obvious reasons. I'm the only one left. And you?"

"I fear nothing, because I have been blessed by Lucifer as his true leader." His tone was silky, deep.

Alarm bells rang in my mind. Did *he* have the five-pointed star, then?

He stepped back from me and pulled a knife from his pocket. The blade glinted in the moonlight, and he drew it across his palm. For just a moment, his skin flashed with bright red—but then the cut was gone again in an instant. Demons healed quickly, but this was different, almost immediate. Like an arrow bouncing off a dragon's hide.

He held up his palm. "I'm afraid to disappoint you, Mortana, but nothing about me is vulnerable. That is what it means to be blessed by Lucifer."

Shit. Was that actually true? If so, why was Orion so convinced otherwise?

"Well, that's disappointing," I said. "I like to leave my mark on a man. Drag my claws down his back." I bared my teeth. "Or mark him as mine with my fangs. I like to deliver pain with pleasure. If you can't be hurt, I'm not sure we'd be well suited."

He moved in again, pressing his hands on either side of my hips. "Maybe we could find a way to work past that."

I arched an eyebrow. "But how?"

The sea wind whipped over us, and my red hair tangled with his. Over his shoulder, I saw Orion standing in the doorway. His eyes looked dark, and darkness seemed to stain the air around him. That was how he looked when he was pissed off.

Why was he annoyed now? I was doing exactly what

he wanted. In fact, I think the king was actually about to tell me something.

I turned my attention back to the king and licked my lips. "How could we arrange that? If Lucifer protects you all the time, how can I leave my claw marks on you like I did on the duke?"

The king's eyes raked down my body. "No. You won't see him anymore." His voice had a desperate edge. "I've watched you for too long to let you go to another man again. When you were with my father, the jealousy ate at me, like it did at my mother. You were the goddess of envy, inspiring it like no one else before. I vowed to have you as my own." He dragged his eyes up to mine again. "But I don't trust you."

Damn. I'd have to play on his desperation to override the sensible side. I shrugged. "Well, perhaps we're not suited to each other. I'm sure there's another demon female who would make a wonderful queen for you. And as for me? Orion can satisfy me like no other male ever has. You can see how all the females look at him, can't you? Everyone wants him."

He reached up and grabbed me by the neck. "No." Ice-cold rage laced his tone, and his fury tightened his jaw. "I *will* have what he has. I'm the king, and I deserve what I want."

Fear was starting to climb up my throat now. Panic clanged in the hollows of my mind, sharpened by my species' thousands of years as prey. My amygdala was telling me to get the fuck out right now—that was a very, *very* powerful demon was about to rip my throat out or take what he wanted from me. But I could also tell I was close to getting the information I needed. He seemed out of control, ready to do anything to have me.

"You know what I want," I whispered. "I want to know all of you. Not just the powerful side."

"I want you now." His eyes gleamed, midnight dark, and he gripped my waist like he was about to rip the fabric. "There is one way—"

"King Cambriel." Orion's voice cut through the tension like a knife. "Do not touch what's mine."

To my surprise, the king simply dropped his grip on me. His eyes glinted with darkness as he slowly stepped away.

I looked beyond the king to see Lydia stepping outside next to Orion. The king pivoted to find the two of them standing behind him.

Lydia was seething, and fury burned in her eyes. Was the king attracted to the jealousy of others, too? If so, he had a feast right here.

I exhaled, trying to hide my frustration. I'd been so close to learning what Orion wanted. But the king had been out of control. And maybe—just maybe—Orion actually cared for me.

My one burning question was why the fuck the king was so scared of Orion.

CHAPTER 29

I met Orion's gaze as he prowled over to join me. His shoulders looked relaxed, but his eyes were dark as night. The king's frenzy had disturbed him.

Lydia shot me a sharp look, and her lip curled in a snarl. "She is not to be trusted," she hissed. "Can't you see that? Nama thinks she's lying about her identity."

King Cambriel glanced at me, his jaw tight, and then he locked his gaze on Lydia again. "Do you think I'm an idiot?" His voice boomed over the party, and the guests inside went quiet as they turned to look. "Do you think I can't detect a threat? Or that I can't look after myself? I am Cambriel, heir of the fallen Seraphim Beelzebub. As the rightful heir to the throne, I am protected by the gods themselves. Obviously, I don't need rumors spread by lunatics like Nama to keep me safe. I thought you were above gossip, Lydia. Not like the other females?"

He stalked inside once more, smoothing out his suit jacket.

Wow, that was harsh. Lydia stared after him for a

moment, then turned to look at me. She gripped her cocktail glass, and the wind raked at her dark hair. The king had just humiliated her, and she looked like she was about to take out all that rage on me. Her eyes went dark as night, and fire blazed from her fingertips, melting her glass. Molten glass pooled at her feet, and my stomach dropped.

"You're ruining everything," she rasped. "I am meant to be queen in the City of Thorns, and you're burning down my plans. Did you hear how he just spoke to me?"

From across the balcony, she lunged for me, and my heart leapt. But before she could reach me, Orion shot out of the shadows and grabbed Lydia by the arm, halting her attack.

Fury contorted her features, and she pivoted to face him. "And where the fuck did you come from, Orion? Who are you, really? You've never managed to explain to anyone why you're here."

A muscle clenched in his jaw. "I don't need to explain why I'm here. In fact, I'm not allowed to. That's what the Trial is for. I passed, and that means the gods want me here. You wouldn't doubt their judgment, would you?"

"Of course not," she conceded.

"Just like Mortana survived the Trial. You know the king doesn't allow blasphemy. I'm sure you wouldn't want to make him angrier."

She shot me one last furious look, then turned and hurried back into the penthouse.

I exhaled slowly. It had felt like the king was about to confess his weakness to me, and I wondered if I'd get another opportunity. After this point, Lydia and Nama would make it their mission to uncover the truth about me.

How long until they simply figured it out?

Orion stepped closer to me, his eyes still black as jet. He leaned down to my ear, and heat from his body warmed me. Whenever he was near, I could feel his power rushing over my skin, a wave of sensual magic. He brushed my hair back from my ear, then whispered, "I had to stop him. He looked like he could have hurt you."

I'm not sure where the impulse came from—if it was from me or all part of the act—but I found myself reaching up and touching his chest. As I did, I heard a sharp intake of breath.

"He nearly confessed the truth," I whispered. "First, he said Lucifer protects him as the king..."

"That's a lie," he whispered. "He uses some form of magic to make himself invulnerable."

I stepped back a little to look into Orion's eyes, wanting to know more. Why was he so obsessed with this? And what did it have to do with Mortana?

But even if the king was easy to manipulate, Orion was not. He wouldn't tell me easily. I pressed myself against him and whispered, "I was close. He's incredibly jealous of you, and I think he was on the verge of telling me how I could leave claw marks on him—"

Orion let out a low growl, then shifted until our foreheads touched. He cupped his hand around the back of my neck. "Did you tell him the truth? That I was the first man you'd ever seen who could truly satisfy you in the way you need?"

My heart was racing faster, my chest flushing. "Did I say that?"

His hooded expression made my breath catch. "Let's make him more jealous, shall we?" He lightly traced a finger over my jaw. "You were close to finding the truth. Maybe we can push him over the edge. I aim to show the king exactly how much you want me."

Was this really just about getting information from the king, or was Orion trying to prove something?

He took me by the hand and led me back into the party. The lights were dimmer inside now, flickering like candles and reflecting off the pool. All eyes were on me as we walked inside—the succubus harlot. I tried to ignore the feeling of being self-conscious as everyone gaped.

Near one of the walls, Orion took a seat in a leather chair, then pulled me into his lap. Only his shocking beauty was able to make me forget the uncomfortable feeling of being stared at. Orion's gaze slid over the room —probably making sure the king was watching—and he stroked his hand down my spine. Hot, sensual magic followed the trail of his touch.

When his eyes met mine again, his hand moved upward, cupping my neck. I leaned in, and my lips met his. My mouth opened against his, and heat swept through my body as his tongue flicked in. I stroked my hand down his chest, feeling his abs tighten under my touch. Every thought I'd had about the crowd around us seemed to melt away, and there was nothing but the deep, sensual pleasure of his kiss. I felt my nipples going hard under my silky gown, and molten heat pooled in my core. His tongue entwined with mine.

As he finished the kiss with a nip to my lower lip, he pulled back. The look he was giving me was molten, hungry. His expression was positively primal, like he was about to rip my dress off, throw me up against the wall, and fuck me right here.

Was that the look he was giving me, or was that what I wanted to happen?

His breath sped up as he pulled down the strap of my dress, just enough that he had a good view of my hard nipples. A growl rose from his throat, and I saw his fangs lengthen like he wanted to devour me.

This was all very out of character for me, but I wasn't exactly stopping him as he reached down for the hem of my dress and slid his hand beneath. My gown was dragged upward as he traced his hand higher, exposing more of my skin. "Are you going to get cocky, love, with the two most powerful men in the city fighting over you?"

"*Get* cocky?" I said, because I was Mortana. "I know my worth."

He tilted me into him, my hips shifting in his lap. One of his hands stroked slowly up and down over my ribs. I could feel his magic, his heat, through the thin material. My breath was hitching, my pulse racing as his other hand slid around my upper thigh. He was touching me like I belonged to him, but his expression held a certain reverence that I hadn't seen before. The seductive scent of burning cedar curled all around us, and desire coiled tight within me.

His eyes darkened to black, and I sensed he knew how much I wanted this. He was responding to me as much as

I was to him. He brushed his knuckles over my thigh, the sensation so maddening I could no longer think straight.

I should probably stop this now.

I mean, we were in a room with other people, for crying out loud...but my breasts ached for his touch.

From behind me, I heard the sound of a throat clearing, and Orion's hand tightened on my ass like he was claiming me. He whispered into my ear, "We got the king's attention."

A cold tendril of disappointment coiled through me. Right. Had this been about the information?

With my cheeks flushing a bright red, I turned my face a little to see King Cambriel looming over us. "Mortana and I were not finished with our discussion."

"The thing is, Your Majesty," said Orion sharply, "I don't really give a fuck."

I gasped. Was the king going to kill him for that impudence?

With me in his arms like an indecent bride, Orion rose. I felt as if the rest of the room had fallen away. It was just me and Orion now, his dark eyes shining with desire.

Without another word, he carried me outside. The sea wind chilled my skin, rustling my hair as Orion walked with me over to the balcony. Clouds had slid over the moon, and shadows swallowed up the night sky around us. The only light out there was from the party and the glittering phosphorescence of the sea.

My emotions were drowning out rational thought completely. My breath hitched, and I simply repeated, "Where are we going?"

"I thought I should take you out of there."

"On the balcony?"

"I don't want to give you over to the king. I want you in my bed, naked and moaning my name."

"Okay," I breathed. "Let's do that." I frowned at him, my heart still racing as I clung to his neck. "Why are we on the balcony? How do we get down from here?"

"You'll see, love." With me in his arms, he climbed atop the railing, and my heart stuttered in my chest.

Now, the sea breeze outside was whipping at us, and panic made my heart race. "Are you crazy?"

His dark eyes locked on mine, and he held me close against his powerful chest. "Do you trust me, love?"

"No."

His beautiful mouth curved in a dark smile. "You're very wise in that regard. But do you trust me at least not to kill you until I can bring you somewhere where I can make you come?"

"I guess?"

I tore my gaze away from him and glanced down at the ocean glittering far below us. Didn't he say only the Lilu could fly? He wasn't Lilu. "Wait—"

Before I could get the rest of my sentence out, he leapt from the balcony, and we started to plunge through the air.

CHAPTER 30

The sea wind whipped over us as we fell into the darkness. Orion was still holding me tightly against his powerful chest, but we were falling toward the sea.

What the fuck, Orion?

Then, with a sound like a snapping bone, our fall stopped sharply. With a slamming heart, I gripped Orion's neck, catching my breath as I stared at the dark wings that spread out behind him. His feathers were tinged a deep silver at the tips, and they seemed to glow like moonlight. "What are you?" I breathed.

"Magnificent," he murmured.

Stunned, I stared at him. "No, really. I thought all the Lilu were dead besides Mortana. And that only the Lilu have wings." I just stared, trying to come to grips with what had just happened. "The female Lilu were succubi. So you're—what, an incubus? You're an incubus. Can you fuck me to death?"

Wickedness gleamed in his eyes. "Is that a request?"

"No, it was a concern."

"I promise to keep you alive." He flashed me a heartbreakingly beautiful smile. "Now you've seen the real me. And you're just about the only one."

"A bit more warning would have helped," I panted.

His muscled arms were wrapped tightly around me, one around my waist, and one under my ass.

"I couldn't risk anyone overhearing me," he said. "They need to think that you are the one flying, not me. You're supposed to be the Lilu."

In the darkness, his pale blue eyes seemed to glow.

I sucked in a sharp breath. "So…hang on, you're secretly a Lilu? And no one else knows?"

"No one except you knows that I am an incubus. And if the other demons realized that, they'd try to kill me." A faint smile. "They'd fail, but they'd try, and it would be messy and disrupt my plans."

My mind could hardly keep up with this new information. "So I'm the only person who knows what you really are?"

The corner of his lips twitched. "Either I trust you, or I'm just making stupid decisions because you robbed me of the ability to think clearly when you were sitting in my lap. When I could hear your heart beating faster and your breath speeding up, it was difficult to think straight."

With a jolt of surprise, I realized he was letting me know what made him vulnerable. "If you're an incubus, then how are you still alive?"

His wings pounded the air, and he held my gaze, his eyes searching mine. I'd never seen him look uncertain before, but he did now. "I've been in the City of Thorns the whole time," he said at last. "I've lived here for centuries. I was locked in the prison underground. The same prison where I locked you up that night. That's where I lived for hundreds of years, and for most of that time, I saw no one except Mortana. Until she disappeared."

"What?" My heart squeezed. "Didn't she leave two hundred years ago?"

He looked out over the sea as he flew, his face a mask of indifference now. "Yes."

"So you were in a dungeon by yourself for centuries." I had so many questions I wanted to ask that I didn't even know where to begin. "Why does everyone think you're a duke? If you were a prisoner that long, how are you so stupidly rich?"

His expression had grown cold. "It's not mine. I demand money from the king."

Every response just invited more questions. "And why does he give it to you? Why is he scared of you?"

A bitter chuckle. "He has good reason to fear me."

Vague. Okay. "And does the king know you were in prison? Does he know that you're an incubus?"

"No. He only knows that I've learned one of his secrets, and he'll do anything to keep it hidden from the rest of the city."

It was hard for me to picture this powerful, dark force of nature in a prison cell for his whole life. Really, it was dreadfully sad. As we flew, the wind swept over us, whipping at my hair. "Was your mother with you when you were a kid? In the prisons?"

"Yes. But it wasn't long before she was executed.

Mortana helped make all that happen. She helped round up every Lilu in exchange for her own protection."

"But how did you survive?"

I felt his fingers tighten on me, nearly imperceptibly. "Mortana liked to toy with me. And when she left, I was simply forgotten. No one knew I was there. Demons don't need to eat. We feel hunger, but we don't require sustenance to live. So I just stayed there." His eyes had darkened, and his expression seemed haunted. "Until at last, I found a way to escape."

I breathed in deeply, watching his wings as they pounded slowly under the dark night sky. "What do you mean, she toyed with you?"

Darkness slid through his eyes, and the wind seemed to grow more bitter. "I mean she amused herself by torturing me in her own way."

Holy shit. No wonder he was desperate for revenge. "And you have no idea what happened to her?"

"No," he said quietly. "I don't even know if *she* remembers what happened to her. I don't know that she has any idea who she is."

"What do you mean?"

He took a deep breath. "She once told me about a spell. It's one we use to forget what we've done, to rid ourselves of guilt. A spell for forgetting. She offered it to me, and I said no." The wind tugged at his silver hair, and his eyes gleamed in the night. "That was why, when I met you, I was so convinced you were Mortana. I thought she'd used the spell on herself. You seemed nothing like her, but I thought there was a chance she'd forgotten everything. I was sure of it until I tasted your blood."

I was pressed right against his chest, like he was clinging to me for salvation. This close to him, I could feel his chest muscles moving slightly as his wings shifted. "Must we talk about her right now?" he murmured. "I'm afraid the mood will be ruined."

But it was hard to let it go when he was a mystery I wanted to solve. "Why did she offer you a spell to forget your past? What was it you wanted to forget?"

"Because at the heart of me, Rowan, I'm evil." His gaze pierced me, the blue in his eyes shot through with shadows. "And sometimes, I'd like to forget that."

It was hard not to hear the ragged edge of pain in his voice. I almost wanted to touch the side of his face, to tell him that he wasn't all that bad. But what did I know? He hadn't told me his history.

The bitter wind was sharpening my senses as we flew. Now, the most pressing question was why I was going somewhere to be alone with an *incubus*, a creature that killed mortals with sex.

"Orion," I began, "we had a deal that if I helped you find out what made the king weak, you would help me find my mother's killer. But I didn't learn anything from the king—"

"I'll still help you"

I stared at the faint glow of silver in his wings. "Okay, and this still seems like a bad idea. As an incubus, won't you kill me? That's what incubi do. They seduce mortal women and kill them."

A sly smile played about his lips. "I may be evil, but I'm compelled to keep you safe, and I will. I won't do anything that hurts you."

"Why are you compelled to keep me safe?"

He swept down lower until I could feel the spray of the ocean against my skin. "I don't know, but it's deeply inconvenient. You're supposed to be my spy. That means putting your life at risk. How can you work for me if I can't tolerate risks to your safety?"

"If you were in prison all that time," I asked, "have you ever actually killed any mortals?"

"Not yet, I'm afraid," he said darkly. "I just obsessed over it for a few centuries."

"Wait, *what?*"

He took a deep breath. "Not the death, but the sex. It's how we feed and grow strong—from lust. So I dreamt of it day after day and night after night—feeding on mortals, drinking from their desire. Demons, too." His wings pounded the air. "I do want to kill that frat boy who attacked you, but I won't be killing him in a way that he enjoys."

I turned my head to see that we were approaching the yawning opening of a sea cave. Angling his wings, Orion swooped inside, and darkness swallowed us.

CHAPTER 31

He touched down in the shadows and lowered me to the floor. When he spoke a word in a demonic language, lights sprang to life in a chandelier above us. The flames cast a warm glow on amber stone walls, and licks of fire rose in lanterns in alcoves.

I turned to look at Orion, whose wings were still spread out wide behind him. In the light, I could see how absolutely exquisite they looked, flecked with pearly white constellations that glowed like stars, blending to silver.

"Nice wings."

With a swirl of smoky, dark magic, his wings disappeared again. "They're all right." A seductive smile played over his lips. "You're the first person I've brought to my grotto."

When I turned to look at it, I realized it wasn't simply a cave. The walls were built with golden stones, and cool, blue water flowed into a pool inset into a tile floor. By the side of the fresh pool stood a bed of flat rock, covered with a mattress and turquoise pillows.

"What is this place?" I asked.

"When I got out of the dungeons, I needed to find a quieter hideaway. In my cell, I craved other people. But now that I'm around them, I'm not used to the noise of the city." The look in his eyes was endlessly sad, and his throat bobbed. "So this is where I go to escape. Except right now, it's where I want to be with you." He took a few steps closer to me.

I reached out to touch his chest, the steel beneath a soft shirt, and he shuddered. "But it must be hard to look at me when I look so much like her."

His eyes sparkled in the warm light. "It's confusing for me, too. But you aren't her. Apart from how you look, you're nothing like her."

"Because I'm not sexy?"

His expression turned fierce. "Because you're willing to risk your own life. Because you put avenging your mother's memory above your own safety. And because you're not afraid to admit your flaws. I guess we're alike in these ways."

"And we've both spent a lot of time alone." My pulse was racing as I looked up at him, still stunned by his shocking beauty. The candlelight wavered over his high cheekbones, sculpting the divine planes of his face. A dangerous pulse beat through my body, making it hard for me to think straight.

I reached down for the bottom of his shirt, and I slid my hands underneath the soft fabric. When I pulled it off him, my eyes went wide. Holy hell, he looked like a god.

His body was thickly corded with muscle, his abs chiseled. He was a warrior dipped in gold.

A thrill lit up my body just looking at him, and I wanted to taste him. When I met his eyes again, I saw them searching mine. I reached for the straps of my gown, and I let it fall to the floor. I heard his sharp intake of breath, and his expression was reverent as his gaze roamed over my sheer blue underwear. With his eyes on me like that, need built within me.

Then he simply looked ravenous. He moved for me and lifted me up against the wall, his hands under my ass. I heard him moan quietly as his mouth met my throat. A hint of his fangs grazed over my skin again. Was he going to bite me? I didn't hate the thought, and I found myself arching my neck, giving him more access.

But instead of the sharp sting of teeth, I felt the warmth of his tongue swirling over my skin. My fingers threaded into his hair, and I closed my eyes. His sensual magic was stroking over my body now, a hot and dangerous caress. With my legs wrapped around him, I felt my hips rocking against his body.

As I gripped his hair, my breath sped up. "But how is it that you won't kill me? Isn't that the whole problem with incubi?"

A dark laugh. "It is a flaw, yes. But I can make you scream with pleasure even if I don't fuck you. It'll take an extreme amount of restraint on my part, but you'll be fine."

My core clenched at his words, and I was already slick with desire for him. "You're quite confident in your abilities." Truth was, I was, too.

He looked up at me with a seductive smile. "I'm an incubus. Along with killing, it's the one thing I know I'm good at."

The cool sea air rushed over my bare skin, and my nipples hardened. The look in his eyes was positively primal now, sliding into darkness.

I arched an eyebrow. "Did I mention that I've never actually had an orgasm?"

"You did." He stroked his hands up my ribs, his thumbs sliding under my bra. "That's about to change."

He caressed me just below my nipples, and my body went tight, heat flooding me. With hooded eyes, his gaze brushed down my body. "You are perfection, Rowan." He leaned down to kiss me, claiming me with his mouth.

As his powerful body pressed against mine, my lips opened for him. The kiss deepened as his tongue caressed mine. His thumbs slid up higher now, sweeping over my breasts—his touch so light that I shuddered against him. Incubi drank from lust, and I was giving him a feast right now. I felt myself melting into him, my knees already going weak. Another brush of his fingers over my breasts, and I clenched with desire.

With a nip to my lower lip, he pulled away from the kiss. I felt dazed as I stared at him.

"I want to see all of you, Rowan," he said, and it came out like a guttural plea. "I want you naked and spread out on my bed."

His gaze slid down to the apex of my thighs, where my sheer panties hid almost nothing. Dark shadows snaked out from his body like smoke, and he bit out a curse in another language. I sensed his restraint was slipping. I could feel the glorious, hard length of him straining against his pants—something else that set demons apart from human men.

He kissed me deeply again, tasting me. As my tongue brushed against his, my mind swarmed with images of the glittering sea. I felt like I was floating above it, still flying.

When he pulled away, his midnight eyes slid down my body, over my aching breasts, and then landed on the little scrap of material between my thighs. Lifting me from the wall, he carried me over to his bed and laid me down on the soft pillows. I was liquid, aching for him.

I thought he was going to lean down and kiss me, but instead, he knelt over me. Demonic magic snaked in the air around him, and his eyes were endless darkness. "Take everything off. I want you to show yourself to me."

My heart raced as my face flushed. I knew how stupid it was to come here with him in the first place, and yet, I needed him so badly that I wanted to do whatever he'd asked. I'd do anything for the pleasure he promised.

A seductive smile ghosted over his lips. "Take it all off. Now."

I reached behind my back and unhooked my bra. When I pulled it off, the ocean breeze rushed over my pebbled nipples.

A low, hungry growl rose from his chest. "Now take off the rest."

I slid my fingertips into the side of my panties. He seemed entranced with my body, which weirdly made me excited by the power I had over him. Because Orion was a powerful, ancient demon, feared even by the king. And the way he was looking at my body, it was almost with a sense of worship.

Basking in the attention, I was moving *very* slowly as I started to pull my panties down one millimeter at a time. Part of me ached to rip them off and spread my legs for him, but I was enjoying this too much.

When my panties were finally low enough to show him everything, I watched every one of his muscles go tense, his fingers clutching the pillows. His dark, intense gaze on my body was a thrill I'd never experienced before, and I wanted him to see exactly how turned on I was. But I still kept my panties moving at a glacial pace down over my hips.

His breath had shallowed, and he moved forward, planting his hands on either side of my head. "Why are you going so slowly, Rowan?"

"No reason." With a sly smile, I slid them down a little more around my thighs. "I just like the way you're looking at me."

He shifted back, then reached for my waist and lifted me. He turned me around until I was on my hands and knees, his body folded over mine. He covered my hands with his, and he whispered in my ear, "How about we go at my pace, love?"

When he'd first called me *love*, I'd hated it. But right now, it made me even wetter.

He moved away from me, but he stroked his hand slowly down my spine. As he touched me, my back arched, my ass rising to meet his touch. He kept tracing his hand down lower, over my ass, then between my thighs. An excruciatingly light touch, making me shiver. I wanted to force my hips back against him...

I gasped and raised my hips up even more. Shameless. I was throbbing with need for him. What I really wanted was for him to pull my panties aside, for him to fill me where I was wet. Aching for him, I let out a moan.

And that was when he pulled his hand away from me.

"Now," he said in a low voice. "Take those the rest of the way off for me, and I'll give you what you need."

CHAPTER 32

I wriggled out of them quickly, and I heard his sharp intake of breath, then a low snarl.

From behind, he leaned over me again, hands covering mine for a moment. Then one of his hands moved slowly down, tracing over my breast, my nipple, making me gasp. Lazily, he moved his hand down to my abdomen.

Oh, God, he hadn't even touched me yet between my legs, and I was already insanely turned on. "Tell me," he whispered in my ear, "that you want me to give you what you need."

I turned my head, my mouth now only inches from his perfect lips. "I want you to give me what I need," I whispered.

Then, *finally*, he moved his hand lower. All it took was one light touch between my thighs to make me moan.

And because he needed his ego stroked, he pulled his hand away again.

"Come on, Orion." I'd never wanted anyone like this before.

"I just like hearing you ask," he said, his voice husky.

Slowly, lightly, he moved his middle finger in a circle just where I needed him. I groaned again, and I found my legs spreading wider, my ass moving against his length. My body was tightly coiled with desire, my toes curling. I wanted more of him—I needed him to take off his pants and fill me. My hips moved of their own accord, my body begging for more pressure. I wanted his hands all over me, and I'd become nothing now but animal desire. "Orion, I need more," I whispered.

At last, he slid one finger into me, then another, and I heard him groan my name. Pleasure was rising in me as he stroked in and out, my body clenching around him. I was moving against him, fucking his hand. Finally, for the first time, I was about to come.

"Rowan." That reverence in his tone, like a desperate prayer offered up to the heavens, started to send me over the edge. I was *writhing* beneath him, surrendering to the pleasure he was giving me.

Was this *actually* going to happen? For the first time, was I going to feel that release?

My hips moved against him as he plunged in and out of me, and my vision started to go hazy, filled with images of a midnight sea outside. My body shuddered.

My mind was going dark, shattering as spasms gripped my body.

At last, I climaxed, calling his name.

* * *

My muscles had gone completely limp, and I pulled the sheet around myself, catching my breath.

When Orion lay down behind me, I felt that his body was still rigid, his muscles tense. I turned, kissing him deeply. Somehow, I still wanted more, but that couldn't happen. He twined his fingers into my hair, kissing me hard, desperately.

Then he pulled away with a groan. "This was more difficult than I'd imagined." His eyes were dark as night. "Rowan, we need to stop now. There's only so much torture I can take in a night."

I touched his cheek, my heart aching at his beauty. "Okay. You did it, by the way."

An amused smile. "I know."

When I turned away from him, tugging the sheets around me, my heart was still pounding hard. Orion's powerful arms were wrapped around me, and I gripped one of them. "No wonder everyone makes a big deal out of orgasms. I had no idea. And no wonder mortals let themselves die at the hands of incubi. It was worth it."

A dark laugh from behind me. "Maybe for most mortals, it was worth it, since their lives were worthless anyway. But not for you, it wouldn't be."

The sound of water lapped gently against the rocks. "That's…sweet. I guess."

"Rowan?" he said quietly. "I don't think you should stay in the City of Thorns any longer."

Disappointment coiled through me. "You're kicking me out now? I thought you were going to help me."

He brushed my hair off my face. "I'm not kicking you

out, but I don't want you to die in the king's fire pit. And I can't keep you safe until I know how to kill him."

I took a deep breath. "So you do plan to kill him. Even though he's the king and you're not his heir."

"Well, yes. I'm also considering killing Lydia and Nama, who are the two people most likely to report you for being a mortal. And I could kill anyone who—"

"Can we save the trail of death discussion for later?" I sighed. "I was enjoying the afterglow."

He pulled up a second silky blanket around me, and I curled into it.

"How often do you sleep in here?" I asked quietly.

"Often. It's where I feel the most comfortable."

My eyelids were growing heavy now, and the candles burning in the chandelier were starting to flicker and gutter out. I let my eyes close. "Orion? How did you escape the prison?"

He brushed my hair off my face, then kissed my forehead. "I dug an escape route. It took a very, very long time."

With his arm wrapped around me, I traced my fingers over his strange tattoo—the snake, formed into a noose. "And no one remembered you were down there?"

"One person did." His voice sounded distant. "But he's dead now."

The candles were growing dimmer, and Orion's chest moved slowly in and out behind me, lulling me to sleep.

"The king?" I asked. "Was he the only one?"

"You should go to sleep, Rowan."

Already, I felt myself drifting off to the gentle sound of

the lapping waves. Man, it would be painful to leave. This place was *magic*.

But sleep started to claim my mind, and I dreamt of sweeping over a sparkling ocean, and lemon trees by a shoreline. Until the dreams started to grow darker—a dark mountain that spewed hellfire. A pit of writhing snakes.

Snakes that coiled themselves into nooses.

I WOKE with a gasp and blinked in the dim light. Now, only a single candle flickered over the grotto. I turned to see Orion sleeping next to me, his chest rising and falling softly. Dark sweeps of eyelashes contrasted with his pale hair.

As he slumbered, the Lord of Chaos looked strangely vulnerable. My throat went tight with emotion when I thought of him in the prison. All that time by himself after his mother was killed. He'd only been a little boy, hadn't he, when they were arrested?

Unable to sleep again, my mind started to turn over the enigma of Mortana.

From what Orion told me, she sacrificed other people to save herself. That was how she operated. I no longer thought Orion was a psychopath. He pretended to be one, but I suspected that underneath it all, his revenge mission was driven by love for his mom.

But Mortana? She sounded like a real psychopath. Someone with one guiding principle—making sure she got what she wanted. Maybe even a sadist? He'd said she tortured him in the prisons.

Why was I suddenly getting so angry about this?

I found my fists tightening so hard that my nails were piercing my palms. Red-hot anger flowed through me at the thought of Mortana, this evil woman who'd stolen my face.

My body felt electrified with rage. Oddly powerful, even. I wanted to rip Mortana's head off her doppelgänger body, but the *weirdest* part was that I felt like I could actually do it.

Wait…what was happening to me?

A flash of searing heat burned my wrist, and I looked down to see something like a tattoo flickering on my skin, black and red—burning like embers in a fire. I stared in fascination as something started to take shape before my eyes. A skeleton key smoldered on my wrist.

What in the world...

A golden light beamed over it. With a pounding heart, I started to realize where the light was coming from.

I touched my forehead, casting my wrist in shadow again.

Oh, fuck. Oh, *fuck*.

Powerful emotions could reveal a demon's true nature...

But I couldn't possibly be a demon. He'd tasted my blood, hadn't he? He'd been sure I was mortal. This had to be a nightmare.

At last, the smoldering skeleton key faded away on my wrist. Only then was I able to breathe, and I gasped, staring at the pale skin on my arm where the key had been. "Holy shit."

Orion's eyes opened, and he frowned at me. "What's wrong?"

I touched my forehead again, but the light seemed to be gone now. Only Orion's eyes glowed pale blue in the dark.

"I, um…I think I was just imagining things," I said.

He reached for me again, pulling me close to him, surrounding me with his arms. "You've had a lot to adjust to in the City of Thorns."

My muscles started to relax again in his arms, and I stared out into the dark grotto.

Diagnostic theories: temporary psychotic break with visual hallucinations, or night terrors from sleep paralysis.

At least, I hoped one of those theories was right.

I lay down again, nestling into his strong arms. I tried to force myself to relax, to let go of that horrible vision. A nightmare. That was all it was.

I turned back to Orion once more, and I caught him looking at me, his eyes half-closed.

"Orion," I whispered, "tomorrow, will you help me find out information about my mom?"

He nodded and murmured, half-asleep, "Yes. Then we need to get you out of here."

"What about the king's weakness?" I asked.

"I'll figure it out."

A nightmare. That was literally what Orion was, wasn't he?

Nightmare: from the Old English maere—an incubus. A creature that robbed you of breath in the night, that fed off you. The monsters that crawled from the shadows to drag you into the afterworld. But despite what he kept telling me, I didn't think he was really a monster. As much as it annoyed and inconvenienced him, he was putting my safety above his own goals. He cared about what happened to me.

When I closed my eyes again, my mind flashed with the image of the burning skeleton key. Why had it been so easy for me to summon my shadow-self here in the City of Thorns?

Dread slid through my blood.

Why did it feel like I knew Mortana?

A horrible thought struck me like a lightning bolt—the secret I'd been keeping myself from turning over in my mind. The thing I'd been running from.

What if it was me?

What if I was the one who'd killed Mom? What if I had a dark side I wouldn't admit to myself? That night was so chaotic, and I remembered being angry at her for making me run, for not explaining what was going on. I remembered thinking she was crazy.

Squeezing my eyes shut, I could feel myself shaking.

What if I was the real nightmare?

"Rowan," Orion whispered, "I can feel that you're panicking over something. What's happening?"

My stomach tightened. "Just what you mentioned. The danger in the City of Thorns."

"I can help you sleep, if you want," he said quietly. "It's an incubus thing."

I wanted to get away from my own terrible thoughts more than anything. "Yes, please."

And with that, a soothing magic rippled over me,

coaxing my muscles to relax. My breathing and my heartbeat started to slow. Confused thoughts whirled in my mind—an image of glowing star, the skeleton key tattooed on my arm, the writhing snakes. But none of it seemed as horrifying now.

In a world of demons and magic, it was starting to become difficult to know what was real and what wasn't.

CHAPTER 33

The demon city was an inverted world, one where I seemed to sleep all day and rose as the sun was setting.

Maybe it was having an orgasm for the first time in my life, or maybe it was Orion's incubus sleep magic, but I slept long and hard. By the time I woke in his grotto, the late afternoon sun was slanting over the ocean, streaming into the cave in horizontal rays of coral.

It was the sunlight that reminded me of a painful reality: sexy as Orion was, he was still *technically* one of my suspects.

I rubbed my eyes, and the smell of coffee greeted me. When I felt the breeze rippling over me, I remembered I was still naked, and I pulled up the sheets around myself.

I smiled when I saw Orion sitting at a table by the side of the pool, coffee in one hand. "I've been waiting all day for you to wake. I even returned to your apartment and picked up some clothes for you."

"Thank you. I don't suppose the grotto has a shower?"

He nodded at the pool. "I have a natural bath. It's warmer than you'd think."

Of course. This was magic demon water, which frankly, was much nicer than Massachusetts water. It was a damn shame the demons had spent so long trying to eat us or fuck us to death, or we could have worked together.

Orion had already seen *all* of me, but for some reason, I still kept a sheet wrapped around me as I crossed to the pool. I dropped it only before I jumped in.

As I sank beneath the surface, the heated pool enveloped me. When I came up again for air, I folded my arms over the side and looked up at Orion.

He gave me an amused smile. "Still shy in front of me?"

"Maybe a little." I sighed. "I love it here. Is the grotto a secret from everyone else?"

"You're the only person in existence who knows it's here, besides me."

The warm water was lapping at my back and my breasts. What I was thinking was that it wouldn't be the *worst* thing in the world to stay here secretly for a while, assuming I cleared Orion off my list of suspects. But maybe hiding in a demon's sea cave wasn't a realistic life plan. And *maybe* trying to move in with someone after a single night was a bit much. "So should we investigate a murder?"

Orion reached for something on the table, then lifted an envelope. "While I was picking up your clothes, I ran into Shai. She gave me this to pass on to you. And as luck would have it, it's got the skeleton key you were looking for."

I rested my chin on my arms as I looked at him. "She

just *gave* you that?" She didn't know he was going to help me. Why would she hand it over to him?

"Well, not willingly. She was standing outside your flat looking for you." He gave a lazy shrug. "So I forced her to tell me what she was doing there."

My fingers tightened into fists. "What do you mean, you forced her? Like, you threatened her?"

His eyebrows rose. "No, of course not. I can't threaten her when she knows I can't hurt her." He dropped the envelope on the table. "So I just controlled her mind with magic."

I stared at him. "You can't just mind-control people, Orion."

A line formed between his brows. "Yes, I can. That's how I got the key. I just told you."

I shook my head, starting to lose patience. "I know you're physically able to. I mean, it's…immoral."

"I am a demon," he said slowly, like I was an idiot.

I dropped my head into my hands. "Okay. But you feel guilt for something in the past." I looked up at him again. How did I explain this? "Guilt is about the realization that you've done something wrong. Like, you've done something to another person that you wouldn't want done to yourself, right? And it makes you feel bad. That's guilt."

He was staring at me like I was speaking a foreign language. "But I don't feel guilty for using mind control on Shai. You asked me to help you find your mother's killer. This key seemed to be one of your only clues, and I got it for you." He opened the envelope and pulled out the skeleton key on a long, black ribbon. "See?"

Maybe it was too much to ask a demon to understand the moral issues with mind control. One step at a time.

But more importantly, they key had my attention right now, because for whatever reason, my mom had a key to a room in the City of Thorns. And it reminded me a lot of the one I'd seen on my arm. "Do you think it could go to a room in the Asmodean Ward?"

"It looks like the keys in the Asmodean buildings. The locks haven't been updated in hundreds of years." He brushed his fingertip over it. "And this one has a faint carving of a skull. It's one of the few things I remember from before I was imprisoned. The keys like this..." He stared at it, lost in his memories. "I think I was scared of them, if you can imagine such a thing."

My mind shimmered with the memory of the key I'd seen flickering in and out on my arm. Had there been a skull there, too?

I hoisted myself out of the pool, my heart slamming hard. As my mind churned, I wrapped his sheet around me like a towel.

His gaze flicked down to the sheet. "You know how you were talking about guilt? Do you feel guilt for soaking my sheet in seawater?"

I looked down. "Sorry, I was distracted. Orion, what the fuck was my mortal mom doing with a key to a building in the abandoned Asmodean Ward?"

He turned it over in his hands. "If we locate the right building, I think we'll find out."

CHAPTER 34

We didn't start looking around until night had fallen and moonlight bathed the Asmodean Ward in haunting silver. For once, I wasn't wearing some sexy gown—just black leather leggings and a dark sweater. We weren't planning to be around anyone else, and it was the best way to blend into the night.

Tonight, the air in the City of Thorns was a little cooler than it had been, a nip along with the ocean breeze. The wind rushed through my red curls as we walked the empty streets.

Side by side, we followed the dark canals. Silent buildings loomed around us, the paint faded and chipped. Inside the once-grand houses and halls, we found portraits with their eyes crossed out, statues defaced. We tried the key in every lock we could find—the front doors, the bedrooms, the closets and drawers.

A sense of tragedy pressed down on every house, the sadness heavy in the air. And when we crossed into the building we'd been in before—the one with smashed busts and abandoned crystal decanters—Orion went very still. He stopped to look up at the ceiling, at the image of the nude woman with the snake wrapped around her. Only a thin sliver of moonlight cast a ghostly light over the place. I hadn't noticed it before, but the curtains and furniture looked scorched in many places, and the glass of a mirror had been blackened.

Lost in thought, Orion was as still as the broken statues. The air seemed to grow darker around him, the room hotter. The weight of an oppressive sadness thickened the atmosphere.

"Do you remember this place?" I asked quietly.

He let out a long sigh. "I used to stare at her. I remember lying on the sofa and thinking I would marry her someday, and that I would save her from the serpent wrapped around her body. I can see now she doesn't actually mind the serpent. I didn't know she was the mother of our gods. I thought she belonged to us and that she needed me." He turned, looking around the abandoned hall. "I remember the day the soldiers arrived."

"The king's soldiers?"

"I wasn't scared of our king's soldiers. I was scared of the mortals. They brought guns with them. But the part that scared me was the looks on their faces. I'd never seen such pure loathing like that before."

I stared at him. "There were mortals here?"

"The king surrendered to them and agreed to let them round up the Lilu like they wanted. It was the last time he allowed mortal soldiers into the city." He breathed in deeply. "I can't say they had any signs of the morality you keep talking about. I think they thought we were like animals."

"I'm sorry." My heart broke for him.

"It's not your fault," he muttered.

"But this must be so painful for you."

"I've thought about that day every day for hundreds of years." He crossed the living room to a patch of wooden floor that had been stained darker than the rest. "This was where they cut out my brother's heart. He fought back because he was trying to save our mother." He traced his fingers over the stained floor. "He was the one..." His sentence trailed off, and he stood again and turned, pointing to the hall. "And that was where they cut out my father's heart."

I could hardly breathe. "I guess this answers my questions about why you have such disdain for mortals."

His eyes gleamed. "It's confusing to me that I have such a high regard for you, but you're not what I expected."

The floor creaked as I crossed the room to the mirror, and I stared into its blackened surface. "What's with all the scorch marks? Did they start to burn this place?"

"That was from me. I couldn't control my fire then, but if I could have, I'd have burned the entire army down. And most of the demons with it for turning on us."

"How old were you?" I asked.

"Five."

The breath left my lungs. "They put you in prison when you were *five?*" I asked, a little louder than I'd intended.

I crossed the room and looked into another of the

scorched mirrors, half my face obscured by the smoke. But I could see my eyes, my cheekbones. Moonlight streamed in through the old, warped windows, tinging my face in ghostly light as I looked at myself. "What happened to the other Lilu? Were they killed right away, or were there others in prison with you?"

"That would be a good question for Mortana."

I felt it again—that rising anger. He'd only been a little boy, and he'd watched mortals cut out his brother's heart right on his living room floor. I felt like my chest was splitting in two when I thought of it.

My anger was rising again, like magma buried in a volcano.

When I thought of little Orion screaming for his father, I wanted to find those very mortals and rip their hearts from their chests. Power flooded me, and I felt like I could pull those Puritan fucks from their graves and kill them a second time.

A dark power imbued my body. I was clutching the side of the table so hard, I was breaking some of the wood. I glanced at my arm, where the image of the skeleton key was flickering—one with a skull shape burning like embers.

It was happening again.

When a demon feels a strong emotion...

When I looked up in the mirror, I saw the faint hint of golden light beaming from my forehead, but the shape was obscured by the scorch marks. I slapped my hand over it, my heart slamming.

Fuck. *Fuck.*

"Rowan?" Orion asked. "Why can I hear your heart

beating like you're about to be devoured? You'll wake half the city."

Orion had said a demon could erase her past, could wipe all her memories. She could get rid of the guilt...

What if I'd erased my own memories?

But I couldn't just stand here permanently with my hand on my forehead, could I? What was I so scared of—that I *was* Mortana? He'd said I was human.

I slowed my heartbeat until my muscles started to relax again.

I was, quite simply, seeing things.

Shaking, I pulled my hand away and shifted so I could see my forehead. Nothing was there. No demon mark, no golden light.

"Orion? I think I've been hallucinating things."

"Ah," he said. "That's because you're here. I'm seeing them, too, the ghosts of my past. In here, they feel more vivid than ever."

I let out a shaky breath and turned to him. "For a second, I thought I was turning into a demon."

He gave me a sad smile. "You can't turn into a demon. You're mortal."

Maybe the tragedy of this place was just getting to me. I reached into my pocket for the key and held it up. "Should we keep looking?"

* * *

WE APPROACHED a stone mansion in a section of the ward I'd never seen before. Canals flowed on either side of the building, gently moving south toward the Acheron River.

An overgrown garden rambled out front, and stone paths curved through uncontrolled shrubs and tangles of vines.

Three stories high, the mansion boasted grandiose columns and ornate carvings of gargoyles. Balconies on the second and third floors overlooked the canals and the garden.

"What is this place?" I asked.

"This was once the home of the duke of the Asmodean Ward."

I shivered as I looked up at it. "Why didn't they put me here, if I'm supposed to be the duchess?"

"When Mortana was the only one left, she stayed in the building where you are now. It became the new residence of the Lilu's representative." He glanced at me, his eyes bright in the darkness. "And she probably didn't want to be haunted by the memories of being instrumental in the death of her own father."

I stared at the mansion, my blood growing colder. If tragedy could cling to a place, this palace was dripping in it. It felt tangible in the air. "The duke who lived here was Mortana's father? What was his name?"

"Moloch."

Orion started leading me through the rambling garden to the front door. Above us, a wooden shutter slammed forlornly against the stone window frame.

He slid his pale eyes to me as we approached the mansion. "The City of Thorns isn't like your world. Here, magic imbues the air. Memories linger. Tragedy can wrap itself around the walls, the floors, the stone and wood. It stays there like a living and breathing thing. So if you are seeing things, I'm not surprised. This world was never meant for mortals, and even demons see things here sometimes."

When we reached the door, I slid the key into the lock. And as my heart skipped a beat, I found that the lock *turned*.

I held my breath as the door swung open, revealing the inside of a palace, one covered in cobwebs. A cold shiver rippled through me as I took in the haunted beauty. Thin rays of moonlight streamed into a hall with towering ceilings. A white marble fireplace was inset into a wall, with a faded mural depicting lions and owls. Statues on columns stood around the hall, their faces smashed. The floor was a mosaic of deep blue and gold, with patterns of delicate rosettes, cracked in many places.

Once, this place would have gleamed with wealth and elegance, but even now, it had its own sort of beauty.

My pulse raced. "Orion?" I asked quietly. "Why would my mom have a key to this place? My mortal mom? Do you think she could have been a servant here at one point?"

"It hasn't been inhabited in hundreds of years."

I shook my head, trying to clear the fog from my mind. "Right. Of course."

"Everyone always thought the duke disappeared during the purges." His quiet voice echoed off the tile as he walked around the hall.

"And that was the last anyone has heard of him?" I asked.

"Maybe. About twenty years ago, a body was found in the gardens outside. The heart had been cut out, and the corpse had been burned beyond recognition. The rumors were that it was Duke Moloch himself, but no one knew how he ended up here, or where he'd come from. There could be Lilu who escaped, who live outside of the City of Thorns without their powers."

A cool wind rushed into the room, rippling over my skin. Goosebumps rose on my arms. "Maybe my mom knew him."

A disturbing thought crossed my mind. I'd never known who my dad was.

"And if he were alive," said Orion, "Cambriel might have seen him as a rival for the throne."

I thought I heard a creaking sound above me. When I looked up, I could just about make out the faded paint, a ceiling decorated with vines and ripe fruit. "Why would Moloch be a rival?"

"Long ago, the demons were ruled by a mad king named Azriel. He was obsessed with the idea of returning to the heavens, of reversing the loss in the heavenly wars. He called himself a god. He started killing his own subjects, burning them to death in the forests, ripping their hearts out. If he'd remained king, he could have slaughtered all of his own. He'd have done the mortals' work for them."

"He sounds terrifying."

"It was Cambriel's father, King Nergal, who challenged him to a trial by combat. By his family's lineage, Nergal didn't have much of a claim to the throne. But only the rightful heir can slaughter a king, and Nergal managed to do it. If our gods exist, they didn't want the mad king to stay on the throne."

I turned to look at Orion, frowning. "And the duke who owned this place—was he related to the mad king?"

Orion nodded. "Moloch was his bastard son."

I closed my eyes, then rubbed them. "I'm just trying to process this. My mom—the normal, mortal mom I knew who made me macaroni and cheese and ate too many pizza rolls—she might have known the bastard son of a mad demon king."

"That seems like a good summary."

What. The. Hell? Why had she never told me about any of this? I'd spent my teenage years thinking my mom was sweet but boring.

How wrong had I been?

CHAPTER 35

I kept walking, exploring, hungry to know more. A breeze rushed in, and I crossed to look at a set of old wooden doors, which opened to a courtyard. Out there, arches surrounded a wild garden, and thorny plants climbed over columns and crumbling statues.

Had Mom ever been here?

As I looked out at the garden, puzzle pieces started sliding together in my mind.

I turned to look at Orion, my heart beating faster. "Mortana was born here, right? She was the granddaughter of the mad king. *She* had a claim to the throne. Maybe this explains some of Cambriel's interest in her. There are two ways to conquer a rival for the throne, aren't there? You can either kill them or marry them."

Orion nodded. "That, and he desperately wants to fuck her. But yes, you're right. Mortana has a claim."

Orion had gone very still again. And when he did that,

it always made me nervous. The air seemed to be growing hotter in here, the shadows thickening around him. His pale eyes bored into me.

"What?" I asked. "I can see you're worked up about something."

"What I'm having a hard time with," he said quietly, "is the number of coincidences. Like I said when we first met, demons sometimes have mortal doppelgängers. But what, exactly, are the chances that a mortal doppelgänger also possessed the key to that demon's house?"

Ice slid through my bones. He'd brought up a very good point. And yet, I had no idea.

I cleared my throat. "I don't know. But you said I was definitely mortal." I was clinging to this desperately now. "You said demons can't breed mortals. And clearly, I don't have any magic. Not even in the City of Thorns."

He held my gaze for longer than was comfortable, then pulled it away again at last. "You did taste mortal, yes."

I sucked in a deep breath. "I'm going to look around and see what I can find, okay?" A sense of dread was starting to rise in me, dark and unnamed fears I didn't want to confront.

And for whatever reason, I was starting to feel uneasy around Orion. If I learned anything about my mom in this place, I wasn't sure I wanted him to be there.

I crossed through the hall, suddenly eager to get away from him, and I found my way to a wide, wooden stairwell that swept to the upper floors. I hurried up the stairs, eager to learn more about this place. With the help of the moonlight, I surveyed the defaced portraits, the scattered clothes and ransacked rooms. I moved quickly and with a rising sense of desperation, feeling like I was on the precipice of a discovery.

I crossed out onto the balcony that overlooked the tangled garden, and a flock of crows burst from one of the gnarled trees below, startling me. My heart fluttered as I watched them take to the dark sky.

When I breathed in, my heart squeezed. I could smell Mom here. A faint, floral smell, velvety and tinged with jasmine. I missed her more right now that I ever had.

When I closed my eyes, I could almost feel her here, and my heart ached. I could see her vividly now, dozing in the chair before the TV, exhausted after work. She always had a hard time sleeping, and every little noise woke her. But it was a different Mom that I felt here—not the mortal one I knew, who watched nature documentaries and drank wine spritzers. *This* Mom wore her hair piled on her head and had servants bring her fruit. *This* one was full of confidence, radiant.

This one scared people.

My throat tightened. I didn't want Orion here as I explored. What if I found something that turned him against me?

My hands were shaking as I started moving again, searching one room after another. I kept going until, at last, I reached the master bedroom, one with a four-poster bed made of dark wood and a high ceiling painted with a constellation. But what stopped my heart was the portrait on the wall—a bust, and a woman with her dark hair piled atop her head. It was just as I'd been envisioning her. The portrait's eyes had been painted over, but I would have recognized the rest of her face anywhere. Her straight nose, high cheekbones, dark eyebrows…

I felt like the world was tilting beneath me as I stared up at Mom's portrait. What the *fuck*?

I couldn't breathe as the possibilities whirled in my mind. Did Mom have a doppelgänger, or…

I had to figure this out before Orion came up here.

I turned around, scanning the room, my heart slamming against my ribs. An ancient-looking wooden desk stood in one corner of the room, and I rushed over to it. I pulled open the drawers until I found a book, its black cover embossed with golden thorns, and a skull key like the one I'd seen on my arm. I don't think I was breathing as I turned the pages and read the ancient hand-written text.

On the first page, written in black ink, was a sort of nursery rhyme.

The Maere of Night
Gave girls a fright,
But one queen loved him well.
He lost his throne
But seeds were sown
In the garden of Adele.
A swindler king,
A golden ring
To keep his heart alive.
Take the ring,
Fell the king,
The city yet will thrive.

What was this? A nursery rhyme? A prophecy?

I glanced over my shoulder, making sure I was still alone. I wasn't sure if the text meant anything or if it was just a rhyme, but I pulled out my cell phone to snap a picture anyway.

When I turned the page, I found an index. This was a book of spells. And in the index, one of the spells had the image of a skeleton key next to it.

Locking Spell

My hands were shaking as I turned to its page. There, at the top, was a key that looked like the one on my arm... and along with it, the explanation I'd been dreading.

Spell to Lock Demon Magic

Used to lock demon powers during purges by mortals. This spell temporarily converts a demon into a mortal.

Holy *shit*. My hands were shaking so badly that I could hardly hold the book.

But I couldn't be Mortana, could I? I know Orion had said something about a spell for forgetting, but...

I'd know. If I were evil, I'd know. I didn't feel evil. Did anyone feel evil?

"Rowan?" Orion's voice had me nearly jumping out of my skin, and I might have yelped.

If he saw what I'd just found—if he knew that was a portrait of my mom—he'd kill me. That execution he'd originally planned for me? It could actually happen. Either I was Mortana, or I was a close relation. He'd vowed to kill her *and* her family. Not just a vow, a fucking blood oath.

I turned around and slid the book back into the

drawer. "I didn't find anything," I said, trying to make my voice sound natural.

"What's wrong?" He moved toward the desk, his eyes glowing brightly in the dark.

He could always just tell, couldn't he? He could hear my damn heart beating.

Sucking in a deep breath, I hurried past him and made my way to the hallway. "I was just seeing things again. Like you said, this place seems haunted. Let's go."

"You're no longer interested in what happened to your mother?" he called after me.

"Just spooked, Orion." I took the stairs quickly, no longer sure what I was doing. I hoped he'd come out with me, that he'd leave this ghostly place behind—and the spell book along with it.

When I got outside, I hurried into the garden. Adrenaline flooded me when I thought of what he'd told me—the body found out here, burned beyond recognition. Someone I thought my mother knew…

As I surveyed the savage garden around me, I suddenly felt desperate to get out of the City of Thorns. Yes, I liked the pools and the luxury. I liked Orion a *lot*. But tragedy haunted every inch of this place, and it was starting to become clear that some of it might be mine.

Did Orion keep looking around up there? If he found that locking spell…

I kept walking through the rambling garden, my nerves electrified. As I ambled through the untamed thorns around me, I shivered. The sound of footfalls made my heart pick up, but as I started to turn around, a hand clamped *hard* around my nose and mouth. A powerful grip was smothering me.

Orion? I thrashed against the hand, trying to pull it off, but he was far too strong for me.

My lungs burned as the air left my lungs. And as I tried to kick at his shins, my vision started to go dark.

CHAPTER 36

I woke in the darkness, tied to a chair. Pain split my head open, and my mouth was dry as a bone.

I smelled faintly of pee, but I didn't want to dwell on that. I needed to think about how I was going to get the fuck out of this situation. Besides the pee, the air smelled like smoke—burnt cedar and maybe iron.

Wait—the burnt cedar was Orion's scent.

"Orion?" I rasped. "I can explain." I really fucking couldn't, but it seemed like a good start.

Ropes chafed at my wrists as I tried to pull against them.

Footfalls echoed off stone, and when I turned my head, I saw a light shining from a tunnel. As it grew brighter, I could just about make out the contours of a small, arched space, like stone vaults underground.

"Rowan." The rasping voice came from the opposite corner, and I turned to see Orion in the shadows. Apparently, he wasn't the one who'd tied me up, because he was wrapped in chains. Blood poured from his shoulders and chest, and a pile of ash lay around him.

"Orion!" I shouted. "What happened to you?"

His eyes were drifting closed, like he was having trouble staying conscious. "Some fucking idiot mortal gave Nama a gun."

"*What?*"

"She shot me and chained me up. I tried burning my way through the chains, but…I just burned the chair. I can't summon any more magic right now, not when I'm riddled with bullets. I'm having a hard time…"

His bright blue eyes closed, and panic started to crawl up my throat.

The sound of footsteps grew louder, and Nama crossed into the room holding a lantern in one hand and a gun in another. Her white hair fell in perfect waves over a scarlet gown. "Hello, friends." She lifted the gun. "This is fun."

I glanced at Orion, but his eyes had closed again. He couldn't actually die unless someone cut out his heart, but it hurt to see him covered in blood.

With all the shit going on, I nearly forgot that I was supposed to be Mortana. Time to summon the imperious attitude.

I tossed my hair over my shoulder. "What are you doing, you fool? Untie me at once."

Nama's eyes widened, and her hand flew to her mouth. "Or what? What will you do if I don't untie you?"

Was she calling my bluff?

She lifted the lantern. "Andras! Gamigan! Lydia!" she bellowed. "She's awake. Bring the mortal with you."

"What are you doing?" I snapped. "You're insane."

"Oh, my slutty little friend," she cooed. "Madness runs in your blood, not mine. There was a reason we had to kill your grandfather. The Lilu are abominations."

Two of the dukes crossed into the room—the platinum-haired greed demon who led the Mammon ward, and a sloth demon with heavy-lidded green eyes from Abadon. And behind them, Lydia sauntered in—right next to Jack Corwin.

Jack? Jack was the idiot mortal who'd given Nama the gun. With his Alpha Kappa sweatshirt and old baseball cap, he looked completely out of place here.

My blood turned to ice, my thoughts whirling out of control. My two worlds were colliding now in the most terrible way possible.

Of course Jack was the idiot mortal in question. Right now, he looked fairly terrified, his eyes shifting from one demon to another. And when I looked closely, I could see that new bruises marred his face. His lip had been split, and purple bloomed over his cheekbones and jaw.

Nama handed the lantern to Lydia.

"What's going on?" I demanded through gritted teeth. I could no longer keep up the pretense of being calm and collected. Right now, my shadow-self was nowhere to be found.

With a smug smile, Nama folded her arms. As she did, the gun went off, and she screamed. Bits of rock and sand sprayed over the room.

Jack held up his hands. "Careful with that!"

Nama frowned at the gun. "These things are confusing." She shook her head. "Anyway, I had a hunch that you spent a lot of time around mortals, Mortana. You just seemed kind of grotesque like they are. You know, like an animal. A filthy, rutting animal."

I curled my lips in a snarl. "Have you lost your mind?"

She shrugged. "So I did a little digging. I spent today hunting around Osborne until I saw a picture of your face in a trophy closet. A track team." She wrinkled her nose and turned to the dukes. "Humans compete against each other in running races, even though they're slow as fuck. But do you really think it's fair for a demon to be on a mortal track team?"

My stomach plummeted, and I watched as she crossed to Jack. She gripped him by the hair, pulling his head back, then pointed the gun at his chin. "Then things got a little more interesting. This little fucker tried to shoot me. Apparently, he fancies himself something of a demon hunter."

Jack was shaking violently. *Holy hell.* Was I on the same side as Jack right now? I didn't like that at all.

Nama slapped him across the face with her free hand. "I beat him until he told me about the picture of Mortana. Except he said her name wasn't Mortana. He said her name was Rowan Morgenstern. And he is quite sure that you're mortal." She let go of him and whirled to face me. "*Apparently,* he can smell demons."

I shook my head, genuinely confused. "What?"

Nama pointed the gun at his pendant—the silver one with the hammer. "The Corwins are witch finders and demon hunters."

Jack nodded, a frantic look in his eyes. "I can smell demons. I could hunt them, if I felt like it." He held up his hands, his face pale. "But I don't! I never have. I just carry the gun for protection. I thought Nama was a threat. I knew your kind are all around, and I knew you might come after me because of what my family did. That was why I tried to shoot Nama. It was just self-defense. I swear—"

"Be quiet, you fuckwit mortal!" bellowed one of the dukes, a man with long black hair. "We did not come here for your trial. We came here to try the succubus. Nama claims that she's not actually a succubus. You're here as a witness. That is your role."

I flexed my wrists in the ropes. "And you all are the judges?"

Nama gestured at me with the gun. "The king seems taken with you, and he won't listen to me unless I have witnesses." She pointed the gun at the other demons. "These are my witnesses. What I really, *really* want is to attend a barbecue in the Tower of Baal, with a mortal whore as the main course. I haven't eaten roasted mortal in a long time."

Oh, *God*.

"Watch it with the gun!" said Jack, his hands up. "Since I've done what you asked, can I leave now? We had a deal. I told you she's mortal. She smells like a mortal, I swear to God. Burn her, have your fun, just let me go."

"Fine!" Nama barked. "I can't kill you since I might need you later. But if I ever catch you hunting demons, I'll rip your guts out through your mouth."

Jack turned and sprinted out through the tunnel.

I kept squirming, trying to pull at the ropes, but there was no point. Since I didn't actually have demonic strength, all I was doing was scraping my skin off. With a thundering heart, I turned to look at Orion. His eyes were starting to open again, and he met my gaze.

"Why is he here, Nama?" I asked.

She grimaced. "I want him to see that you've been lying to him. You're nothing but a filthy little doppelgänger, aren't you? I want him to realize that I was right all along. I'm the right person for him. And if you were *actually* a demon, you wouldn't have such a hard time getting out of rope bonds, would you? It's just *rope*. Any demon can break it."

"Maybe I don't care to prove myself to you," I said breezily. "Maybe I don't want to be part of your stupid little game."

This was the very definition of being caught between a rock and a hard place. If I told them about the locking spell, I'd die at Orion's hands. If I were a mortal, I'd die at theirs.

My body shook. "You think that he'll love you after you shot him?" I asked. "You're insane."

She crossed to me, her eyes wild and fanatical. "He'll see that I did it because I love him. All of this, everything that I'm doing, is for him. For us. We're meant to be."

Lydia crossed her arms. "Can we get on with it, Nama? Your obsession with him is frankly depressing, and it's making me regret sharing a gender with you. I should have listened to Legion. The duke of the Sathanas Ward said you were a lunatic."

"What, exactly, are we getting on with?" My voice was shaking so hard they had to know by now that I wasn't

Mortana. I sounded *terrified*. "I told you that I'm not participating."

Orion's eyes opened just a little wider, pure black now. I could feel the room growing hotter.

"Maybe you need a little motivation." Nama pointed her gun at Orion. "Here's how the trial will work. I'm going to keep shooting Orion. His knees, his hand. Maybe his pretty face."

"You just said you loved him!" I shouted, sounding frantic. I couldn't keep up the act anymore.

Her face beamed. "Yes, Mortana. And if I can't have him, no one else will. That's how much I love him."

Lydia pinched her nose. "Oh, my God, Nama."

"So here's how the first trial works," Nama went on. "You prove that you're a demon and save him. Or you can stay tied to your chair like a weak little mortal and show him that you're an animal."

I gritted my teeth, my entire body shaking. "What if I don't care what happens to him?"

Nama grinned, her eyes maniacal now. She turned to Orion. "Then you prove that you don't deserve him! You don't even care enough to get up to help him. And I care enough about him to do all this."

"Excuse me," the Duke of Mammon interrupted, his golden rings gleaming. "We're not putting her on trial to see if she cares about Orion. I just want to ensure we're not giving our hard-earned tax revenue to a mortal. If she's a demon, I don't give a fuck if she cares about Orion."

"*I do*!" Nama bellowed, then whirled, aimed the gun at me, and pulled the trigger.

CHAPTER 37

Pain exploded through my leg, the agony so shocking I could no longer think straight. My mind went dark for a second, and when my vision cleared again, I saw that she'd turned the gun back on Orion.

Nama's laughter echoed off the stone walls. "Now let's try Orion, my beloved. Show us how strong you are, Mortana. Show us you can use that fire magic of yours."

She pulled the trigger and shot Orion in his kneecap. I watched as his eyes went dark, and a blast of heat pulsed through the room.

I could feel it again—that rising anger. The rage. Pure strength coursed through my body, and an ancient fury that could melt rock to stone. Darkness spilled through my blood like ink. My shadow-self was rising to the surface like molten lava, and I could no longer feel the pain of the bullet in my leg.

Mortals and ruthless demons had murdered Orion's family in front of him when he was just a boy. They'd locked him in a room alone with his haunting memories.

Most people would be broken by that. And now they'd dragged him here to a tunnel to torture him some more.

Fury ignited in my blood, and I could feel the ropes straining at my wrists. A light was beaming from my forehead, my chest growing hotter. Brighter. Deep down, the buried truth—the one I'd hidden from myself—was that I was stronger than all these fuckers.

And I'd kill to protect those I loved. I'd make them regret that they'd been born.

Nama aimed the gun at Orion's face. "It's so pretty, Orion. You know, I think that's your problem. Your face is too pretty, and I need to make you feel—"

I would bathe my enemies in flames. I'd stop when they lay as piles of ash.

The rope shredded behind me, and hot wrath erupted.

I didn't know the fire was streaming from my body until I smelled the burning flesh. Only then did I see the flames that filled the vault, a pure inferno of death. A vortex of molten heat.

They wanted to put me on trial?

I was Hell itself. I would burn the wicked from this earth. I was born to rule.

The flames snapped back into my body, and I gasped, looking down at myself. Pure power imbued my body, and my legs started to shake.

Magic. Powerful, terrifying magic.

The locking spell had been unlocked. I felt unsteady on my feet, in shock from what had just happened.

I was in a nightmare.

My clothes were singed, partly burned off, and my legs bare from the thighs down. Enormous piles of ash lay on the floor where three of the demons had been standing. To my right, soot covered Lydia and her seared clothes. Ashes filled the air.

Lydia gaped at where the other demons had been standing. "I guess Nama was wrong," she said in a daze.

With a slamming heart, I stared as she ran out of the tunnel. I looked down at my hands, at my glowing fingers. Flames flickered from them like candles. I felt a jolt of magic sizzle through my arms, electrifying me down to my fingertips.

When I turned to look at Orion, a new horror coursed through my bones. The chains had melted off him, and he rose to his feet, his eyes black as night. Seems he had strength in him, after all. His clothes had been burned off in places, exposing arms and thighs thickly corded with muscle.

The pure hatred in his features made my heart stop. Time seemed to slow down, and a phantom breeze toyed with his silver hair.

But it was the mark on his forehead that made me want to murder him.

A five-pointed star.

There he was—the fucking Lightbringer. The ruler of demons.

Battle fury rippled through my body, and I could feel the air heating up around us, but I had no idea if the source was Orion or me. I only knew the stones were starting to glow beneath us, red hot. The silence pressed on us, heavy as soil in a grave.

My shoulder blades tingled with some ancient instinct to unleash my wings.

Orion's lip curled, and shadows coiled around him like smoke. "Mortana," he snarled, his voice a frigid blade that cut me to the core. "There you are."

"There's the Lightbringer," I hissed. "You've made a remarkable recovery."

"I wasn't that hurt. I wanted to learn the truth about you as much as they did. And now I know. You managed to disguise yourself as a mortal."

I pointed at him, feeling like the betrayal was eating me alive. "I know what happened now. You killed my mom. You made a blood oath to murder everyone in Mortana's family, and that included my mother. This whole time, you were pretending to help me find her killer, and you knew it was you."

He shook his head slowly, and I wasn't sure what that meant. I only knew he looked like he was going to rip my head from my body.

I wasn't sure which of us moved first, but in the next moment, he was pinning me up against the wall, and my feet were off the ground. His hand clamped around my throat, and he pressed me hard against the stone. Endless darkness burned in his eyes. "Mortana," he snarled. "It is deeply unfortunate that the most beautiful person I've ever seen is also my worst enemy."

But I wasn't a weak mortal anymore, and I could fight back. My self-defense classes came roaring into my mind, except now with the strength of a god. I raised my arms, slamming my hands against his wrists. At the same time, I brought my knee up hard into his groin.

He dropped his grip on me, and I lunged forward, aiming for his face with my fist. But he grabbed my hand

and twisted it behind my back, and when he shoved me against the wall with bone-breaking force, the air left my lungs.

"Did you know?" His quiet voice was like an ancient curse. "Did you know how I would feel when I learned the truth? Is that why you did it?"

"I don't know anything." I kicked back into his shin, hard enough that I heard a crack. "I have no fucking idea what's happening, Orion."

I whirled to try to punch him, but he was lifting me in the air. He threw me hard across the room, and I slammed onto the floor. The blow winded me. As a mortal, I'd be dead. As a demon, it was just a setback.

No wonder demons thought mortals were weak. I felt invincible.

From above, Orion looked down at me like a conquering god waiting for a sacrifice. "I know exactly who you are. You're my worst enemy, and you always have been."

I thrust my hips up and slammed the back of my heel into his knee where Nama had shot him—once, twice. With a growl, he stumbled back. From the ground, I kicked at his calves, sweeping his legs out from under him. When he fell backward, I leapt atop him. I clamped my hands around his neck, my thighs around his waist. I wasn't squeezing yet, but I was threatening it. I felt my claws emerge, ready to rip his heart out, and I pressed them against his chest.

"I don't know if I'm Mortana!" I shouted at him. "If I was once Mortana, she's as foreign to me as a stranger. I'm not what you think I am. You said Mortana only cares for herself, that she's driven by self-preservation. And you said emotions make a demon reveal her true self. But it wasn't self-preservation that unveiled my demon side. Every time I started to feel it rising, it was from wanting to protect you. It was thinking of you as a little boy in that prison." My chest ached from the hurt of all this. "My demon side came out because I wanted to protect you. I burned through the locking spell because I wanted to keep you safe. So I don't know who I am, but I do know that I'm not the monster you're looking for. But you? You're the one who betrayed *me,* Orion. You were pretending to help me find my mom's killer, when all this time, it was you," I snarled.

He stared up at me, transfixed. "What makes you think it was me?"

"I remember you from that night."

"No, you don't." His lip curled. "I never lied to you about what I am. I don't hide my faults or what I've done. If I'd killed your mother, I would have told you as soon as I met you. Except now I have a new flaw, and it's my worst one."

"What?"

"I could have killed you five times over in the last two minutes. I could kill you now. And something fucking idiotic is stopping me." His jaw tightened. "I have never loathed myself more than I do right now, and believe me, that's saying something, because I have plumbed some *amazing* depths of self-loathing."

"Stop changing the subject." Tears streamed down my face. "You have the five-pointed star. I remember it from the night my mom was murdered in the woods with *fire* magic just like yours. It was you."

"You might want to look in the mirror, Mortana," he spat. "I'm not the only one with fire, and it seems Lucifer has blessed us both. You and I are both marked as the Lightbringer. But if you think you'll take the throne from me, you're mistaken."

Dread bloomed in my chest. Horrified, I rose and stumbled away from Orion. With tears streaking my face, I reached into my jeans pocket for my phone. It was half-melted, no longer working, but in the black gleam, I could make out a reflection—one shining from my forehead.

A five-pointed star. The image hit me like a fist to my throat.

Without another word to Orion, I started running through the tunnels at full speed.

But I wasn't running from Orion now. I was sprinting from the memory I'd been running from all this time. The reason I was so obsessed with finding my mom's killer. This had been my worst fear—the darkest truth buried in the depths of my mind, the thing I so desperately wanted to prove wasn't true.

What if I killed Mom?

We'd had a fight that night. She'd kept wanting me to move from one apartment to another. She'd seemed paranoid, delusional. She'd thought someone was after us but wouldn't tell me who, and I only remembered that I hadn't wanted to go with her.

Orion had said he couldn't control his fire when he was younger…

I thought she'd lost her mind. I remember yelling at her, and I was so angry—

Sickness rose in my gut, and I hardly knew where I was running. I felt like the walls were collapsing around me.

Was I Mortana—and I'd forgotten?

Deep down at my core, under the lies I told myself, what if I was truly evil?

I ran and ran until I saw the moonlight in Osborne. I slipped into the shadows, my feet pounding along the waterfront. I sprinted past the brewery, the Cirque de la Mer. I didn't know where I was going, just that I needed to move.

But I could never outrun what I was really fleeing.

CHAPTER 38

I leaned back on my bed in my basement apartment, staring at the wall. I poured myself another paper cup of cheap red wine, no longer caring that the spiders were crawling all over my bedspread.

Let them crawl.

I'd been down here for nearly a day, and I was on my second bottle.

If Orion wanted to come find me and throw me in prison again, it wouldn't be hard. I hadn't bothered to hide. I'd just come back to where I'd started—the mildewed basement I shared with six other people. Now, I had less fear but a lot more self-loathing. If Orion dragged me back, I'd go dressed in old leggings and a David Bowie T-shirt covered in wine stains. And I'm not sure I'd put up that much of a fight.

My gaze wandered around the room, then landed on the fire extinguisher. I broke out into a sort of hysterical dark laughter and spilled some of my wine on the duvet.

Guess I could get rid of all the fire safety equipment now.

My phone buzzed—another text from Shai, desperate to know what was going on. I hadn't been answering, because frankly, I had no idea what to say.

I was a demon, yes. But I wasn't going to deliver that news over text. Still, I should let her know I was alive.

I flicked open my new, extremely cheap phone. Unable to come up with anything better, I texted her a smiley face and a bottle of wine emoji.

That should cover it.

My head was swimming, and I was starting to feel faintly nauseated. When had I last eaten?

The room seemed to be wavering. Apparently, being a demon made you faster and stronger, but it didn't raise your alcohol tolerance.

And yet, I didn't want my head to clear. I couldn't face the possibility that my own fire magic had killed Mom.

When my phone buzzed again, I found a frantic all-caps message from Shai:

ARE YOU OKAY??! WTF IS HAPPENING? TWO MORE DUKES ARE DEAD?? I saw Legion in the Sathanas Ward. I got up the courage to ask him where Mortana was. He said no one had seen you, and rumor was that you'd burned two dukes. ARE YOU OKAY?

I dropped my cup of wine on the bedside table and started typing back to her.

I'm fine!

You know what? Fuck it. I was always so worried about what people would think or that I'd make them uncomfortable with the darkness I carried with me. I never wanted to burden anyone with my most disturbing thoughts. Maybe I could actually learn a thing or two from Orion. Maybe I could try…just coming out and saying things.

With a strange feeling of giddiness, I typed:

Turns out I'm a demon. I have fire magic. And a star mark. What if I'm the one who killed Mom? What if I'm evil?

I watched as the dots moved on the screen while she wrote back to me, and my heart pounded as if the judgment of St. Peter awaited me.

Evil people don't worry that they're evil, Rowan. They don't care.

My chest unclenched, and I dropped the phone. Holy shit. Of course she was right.

Why hadn't I been able to think clearly enough to consider that? A psychopath doesn't worry that she's evil. She doesn't feel anxiety. And me? Even as a demon, I had plenty of that.

I rose from my bed and yanked open my basement door. Orion described someone who at her core did not care for other people. And what I'd said to him was true—my emotions rose to the surface when I felt like I desperately wanted to protect him.

And I couldn't be Mortana.

I mean, I remembered being a kid. Crying in the ball pit at Chuck E. Cheese and peeing my pants in the second grade. Mom sending me to school with waffles for a year because I refused to eat anything else, and other kids laughing at my bony knees. The nights Mom spent petting my head because I had nightmares and kept asking for water.

I remembered being the fastest kid in my gym class but never being able to climb the ropes, and having a crush on Matt Logan even after he told me I was annoying. I remembered watching *The Price is Right* with my mom over early lunches and getting excited at the prizes.

I remembered getting Communion when I went to church with my friend Amy, even though I wasn't Catholic. I'd immediately puked over a statue of Santa Lucia.

And…now I understood why I'd puked, I guess.

Maybe magic could suppress memories, but could it really fake a childhood? With that level of specificity? I wasn't a five-hundred-year-old demon. I was Rowan Morgenstern, and that was all there was to it.

And most of all, I remembered how much I loved my mom because I'd felt safe near her. No matter how mad I'd been at her, there was no way I'd killed her. At least not on purpose.

When I went outside, I was surprised to find that it was night—I'd completely lost track of time. I blinked at the moon over Osborne, feeling oddly at home under its light.

Holy shit.

I was Rowan Morgenstern, but I was also a succubus, wasn't I?

A creature of the night. I belonged out here.

I glanced at the key tattoo again on my arm—now permanent. I still didn't know what had happened, but I could only guess that Mom had given me the spell to make sure I was always safe. That my blood tasted mortal, just in case.

I started walking toward the waterfront. It was colder here than in the City of Thorns, and goosebumps rose over my skin. The air tasted of salt and smelled of seaweed. By the cold sea, I let the shadows swallow me. I didn't actually have to be scared of being outside at night anymore. The mortals couldn't hurt me. The demons wouldn't dare.

The thing was, if I was a demon, I didn't really belong out here in Osborne, did I? If I didn't get within the city walls again, I only had about another day or two before my magic faded.

I wasn't mortal. Neither was Mom. She was Lilu—one of the exiled. She'd been living out here in hiding, always looking over her shoulder. Banished just because she was a succubus.

And my dad? If he was, in fact, Duke Moloch, he'd been killed just after I was born. About twenty years ago. Maybe he'd gone back to try to save me.

My mind snagged on the nursery rhyme I'd found, the one in the book. Had that meant anything?

The Maere of Night
Gave girls a fright,
But one queen loved him well.
He lost his throne
But seeds were sown
In the garden of Adele.
A swindler king,
A golden ring
To keep his heart alive.
Take the ring,
Fell the king,

The city yet will thrive.

It sounded like a nursery rhyme, but I was sure something important had been written into that poem. A secret I needed to unlock.

From deep within my brain, an ancient instinct was rising to the surface, and magic tingled down my shoulder blades.

I needed to take to the skies. I needed to be free.

My back arched, then wings burst from my skin. When I glanced over my shoulder, I saw them, black and feathered, flecked with gold. Beautiful.

This was a release—the unveiling of my true self. My wings started to pound the air, instinct carrying me higher and higher into the briny wind.

Orion hated me now. He was convinced down to his marrow that I was Mortana.

But I was going to find out the truth. I was going to learn exactly what happened to Mom, and who I was.

What makes a person who they are, their essence? Was it a soul or their memories? I didn't know. I only knew I wasn't the monster Orion imagined me to be.

I breathed in deeply and stared at the locked gates of the City of Thorns.

Deep within my bones, I knew that was where I belonged. I'd always known.

I was a Lightbringer—blessed by Lucifer. And whether he liked it or not, I would fight him for my place in the city I was destined to lead.

AFTERWORD

Thank you for reading City of Thorns. Please check out our website, cncrawford.com, if you want to learn how to get updates about book two (Lord of Embers).

You can also follow me on Instagram, or join C.N. Crawford's Coven on Facebook for news about the series.

On the following pages, I've included the opening chapters of another one of our novels, The Fallen.

Our full list of books can be found on Amazon or Goodreads.

LILA

Excerpt from The Fallen

When I was a kid, I dreamt of living in the castle that loomed over our city, a place of magic and intrigue. As I got older, I started to learn that even the slums had their own kind of magic. If you knew where to look, you could feel the power of ancient kings thrumming under the stones beneath your feet.

Tonight, warm lights shone through some of the windows through the fog, and the sound of a distant piano floated on the wind, winding between narrow alleys. No one was out here, just me and the salty breeze, the shadows growing longer as the sun slid lower in the sky. The mist curled around brick tenements that groaned toward each other, crooked with age. Fog skimmed over the dark, cobbled street.

I didn't care what anyone thought—this city was beautiful.

I shoved my hands in my pockets, glad the day was over. Like every Friday night, I was heading for the

Bibliotek Music Hall. Some lovely chap would buy me a drink. I'd dance till the sun came up and the blackbirds started to sing.

I knew every alley, every hiding spot, every haunted corner where pirates once hung in gallows. I'd grown up to the sound of the seagulls overhead and the lapping of the Dark River against the embankment.

But tonight as I walked, the sense of wonder started to darken a little. The shadows seemed to thicken.

Every now and then, the crowded streets could feel like a trap. Because as much as I loved the place, it wasn't necessarily populated by gentlemen.

And right now, the familiar magic was being replaced by a sense of menace. It lingered in the air, making goosebumps rise on my skin, but I wasn't sure why.

I picked up my pace, envisioning the fresh bread and cheese I'd get at the Bibliotek Music Hall. Maybe I just needed a proper snack.

But why did I feel like someone was following me?

When I sniffed, I smelled whale oil, pitch pine and turpentine. Ah. Bloody hell. That was what had me on edge. The Rough Boys—a gang who lived on an old boat in the docks—always reeked of their ship. I could smell them from here, even if I couldn't see them yet.

Were they following me? Had I stolen something that belonged to them? I spent my days on the docks, in and out of ships and warehouses. I pilfered tea and other valuables, passing them off to a network of thieves.

Not glamorous, admittedly, but it was honest work.

Okay, fine. It wasn't honest either, but it meant I got to eat.

I glanced over my shoulder, and that was when my pulse kicked up a notch. I swallowed hard. Three of them stood at the end of the street, fog billowing around them like ghost ships on a misty sea. I recognized them right away by their signature look—shaggy hair and pea coats.

"Oi! Pussycat!" One of them shouted for me, voice booming off stone walls. "I got a message for your mum! She needs to pay up."

"No thanks!" I shouted.

I knew how they sent messages—with their blades, carved in skin. Mum owed them money, which meant I owed them money. And if I didn't pay up they'd take a knife to me fast.

I whirled and raced through the narrow street.

"It's not exactly optional!" One of them shouted after me.

Where were the bloody coppers when you needed them? Always around when I pinched something, but never when cutthroats were after me.

At least I knew these streets as well as I knew my own body. If I could keep up the pace, I could lose the bastards.

My feet hammered the pavement, arms pumping as I ran. My brown curls streamed behind me. Puddles soaked into my socks through the holes in my threadbare shoes. I wanted to look behind me, to see how close they were, but that little movement would cost me. I knew if I slowed down, there'd be more of their gang crawling from the shadows. Fear was giving me speed.

The Rough Boys took people's noses, eyelids, ears. If I could avoid it, I'd prefer not to walk around like a mutilated horror show for the rest of my life.

So as they chased me, I dodged from one dark alley to the next, rounding the labyrinthine corners, keeping to the shadows, trying to lose them.

But the Rough Boys were taller than me, and just as fast, sprinting like jackals over the stones.

"Lila, is it? Pretty lady." One of them shouted. "We just need to have a little chat."

Did they think if they called me pretty I'd simper over to them, blushing?

I was good in a fight—better than most men, even—but a fight with a gang in their territory was always a losing prospect. There were always more of them ready to slink out of alleys. My sister Alice taught me never to draw your knife unless you knew you could win.

Except I couldn't run forever, and I needed just a moment to catch my breath. At twenty-five, I was already getting slow. Embarrassing.

Breathless, I took a sharp turn onto Dagger Row. Then I darted into a shadowy alley between two brick walls. I hid deep in the darkness, listening with relief as the cutthroats ran on past. Oblivious.

A smile curled my lips. *You lived another night.*

Perhaps I'd make it to twenty-six with my face intact.

For just a moment, I rested, hands on my thighs. Crowded tenements rose up on either side of me. Dirty water ran in the gutters. I straightened again and peered out from the alley.

No one around.

I pulled the hood of my coat tight, then started walking at a fast clip.

The winding streets had taken me on a jagged path

back toward the river. Before I crossed onto the next street, I peered around the corner to the right. I shivered at the sight of Castle Hades.

The ancient fortress was still breathtaking, every time I looked at it. Its dark stone loomed over a bustling city of merchants and beggars, holy sisters and street crawlers. We all looked up to it with awe.

The castle's four central towers rose up like ancient obelisks against the night sky. Two enormous rings of stone walls fortified the exterior, and a moat surrounded it. Once, the castle had gleamed white in the sun, and lions roamed the courtyards. Just fifty years ago, ravens had swooped over its twenty-one towers, and true Albian kings and queens danced in the courtyards.

Back then, we used to think the ravens protected Dovren. That they were good luck.

But the ravens had done nothing when invaders arrived on the Dark River—an army of elite warriors, headed by the ruthless Count Saklas. The ravens didn't help at all when Count Saklas beheaded our king in his own dungeon.

Now, the count ruled the whole kingdom from the castle's stone walls. Our citizens hung from gallows and gibbets outside, macabre warnings. Anyone who opposed his rule got the death penalty.

Pretty sure the bastard killed the ravens, too, because of course he did.

Two years ago, the last time anyone saw my sister Alice, she was carrying red silks into the castle. Then, she just disappeared. No idea what happened to her. It felt like the castle had swallowed her up.

Shivering, I turned away, thinking warmly of the Bibliotek Music Hall. My friend Zahra would be waiting for me, probably already with a cocktail in hand. In my pocket, I had a tiny nip of whiskey, and I pulled it out to take a sip and warm myself up. Cheap and strong, it burned my throat.

Maybe the count had conquered my country, but we still had the best music in the world. And we knew how to throw a party.

But just as I was starting to let down my guard, the sound of footfalls echoed behind me. I whirled, and fear jolted me as dark shadows emerged from the fog.

Bloody hell. The Rough Boys had found me again.

LILA

"Lila!" they shouted. "Got a message, don't we?"

It looked like I'd be taking the fast route to the music hall, then. Breaking into an all-out sprint, my feet pounded the cobbles, echoing off the buildings around me.

Even as my lungs burned and my legs ached, I knew I was going to run until I collapsed, and died, or reached the music hall. Because I would *not* be losing any parts of my face tonight. I was rather attached to them.

Heaving for breath, I sprinted up Savage Lane. Here, the shops were shuttered for the night, windows dark. I still had ten streets to go.

As I ran, the sound of my breath formed a rhythm along with my feet.

Nine streets.

When I was a kid, my sister Alice and I played a game: we'd run through the alleys pretending a phantom called Skin-Monster Trevor was chasing us. I'm not sure where Alice got the name, but I imagined him as terrifying. If he caught us, he'd leave behind nothing but a pile of bloody bones. I could almost hear Alice's voice in my mind, telling me to run. *Lila! Trevor's coming for you! He'll kill you!*

Only it wasn't a phantom chasing me now. It was real flesh and blood men who wanted to carve me up.

My gaze darted across the street, where a narrow alley jutted off from the main road between abandoned shops. I veered into it.

From behind, the gang's boots pounded the stones.

With burning lungs, I careened out of the mouth of the alley onto Magpie Court—a cramped little street lined with slum houses, where everything stank of piss and old fish.

Almost there... almost to Bibliotek ...

"Stop running, little pussycat!" they shouted from behind me. "Lovely Lila!"

What a charmer. But I wasn't about to stop and deliver myself into their hands, was I?

I turned the corner. Ahead of me, gas lamps lit the road with wavering light. This was Cock Row, so named because it bordered a park of shadowy trees, where the bunters worked—the street whores. Opposite the park, the enormous music hall stretched out over the entire square.

I was almost to the doors now. I stole a glance over my shoulder and relief flooded me.

No sign of the Rough Boys. I'd lost them again. Ha! Slow bastards.

I actually laughed with relief. *Not bad, Lila. Not bad at all.*

With my hand on the doorknob, I glanced up at the

Bibliotek Music Hall, at the beaming windows crowded with dancing people. Three stories of red brick rose up before me. On the first floor, a stone facade had once been painted a vibrant red, but now it had faded and peeled into something more beautiful. I liked it that way. Music pulsed through the walls, brassy and booming. This decadent place had everything I could ever want.

Except, apparently, a *very* key feature right now: a way in.

I tried to turn the doorknob again, and a tendril of dread curled through me. Locked.

My heart thudded against my ribs. Why was the door locked? Was someone having a laugh?

No, everyone loved me in Bibliotek. Finn or one of the other doormen must've closed it down to take a piss, which was *distinctly* bad timing as far I was concerned.

I banged on the door. "Hello? Finn? Anyone?"

When they didn't answer, I shoved my hand into my pocket for my lock picks. But before I could get started, my stomach lurched. Boots thumped on cobbles.

The Rough Boys were running down the narrow pathway, gunning for me. A whole pack of them now; they'd brought reinforcements.

My gaze flicked to the torches that hung from the reddish stone, and I grabbed one of them.

As I held it out at them, its warmth beamed over my face. "Step back!" I shouted.

Smoke billowed before my face.

The turpentine they reeked of—from their ship—was in fact very flammable. The whale oil, too.

A pair of cutthroats stepped from the pack. The one

on the right was a good foot taller than the other, but both were pure muscle, both had shaggy blond curls. They might even be brothers.

I whirled. As they tried to surround me, I used the flaming torch to try to keep them at bay.

The tall one raised his hands, though he didn't actually look one bit afraid of the fire. "Easy there, darling. All we need is two thousand crowns."

"Oh that's all, is it? That's about a year's rent!"

One of the men behind him said, "Your mum borrowed it from Diamond Danny, and he charges interest. And time's up now, isn't it?"

Another of Mum's terrible decisions coming home to roost.

The smoke curled around my eyes, making it hard to see.

Shorty pulled out a curved dagger and twirled it against his fingertips. "Since you can't pay up, we will need to send your mum a message so she understands the severe-ious-ness of the situation, as it were."

I swung the torch before them, trying to ward them off. Plumes of smoke filled the air.

"Don't worry doll," one of them said. "We'll just be taking a few bits of you with us. Flesh tokens. Nose and a few other bits."

Where the hell was Finn? If I lost my nose because he was having a crack at one of the barmaids, I'd haunt his sleep every night till he died.

"I'll get you the money," I stalled. "I promise. I just don't have it right now."

The tall one grinned, giving me an unfortunate view of

his rotten teeth. "Courtesan, are ya? Too pretty to be one of them street bunters. Won't get much work without a nose though, will ya? Bit of a pickle."

I gritted my teeth. "Has it ever occurred to you that this city needs a new banking system with more reasonable penalties?"

Shorty nodded at me. "Nah, she's not a courtesan. Lila's a dock thief isn't she? Steals from the ships. Little magpie. Works for Ernald."

I didn't want to drag my boss into this. "Don't worry about Ernald. I'll get you your money in no time."

I had no idea how. I just needed time to think of something.

The tall one shook his head and pulled out another, longer knife. "Sure, but we'll need a few bits of your face to get the message across to everyone. Your mum. Ernald. Otherwise, every beggar in Dovren will mess Diamond Danny around, won't they? Think they can borrow money without paying it back. He don't like people making him into a mug. So we've gotta send a message, take a few pieces of you with us. A few flesh tokens."

Now, all my muscles had gone totally rigid, and fear twisted my stomach. "Please stop saying 'flesh tokens.' It is a deeply unpleasant phrase." I swung the torch in an arc. They leaned back a little. "Deeply unpleasant."

"Easy there, little doll," the tall one said in a soothing tone. His knife flashed in the torchlight.

"Finn?" I shouted again, panic ringing in my voice. "Anyone?"

The music from inside was drowning me out.

The tall Rough Boy started moving away from the

other, and my blood roared in my ears. I couldn't keep them both at bay with the torch forever. It would only take one of them to grab me from behind.

Think fast.

I pulled the cheap whiskey from my pocket, took a searing sip, then blew on the torch. With the alcohol on my breath, a burst of flame exploded in their direction.

I didn't stick around to watch him go up in flames, but I did hear his screams. I pivoted, then kicked the door as hard as I could. I'd hoped to break it open, but instead my foot went through the old wood. Splinters rained around it, but it remained shut. Locked.

The smaller Rough Boy slung his arm around my throat from behind, squeezing. I dropped the torch on the pavement. I elbowed him twice in the ribs, as hard as I could. When he released his grip, I brought my elbow up hard into his jaw. Then I shoved my hand through the broken door, unlatching the dead bolt from inside.

I bolted up the stairs and into a music hall crowded with dancers, and the raucous sound of horns and a bass drum. No one had even noticed the scene outside. I elbowed and shoved my way through the crowd as hard as I could.

In here, the ceiling towered high above us. The lurid colors once painted on the inside of the place had faded, sedate now. Velvet curtains draped from a towering stage. High above me, candles hung in chandeliers. Two stories of balconies swept around overhead, private rooms where only East Dovren's fanciest denizens were allowed entry.

And all around me, people danced in their best clothes,

faces beaming with happiness. The Bibliotek band was playing on the stage, a trumpeter blaring a solo.

I turned back to the entry, hoping that they'd given up.

But, no. My stomach sank. Three of them had barged in, eyes trained on me.

I needed to find my friend Zahra—fast.

COUNT SAKLAS

I turned the corner onto a dark, crowded lane where music and shouts rose from the pubs. My sword—Asmodai—hung at my waist. Forged from stars, it was one of the few things that brought me pleasure.

For a moment, I peered in the window of a pub called the Green Garland. Men and women crowded around tables, drinking, singing. Steam clouded the window.

After a thousand years on earth, I'd still never learned to enjoy the things mankind did.

Compared to an angel's senses, mortals' were dull. They perceived only a fraction of the light, heard only the loudest of noises. Their lives were so short, a few beats of a moth's wings. And for some reason, they liked to spend their short time dulling their unremarkable senses even further. It seemed they reveled in madness, in stupidity.

I thought the knowledge angels had bestowed upon them was wasted.

Though they were drunk, my presence seemed to

unnerve them anyway. They shifted away from the windows, and they drank even deeper from their pints. Maybe it made sense. Maybe that was how they coped with mortality—trying to forget it existed.

With me nearby, they drank more. Even if they didn't know who I was, they felt the Venom of God in their presence.

I turned away from the window. Emptiness hollowed out my chest. It had been a long time since I'd felt a real thrill. Even war no longer delighted me. In the last battle, the mortals had used poisons and great arcs of fire to murder each other in droves. Injured soldiers had crawled through mud and bone and blood. That was what mortals had done with the secrets the angels taught them.

The horror of it all had broken the soldiers' minds. Not a fun madness like they got from drinking in pubs. No, it was a sort of madness that made them scream in the night, made their hands shake and cheeks pale.

I turned the corner onto Parchment Row, where yellow lights illuminated window panes in black buildings.

A young woman lingered in the mouth of an alleyway, and she watched me carefully as I approached. She wore a dingy black dress, and blond hair framed her heart-shaped face.

"Half a crown," she said, hopefully. "Make your dreams come true."

Now *there* was an interesting idea, because I certainly intended to make my dreams come true. But if she had any idea what really played out in my dreams, I had a feeling her mind would break, too.

I ignored her, walking past.

But her hand jutted out, and she grabbed my arm. Slowly, I turned to look at her, leveling the full force of my divine gaze on her. Her smile faded, and she started to tremble.

A moment of dread before her fear faded, then her features started to soften, pupils dilating. Her heart raced faster, cheeks growing pink.

Among mortals, I was known as both a destroyer and a seducer.

It's just that I never wanted to act on the seduction. Not only did I not possess the desire, but seducing a mortal woman would make *me,* for a time, mortal. The name *Seducer,* in my opinion, was completely misplaced.

"Half a crown," she said again, breathlessly. "Or less. You smell nice."

Then she dropped her grip on me, and stepped back into the alley, facing the wall.

Slowly, she lifted her skirt, all the way to her waist, exposing her bare body beneath, the naked curves of her hips, her legs. Thrusting her bottom backward, she looked at me hopefully over her shoulder, her pale eyes wide.

"Put that away." I started walking again.

My gaze set on my intended destination: Alfred's Rare Books. I pushed through the door into a narrow, cluttered space.

Stacks of books crowded every surface—tables, desks, bookshelves. All haphazardly arranged. Candlelight danced back and forth over the warped wood floors, the dusty shelves of books.

At the back of the shop, a dark-haired man sat next to

a guttering taper, a pen in his hand. He surveyed me through a thick set of spectacles.

"Alfred?" I said.

His hands shook. "Count Saklas. Welcome."

I pulled out a pouch of gold. "You have the Mysterium Liber for me?"

His eyes shifted around the room, which set me on edge. My hand twitched at Asmodai's hilt.

I stared at Alfred. "The book. Where is it?"

Gripping the pen, his hand was trembling so much he unconsciously scribbled jagged lines all over his ledger. It wasn't unusual for people to react to me with terror. It was the natural way of things. The strange part was that his attention was not on me.

Something was off.

I was drawing my sword just as the first bullet hit. Another, and another slammed me from behind, knocking me forward into Alfred's desk.

But the bullets passed through me, and already my immortal body was healing. I whirled, sword drawn. The gunfire fell silent as they realized the mistake they'd made.

Five men: all sleek hair and black shirts. They stood behind me, guns drawn.

"For Albia!" one of them shouted, but I heard the terror in his voice.

A dark smile curled my lips. Now these men, without question, deserved to die.

The first arc of my sword went through two necks, and for just a moment, I felt a flicker of that pure, divine destruction that had once blazed from me. These mortals